# My Captain, My Earl

## A Hold Your Breath Novel, Volume 3

A THOUSAND REASONS TO HOLD YOUR BREATH,
AND ONE TO LET IT GO.

# K.J. Jackson

First Edition: January 2015
ISBN: 978-1-940149-08-0
http://www.kjjackson.com

# DEDICATION

– FOR MY FAVORITE KS

# CHAPTER 1

She pondered the inert body on the cabin floor. The battle was over, or at least it would be in short order. They had put up half-hearted resistance, the crew of the Rosewater, but she could still hear remnant clangs of steel against steel above deck.

She hadn't wanted to attack in daylight, but the ship had spotted them and made a run for it, and they were too close to the island of Saba. Too close to chance the Rosewater slipping away to safety. She wasn't about to let that happen. Not with her father's life on the line.

The cleanest of Katalin Dewitt's dirty fingernails slid under the red bandana covering her head, scratching the sweat at her temple as she contemplated the figure sprawled on the floor. Now she had to figure out what to do with the body.

She shoved the toe of her boot into his ribcage. No movement. But his chest swelled with a shallow breath under the rag of a white linen shirt he wore.

Telling, the man had taken up arms against his own ship. Or more correctly, he had used a mop handle against his own crew, at least until he could get his hands on a cutlass. And he knew what to do with that blade once it was in his hand.

The man could fight. Fight well. Mop handle or sword, he inflicted damage quite well. Almost too well for him to be useful to her.

Katalin closed the door to the captain's quarters, stepping over the man and sitting down on the curved wooden chair by his head. She adjusted the cutlass at her waist as her eyes swept over him. A bushy, scraggly brown beard covered the lower half of his face. He was woefully unkempt, but big, and she could see lean muscles through his thin shirt. Strong.

The man might be useful as another deckhand now that she was about to set Roland on to captain his own ship. She would have to send a good third of her crew with him to handle the Rosewater.

Roland had rightly earned his own ship from the years under her father, but her father had never allowed it to happen. But Roland deserved it and knew it, and Katalin knew that would only mean trouble in the future.

For the most part, Roland had kept his discontent in check, but Katalin recognized that it was festering and growing. Soon enough, the man's discontent would replace his loyalty.

Time to give Roland what he deserved and cut him to the winds.

She ticked off the list of the men she would send with Roland as she watched a trail of blood trickle along the cheekbone of the man on her floor. The gash on his temple would need to be sewn if he was to become part of the crew—she couldn't have that wound splitting open time and again.

Taking a deep breath, she leaned forward, watching him as she balanced her elbows on her thighs and took off her bandana, scratching free the hair that had been in matted braids for weeks now. Hiding her hair was easier than having the crew stare at it, but she was going to have a devil of a time untangling it when they got to land.

The man jerked, shaking the wood planks under her feet, but his eyes remained closed. Katalin wondered if it had been a mistake to have the man dragged down into the cabin.

He obviously wanted off of his ship—he couldn't wait to jump onto the Windrunner—but that meant very little. And the last time she took on a man into the crew that hadn't met her father's approval, it had not gone well. That sailor had lasted only a month before the crew had taken care of him themselves.

The sounds of clashing steel from above petered out. Standing, she tied her bandana back into place and gave the man one last glance. She had to get up on deck to talk to Roland. The stitching would have to wait.

~ ~ ~

Katalin didn't want him on her bed, but she also didn't want to sit on the floor and sew him up, much less do it with him in a hammock. She was hoping he would remain passed out until the stitching was done—she didn't need him flopping about—but at the first poke of the needle, he roused. Three more pokes, and he groaned as his eyes opened and he rolled away from her onto his side, tearing the needle from her hand.

Sighing, she pulled his shoulder, trying to shift him onto his back. He was surprisingly solid, and strong, against her hand.

She grabbed with both hands, rising up as she pushed down on his thick shoulder. He fell to his back, the needle half in and out of his temple. His unfocused green eyes searched, then found her face.

"What the hell…" His voice came out thick and gravelly, like sharp rocks were ripping through his throat.

"I had hoped ye sleep through it, matey." Katalin pinched the needle and yanked it free from the skin. "But ye didn't. So no caterwaulin'."

"What?" His eyebrow arched up toward the slice on his temple as he tried to look up.

Her hand went on his forehead, stilling it. "Yer temple. It be sliced. Ye need to be still fer the next five stitches. Can ye do it?"

His eyes dropped to her face. "Aye."

She nodded and quickly pushed his brown hair out of the way and set needle back to skin. True to his word, he didn't flinch once as she closed the wound. But she did feel his eyes pinning her as she worked on his temple.

Katalin leaned in, biting off the thread, and then pulled away, sitting straight as she arched her back, her eyes running down his body. "Is that it? Any more gaping wounds?"

He shook his head silently.

"Good. That's not me favorite thing to be doin'." She set the needle and thread down in a wooden box nailed to the small round table next to her.

"I will not become a pirate."

His words cut into the thick salt air, making Katalin's head spin toward him.

"What ye say?"

"I will not become a pirate."

She laughed. "Admirable one, ain't ye? No worries on that, matey, no one is asking you to be one."

"No?"

"No."

"Then why fix my wound?" He sat up. "I would like to speak to the captain of this vessel."

Katalin set each of her palms on the breeches covering her knees, spreading her legs wide as she leaned forward, blocking his movement from the bed. Her eyes narrowed at him. "Ye be speakin' to the captain."

He looked over her shoulder and around the cabin. His eyes landed on her, confused.

"Ye don't understand words, boy? I am the captain."

He guffawed. "No."

Katalin rolled her eyes. She rarely had to admit to captaining the Windrunner to anyone new. And in the unfortunate instances where she had to, the reaction was always the same. Aghast. Scorn. Faces scrunched in derision. "Yes. And ye can get past it this very moment, matey, for the fact of it ain't goin' to change no matter how long ye look at me like that."

"But you are a woman."

"That be true."

"Ludicrous…" he muttered, his voice trailing off. Long seconds passed before the disbelief lining his face melted off, wariness taking root. "What do you want of me? Why sew my wound?"

"It is simple. Serve the ship. That is all. I would like the extra help, now that Roland and a good slice of the crew took on the Rosewater. Ye look strong. Healthy save for that gash. I be likin' yer help on deck, but the crew will survive fine without it. Serve the ship, and I will get ye to port, and then ye are free to make yer way as ye wish from there."

"Or?"

"I can skim the northern coast of the island we will be passing later today, and ye are free to swim to shore. The current in these waters will carry ye close to the land, so even with yer injury, ye should be able to make the swim fine."

"What is on the island?"

She shrugged. "A small settlement. They don't take kindly to pirates. But ye are not one, so ye should be fine."

She could tell he was seriously contemplating his options.

He scratched the back of his neck. "And what would I do on this ship?"

Katalin leaned back in her chair, crossing her ankle onto her knee. "Ye are strong. I have seen that. It be useful. Ye would do whatever is necessary as deemed by the crew."

"I have lived that life on the last ship I was on, woman, and I did not take kindly to it."

In a flash, her foot stomped down, and she jerked forward, her face in his. "I do believe ye misunderstand yer very precarious position right now, boy. This is not a passenger ship. This is a vessel for swiftness and attacking, and I be happy to deposit ye down with the rowboat we be affording the survivors from the last ship ye were aboard. I be quite positive they be rippin' ye apart and eatin' ye before their boat makes land, but that is not me concern."

Her ear craned to the small round window above his head as the sounds of a small ruckus and splashing filtered into the cabin. Her mouth took on a hard line, but she sat back, resuming her earlier relaxed posture. "That said, I have no intentions of attacking another ship on this voyage. The Rosewater was the only one we be after, and now that be done. I am done. We be headin' to port. So make yer decision, boy, and make it swift. I be needed on deck."

She stared at him, watching his anger rise at her words.

It was clear this one had too much pride. Too much entitlement in life. He was damn lucky she was giving him this opportunity. No wonder he had taken up steel so quickly against his last mates. He thought he deserved better.

Clearly this was a mistake. He would do her, the crew no good. She needed to go check on that rowboat to see if she could still toss him aboard.

Katalin stood, pushing her cutlass further back around her waist. Setting the wooden chair to its spot in front of the wide desk, she went to the door. She was a step out of the cabin, her path blocked by Chomper the goat, before the man's words made her pause.

"I will stay aboard."

She rubbed Chomper's black ear before she turned back to him. "I already made me decision, boy. Yer off."

He swung his legs off the bed, but did not stand. "I apologize. The gash on my head has made my thoughts fuzzy. I meant no disrespect to your leadership on this vessel. You are a woman captain, and it is an unusual sight, but that does not mean I should have shown disrespect. I do wish to stay aboard, if you will allow it. I believe I can be of help to the crew, and to you, the captain. I am capable of following orders."

Katalin's head cocked at the man. That was unexpected. He spoke with more grace and humility than she imagined existed in the word. Peculiar. Not the slightest trace of sarcasm on his face or in his tone.

She stepped back into the cabin.

"Ye just saved yerself from the rowboat, matey." She went over to the edge of the desk, grabbing a green apple from the basket she had fixed to the desk long ago. She took a bite, still eyeing his large frame. He swallowed the mass of her bed, even with his bare feet on the wood planks of the floor. "I be Captain Kat. What be yer name?"

"Jason."

"Jason? That won't do."

"No?"

She took another bite of the apple, chewing slowly as she watched him wait patiently. "Two syllables. None aboard have that luxury. We already have a Jay in the crew, so Jase it is." She turned to leave once more, but then looked at him over her shoulder. "Ye can rest on the bed for a spell before we put ye to scrubbin'."

She walked out, Chomper turning and following her.

"Captain Kat?"

She stopped and popped her head back into the opening. "Aye?"

"Captain Kat has three syllables."

Her cheek cracked in a half smile. "Yes, but I be the captain, and I make the rules, Jase."

# CHAPTER 2

Jason stepped up onto the quarterdeck, bare feet soft on the wood planks. Eyes to the black sky, he took fresh air into his lungs, letting it sink deep into his chest after the stench from below deck.

That he was able to escape the smells below, and not have to still sniff the putrescence of his own beard was a blessing he had thought never to have again. Removing the offensive mound on his chin had been the first thing he had done a week ago on the Windrunner—knives were thankfully not kept far from his reach on this ship.

He took several steps on the wood planks, wondering who was on watch tonight. It wasn't until he had rounded the wheel that he saw the figure leaning on the rear railing, arms spread wide, head tilted up to the three-quarter's moon.

He stopped. Hours before dawn, the captain was wide awake, watching the movement of the stars. He had thought to come up and chat with whoever was at the helm, but he hadn't anticipated the captain being awake at this time of night.

The red bandana that usually covered her hair was missing, hanging from her fingertips, and in the low moonlight, Jason could see thick braids wrapping her head like a crown.

Catching the wind, white sleeves puffed down to her elbows from the dark blue vest she always wore. He had not seen the back of her very often in the last week—but even in the darkness, he could see the short brown breeches she wore curved tightly to her backside.

She adjusted, kicking the toe of her tall boots at the railing. Jason froze, looking downward, only to the see the goat that was always two steps behind the captain sitting by the wheel. The goat was looking up at him curiously. Buggers. The last thing he needed was the goat to bleat his presence to the captain.

Jason made the slightest step backward with his foot, but it was enough noise to make the board under him creak.

She jerked around. "What?"

He had just been caught lurking and there was no denying it. He stepped forward out of the dark shadow casting down from the main sail. "Captain Kat. I apologize. I did not intend to disturb you. I did not see you were on the deck when I came out here."

"Do not fret on it, Jase." Leaning back on the railing, she quickly worked on tying the bandana that had been floating free from her fingertips back around her head, tucking in the thick braids. "Were you below or above Frog?"

"Below."

"It is quite horrid, is it not?"

Jason chuckled. "It is other-worldly—like nothing I have ever witnessed in my ears. But everyone below is asleep. It makes me think I am going mad. You heard him?"

"We all hear him, Jase. We have tried everything—even tied ropes around his head to keep his mouth shut against the snores—all to no avail. It is easier to learn to sleep through his snoring than to get him to stop."

"That will be quite the feat."

"It is." She nodded. "Did you not wonder on the swath of empty hammocks surrounding his? Usually only the drunkest of the bunch can handle proximity to him. So everyone below is either drunk, deaf, or immune."

"What are you?"

She smiled. "I am, fortunately, immune. I have slept through Frog's snores for as long as I can remember."

"So if it is not the thundering below, what has you awake?" Jason asked. "I did not expect you to be up here, Captain."

She shrugged, turning from him and tucking the remaining few strands of hair up under her bandana. "I like the night. I always have. The moon when it is fat. A solid wind in the sails.

Stars leading the way home." She looked over her shoulder at him. "So I often take the helm at night. It is the only time I feel half alone."

"I apologize again." He started to turn away from her. "I did not wish to disturb your solitude."

"No. It is fine." She waved her hand. "Talking to one man is very different than herding the rambling minds of that crew below." She moved to sit on the wooden crate next to her, leaning back on the railing as she kicked an adjoining crate his way. "Sit. It is cruel punishment to send you back down to listen to the rumblings of Frog."

Jason paused, staring at the crate. This was the closest thing to an actual conversation that he had experienced in more than two years. He had begun to wonder if his mouth could still form coherent sentences. But she was a young, unchaperoned woman in the middle of the night.

The thought struck him, and it made him chuckle to himself. She was also the woman captain of the pirate ship he was stranded on—and he was worried about propriety?

He stepped forward, grabbing the crate and wedging it against the railing a short distance from her before he sat. He could feel her eyes on him the entire time.

Since after that first day when she stitched his head, he had had almost no contact with her. The crew had kept him more than busy the past week, and there had been no need.

He paused, suddenly at a loss now that he was sitting next to her. What did one say to a young woman with the peculiarity of captaining a pirate ship?

"You have surprised me, Jase. After our first encounter, I did not think it possible for you to survive on this ship. Survive with this crew."

He nodded, his eyes squinting at memories from the last ship he was on. "Your crew is far above the kind that was on the Rosewater."

"But my crew can be harsh. It is our way. But you have escaped that. You have been true to what you said you would do.

You have kept your head down, followed orders, done all that has been asked of you and more."

She leaned forward, head cocked as she looked at him. "I did not see it in you at first. I did not think you capable."

"No?"

"No. Your ire—your hackles prickled too quickly when we first talked. A man with that much unwarranted pride rarely does well on the Windrunner."

Jason's eyes swung to the vast blackness of the night ocean. He had seen too much of it in the past years. "I will be honest, Captain Kat, I am just looking survive. Survive so I can get to dry land. This is the first hope of that I have had in two years."

"Two years? How did you get on the Rosewater?"

"Unfortunate circumstances." He stood abruptly. "I should retire."

"Avoidance does not make the truth disappear." She looked up at him, the challenge clear in her dark blue eyes, even in the moonlight.

He stood for a moment, then sat heavily, the crate creaking. It was not like he needed to hide the truth at this point in time. "I was gathering evidence of treason against several men when I was bound and gagged and tossed into the hold of a ship. I presume they discovered my investigation. I have been a slave to three more ships since then. The Rosewater was the last one."

"No wonder you took up a weapon so quickly against your Rosewater mates."

"They were not my mates." His fist curled. "Captors, at best. Demons from hell, at worst."

"Truly? If I recall, they did not seem to have much skill in the way of fighting."

"No. They were worthless. But I was one against the number of them, and they liked their cat-o-nines."

She whistled low, shaking her head. Her eyes came back to his. "That much anger, it makes it interesting that you have done well on our ship. I have heard nary a negative word from the crew about you."

"Your crew has respect amongst them."

"Aye." She nodded. "That is also our way."

When she said the word "aye," it suddenly occurred to Jason the oddity in his conversation with the captain—her accent was gone. When they first spoke a week ago, and in every order she gave the crew, her odd sailor accent and mariner talk swallowed most of her words.

But not now.

And that was exactly how he had been lulled into conversation. He could have just as easily been sitting in a London drawing room chatting with a lady of the ton—well, maybe not a lady of the ton, but a gentle lady of the countryside, yes. But they were a wide ocean away from the drawing rooms of his past.

What was she?

"Your talk. Your language, Captain Kat. It is not guttural. It actually has remnants of refinement."

She laughed. It was a warm, throaty chuckle that disappeared low over the water. "I slipped with that, but thank you, I think."

Her eyes moved to the stars as she propped her head on the thick wood rail behind her. "Truthfully, this is how I hear language in my mind. I dream like this. Think like this. But I maintain the accent for the crew, lest they think I am edging into a proper lady. They get uncomfortable when I slip. My father had several English tutors for me that were extremely proper with their grammar. He grew up in England and wanted me to learn to speak like an Englishwoman—for what purpose, I know not—I have no intentions of getting anywhere near that part of the world."

She shrugged. "It is possible he eventually wants to return to England. I do not know. But he always demanded—still does— that I only speak with the utmost propriety in front of him. But that does me little good with a crew of salty dogs."

"And there is no need to toss your accent for me?"

"No, Jase, there is not." She laughed again, her eyes still to the darkness above. "You are ridiculously far from being a mariner. We have never had a proper Englishman aboard, save for the tutors. So I find you a curiosity. Plus, it is nice to be able to be natural in speech with someone other than my father."

"You maintain quite the facade with the men, do you not?"

Her eyes swung down to him sharply. "Rude. I would take offense and have you flogged were you part of my crew." Then her eyes softened. "As you will be off the ship within a fortnight, I will allow it to slide."

Jason braced himself. The last thing he needed was to have her change her mind and throw him in another ship hold instead of bringing him to land. He was suddenly acutely aware he was treading in dangerous waters speaking to the captain with such informality.

But then her posture relaxed, and her eyes went to the crow's nest. "It is also why I like the night. The simplicity. No airs to put on. No pressure. The stars. Open waters. Salty breezes. Freedom, if only for a few hours."

"I think this is the first time I have met someone who has strived for a veneer of downward rather that upward mobility, even if it is an act."

She shrugged. "Whatever serves the ship. And the ship demands I lead the crew. Just because I accept what I must do, Jase, does not mean I choose it when given the choice."

She went quiet, and the lapping of the ocean against ship tempered them into a comfortable silence.

Deep in the moving shadows, Jason watched her watch the sky, trying to place her into some sort of category of women he had known in his life. The proper lady she bore little resemblance to, except for her speech. God forgive her, she wore a shirt and breeches. But that didn't necessarily put her into the whore category, either.

She was a leader—a good one, he had to admit—from what he had observed over the past week. The crew respected her. He had never heard them say one ill word about her and her decisions—even if she was nowhere within ear-shot.

She was fair. She treated the men with respect, but nor was there the slightest coddle of womanly attentions to them.

His eyes swept over her form. There was definitely a woman's body beneath the linen shirt, vest and breeches. This was the first time he had been close enough to really study her, but the shadows hid much of what he was curious about.

She wasn't exactly clean, but then again, none of them were. It was hard to tell if she was pleasing to the eye through the dirt and the bandana covering her entire forehead and skull—he guessed so, by the classic lines of her jaw and cheekbones. Her eyes were stunning, if nothing else.

"Why do you hide under that?" Jason pointed at her head.

"What?" Her hand went to her head, touching the red cloth. "Oh, do you mean the bandana?"

He nodded.

"Would you think of me as a woman if you had to look at my hair all day?"

"I do think of you as a woman."

"A woman before a captain?"

"Yes."

"Dear God, I pray you are the only one on board with that thought."

"It matters that much?"

She looked at him, fingernails plucking the edge of the wood crate. "Yes, it matters. It matters to the hierarchy of the ship. To the respect I must demand. To the respect I have earned."

"You think the respect hinges on your hair?"

"No. But I will not allow a reason that is not a reason to affect my control on this ship. I decided long ago I either needed to crop it to my skull or keep it hidden. I chose hidden."

Jason latched onto the tiniest thread she just offered—a thread of something genuinely personal about herself. He leaned forward. "What on God's earth could have led you to this life?"

"I was not led." She stood, turning to lean her belly on the railing as she watched the waters. "I was born into it. It is all I ever remember. The only life I have lived. I have no mother. My father is a captain, always has been, so I grew up on this ship."

"But how did you survive? Being a fem—" He cut himself off, eyes shifting to the rigging off the mast.

She laughed. "Being a female? It is a fair question. I take no offense at it. I know I am a woman—and an oddity. The crew may respect me, but truthfully, the only reason I can do what I do is my father. He is a force among men. A giant. I have survived unscathed thus far because of the loyalty—and fear—he inspires. No man has ever dared to touch me. And when he could no longer captain, his crew became my crew."

"Can I ask you a question?"

Her head swung in his direction. "You have not curbed yourself thus far, Jase, so am I to stop you now?"

"Have you killed? You are a pirate."

"You are trying to figure me out?"

"Yes."

"Let me first correct you on a fact you have already convinced yourself to be true, Jase. We are privateers, not pirates."

"Upon whose authority?"

"Upon the letter of marque and reprisal from your very own England."

"Those ended with the war."

"Did they? Are you sure? You have been ocean-locked for a long spell."

"What need is there now for privateers?"

"There will always be need as long as governments are greedy, Jase. I would think a man of your age would have already figured that out."

He stood. "Do not speak of my homeland with such disrespect."

"And do not take a tone with me, boy." She glared up at him. "Your loyalty is quaint, but it is not my country, not my loyalty. I can see it for what it is."

"But that same government gives you breadth to attack the innocent."

"Posh. No innocents. We do not prey on honorable causes. We only come out occasionally. My father's health no longer allows him to captain, but the crew—even though they are all wealthy in their own right—they need the adventure. These runs keep them happy. Keep my father's…investors…happy. Keep my father safe from their threats. So we set sail, take down ships that need to be taken down, and return home."

"That simple?"

"That simple."

He looked down at her, realizing that not only was he a good head-and-a-half taller than her, she was noticeably slight. That she managed to captain a crew the size of hers without trouble was actually quite remarkable.

"How long have you been captain of the Windrunner?"

She crossed her arms over her chest, turning to him. "Two years, now. There have been no complaints."

"I do not imagine so. Kill to keep everyone fat and wealthy, and all is well?"

"I do not take a share of the prize, boy. It is blood money."

"So you do kill for it."

"I try very hard to spare lives—even for those that do not deserve that courtesy. But the deaths—I make no apologies for. I do this to keep my father safe, safe from threat."

She moved closer to him, anger in her steps as one hand went to the railing and the other to the silver hilt of her cutlass. "You are no different, boy. Tell me you would not have killed members of the Rosewater's crew if you had first managed in-hand a true weapon instead of a mop handle?"

Jason's jaw clenched. "Maybe. But that was for protecting my own life. Not another's."

"So you would not kill for someone you loved?"

He shrugged.

"No answer, boy?"

"Yes. Yes, I would kill for someone I love."

"Then please, cease your judgment of me, boy." Her arms re-crossed against her chest as she tilted her head, craning her ear to the deck. "I do believe Frog has repositioned and is currently quiet. I think it would do you well to get more sleep in before the crew puts you to work at dawn."

Realizing his insolence had, again, put him in treacherous waters with this captain, Jason took the suggestion for what it was. A command.

He gave her a crisp nod, and walked to the steps descending from the quarterdeck. He started down the stairs, but before his head disappeared from her view, he stopped.

"Captain Kat."

"Yes?"

"Is your name really Kat?"

"No."

He waited, poised on the steps.

She sighed, uncrossing her arms as she walked to the wheel. "It is Katalin. Katalin Dewitt."

Surprised she answered him, Jason gave another nod and descended.

# CHAPTER 3

Two days later, Jason slogged a heavy slop bucket from the ship's galley across the deck. The bright sunlight hitting him after being below deck, it took him a few blinks to realize the crew had converged on one side of the ship.

Setting the bucket down, he walked to the jostling bodies and stopped at the outer back edge of the crowd that had gathered. Between the yelling and shouts around him, he could hear a heated argument going on in the front of the crowd.

Jason leaned toward Clegg, one of the scrawniest of the crew, who was hopping, trying to see over the heads of the men in front of him. "What is going on?"

The sailor didn't take his eyes off of the wildly waving arms in the front of the crowd. "Not sure. Longboat not be there." He pointed to the side of the ship. "I 'ear a scream an' splash an' the boat not 'ere no more. 'Eard something 'bout Cap'n. Not rightly sure what that be."

Jason pushed his way through the crowd, stopping once he got to Poe and Frog at the railing, throwing arms and spit and bellowing at each other. A small pair of boots sat on the deck between them.

Jason snatched a flailing tattooed arm from each man. Both went instantly silent, fierce faces turning to him.

Jason dropped their wrists. "What is happening? Where is Captain Kat?"

Frog opened his mouth first, mostly to cut off Poe. "Cap'n be limber, so went onto the boat to untangle rigging that caught. Then bloody dumb arse, Poe," he smacked the head of the man next to him, "cut the bloody wrong rope while Cap'n still be on there and it fell."

Jason pushed between them to look over the railing. An upside-down longboat bobbed in the water, several ropes along the back still attached to the ship.

Jason looked at Poe. "Captain has not come up?"

"Nope," Poe said. "She be a good swimmer. Don't know where she be."

"Why is no one down there?" Jason looked back and forth between the two. "She could be trapped."

"Good idear, matey," Frog said. "Ye get down there."

Jason looked down at the rolling waves and swallowed hard. "Give me a damn rope."

Within minutes, Jason let himself down the side of the ship slowly, hand wrapped tight on the rope. Edging into the water, he refused to give up his death grip on the lifeline until a rope from the longboat floated near him, and Jason grabbed it, pulling himself to the boat.

Hand searching in the water, he found the edge of the longboat and moved alongside it, scanning the surface of the water.

"See anything, mate?" Frog yelled from above.

Jason shook his head.

"Check the other side of the boat."

One hand on the rope and the other moving him along the edge of the longboat, Jason searched the water. Still nothing.

"Dive under, matey. She be under it, maybe."

Two deep breaths, one to steady himself, and the other to fill his lungs with air, and Jason ducked his head under the water. He opened his eyes, the salt instantly stinging, but he kept them open, searching through the shadow of the boat. He kicked upward, finding the shallow air pocket left under the boat, and gulped air.

Heavy—panicked—panting greeted him. He turned to the sound.

"Captain?"

Her back to him, she spun, sheer terror on her face.

"It's caught. My foot—" Her words cut off as her breath went out of control.

"Stop. Slow down. Breathe."

Shaking her head furiously, she jerked out of control, shoving the immobile wooden plank seat that was behind her. Water went splashing, and the boat rocked, sliding further down in the water, tightening the air pocket around them.

One hand still gripping the side of the boat, Jason dropped the rope and moved to her, grabbing the back of her neck, forcing her face into his.

"Breathe, Katalin, breathe. I will untangle you."

She tried to jerk away from him, screaming, but his hand held her solid.

"Katalin. Breathe, dammit it. Stop fighting it and let me untangle it."

Her wild eyes found his, stopped, focused, and then she stilled.

Gulping air, she closed her eyes tight and nodded.

Jason let his hold on her neck relax.

She nodded.

"Is it a rope? Do you have a knife?"

Her eyes stayed tight against the world. "Waist."

Jason's free hand went down her body, circling her waist before he found the hilt of a blade. It slipped out of his hand as she kicked, her arm hitting his as she treaded water.

He kept his swear to himself, hoping the blade didn't just sink to the ocean floor. His hand followed the same path along her body, finding the blade again and pulling it free.

"Your right or left foot?"

"L-left."

Before giving himself a chance to think about it, Jason sucked a deep breath of air and went under. He grabbed her left leg with both hands, following deeper into the water until his fingers felt skin and ran into the rough rope her ankle strained against. Three quick saws at the rope, and her foot jerked free.

Surprised it had been that easy, Jason grabbed the wooden seat the rope had been wrapped around, and followed it to the edge of the boat, pulling himself into the small air pocket again.

Katalin's eyes were open when he broke free of the water, gasping for air, but she still looked panicked, her breathing hard.

"You are free, Captain."

She closed her eyes, nodding her head. "Just give me a moment—the crew cannot see me like this."

It took minutes, and Jason watched as the panic slowly slid off her face and her breathing turned even. It looked like it took intense control to make it so.

Her eyes opened.

"Are you unharmed? Calmed?"

"Yes. Let us go."

With a quick breath, she dove under the water and the side of the boat.

Jason followed, hand still gripping the lip of the boat.

~ ~ ~

Chomper's snort next to her ear sent Katalin upright. On the quarterdeck, she had been flat on her back, a blanket under her with her hands wedged under her head, staring at the night sky until the wet snort tickled her ear.

Other than to follow her if she moved above deck, Chomper was usually quite content to be sleeping at this time of night. Something was amiss.

Her eyes first scanned the surrounding waters.

Vast, empty ocean.

Chomper nudged her arm, and she put her hand on the goat's nose, the whiskers scratching Katalin's palm as she watched the top of the steps from the main deck. Within a second, a head popped up.

Jase.

His eyes met hers as his bare feet landed on the deck.

He didn't wait for an invitation to join her. Just walked toward her.

Katalin didn't care for his presumption.

Maybe where he came from, saving a life earned one certain rights. But this was a ship. Her ship. Rights were given as she saw fit.

She stood, muttering a nonsensical blasphemy under her breath. As if saving her life gave him any right.

Chomper clomped over to him, took a sniff, then came back to Katalin's side, settling by her blanket. She bit onto a corner of the cloth and started gnawing it. Katalin put her foot on the fabric, effectively blocking the goat's path. Chomper could have a corner, no more.

Jase stood a distance from her, watching the scene, slight smirk on his face.

She spread her legs in wide stance, hands on her hips. "Ye need something, matey?"

He took a step toward her and she eyed him. Although an improvement from the tattered rags he landed on the ship with, the clothes he had found on the Windrunner fit his tall frame awkwardly—grey slops that were too large with a rope tied at his waist, and a white linen tunic that sat too tight across his wide chest. She had to admit he looked much better without the ragged beard she had first seen him with, and his bare arms were oddly free of the ink that covered most of the skin of her crew.

She gave herself a mental shake. Wide chest? Since when had she noted how big a man's chest was, save for the muscle he could contribute to the ship?

She inhaled a deep breath, hands not moving from her hips.

Since he had talked to her the other night. Talked to her like a real person. Not a captain. Not her father's daughter. Talked to her without an agenda.

No agenda except getting to dry land.

And then he had gone and saved her from drowning herself.

That was when she had started seeing his chest. Seeing how his bronzed arms flexed as he hauled heavy wet ropes. Seeing him as something more than an annoyance she had to keep in check for a few weeks. It didn't help that he did whatever was asked of him, no matter how menial, and that the crew liked him.

She took another breath.

No attachments.

Never any attachments.

He ventured one more step to her. "What happened to you today?"

"What?"

He took another step, his deep voice lower than usual. She could hear the concern in it. "Under the boat. Your fear. You were panicked."

"No. I was not." She dismissed him with a jerk of her head. "I am not sure what you thought you saw under that boat, Jase, but I was fine. I was just trying to free myself."

He moved to within an arm's length of her. "Truly, Captain Kat? Had you been in your right mind, that rope was easily cut through. You had your knife, but you were floundering— incapable of moving down there to free yourself. You were not just panicked, you were in terror."

She spun from him, moving to the railing to watch the waters and avoid his eyes. "Ye be mistaken, boy."

"I do not believe you, Captain. I saw what I saw."

Jason went silent behind her, but only for a moment before he joined her at the railing, staring down at her.

"Avoidance does not make the truth disappear, Captain."

She sighed, eyes to the heavens before she looked up at him. "You are correct, Jase. I was in trouble. Thank you for your assistance. Is that why you are up here? Gratitude?"

"No." His eyes didn't leave her. "You saved my life. I saved yours. I am sure we are both grateful. But I could care less about a thank you. What I do care about is when I see a woman terrorized. It is not right."

"I am not exactly the type of gentle woman you are accustomed to, Jase. I need no saving."

"You did today. Why?"

He hovered. Silent. Waiting.

She tried to avoid acknowledging him without moving away. Impossible. She could hear his breathing. Feel his eyes on her face.

She exhaled, clasping her hands as she set her forearms on the railing, leaning forward. Head down, she kicked at a wood plank with the toe of her boot. "I told you I grew up on my father's ship."

"Yes."

"My father did the best he could with a baby on a ship. But he was in the business of raiding vessels, and a baby in the middle of a battle was, in his mind, craziness."

"That is crazy, Captain Kat."

Her head tilted up to him. She couldn't meet his eyes and focused on the V of his shirt where the white linen gave way to skin. "Yes, well, crazy begot more crazy. Before battles he used to seal me in a barrel, tie it to the ship, and set me in the ocean. He thought it was the safest place for me—and I imagine it probably was. He did his best. It made sense for a baby. A baby does not know what is going on."

Her voice had petered to a whisper, and the lump in her throat threatened to cut off her words. She rushed on, eyes lost in memory. "But then I grew. I knew what was going on. I was so little, four, five, and I would bob in the blackness of the dark barrel, terror in every second. I never knew what was happening. Cannons, gunfire, screaming. I never knew if the rope had been severed—if I was floating lost from the ship in the ocean. If I was going to sink. If I was going to be forgotten. Time and again he would do it. I would fight him, kicking and screaming. He would still shove me in. Seal the top."

Her throat choked the words.

"When did he stop?"

It took her a long moment to find her voice. "When he taught me to fight. When he thought I could defend myself. But he never stopped wanting to put me in that barrel. It meant safety to him. It meant terror to me."

Her eyes went up, meeting his. "So I do not do well in tiny spaces. Especially tiny spaces where I am trapped on the ocean. That is what you saw today." She pushed herself up to stand straight, sucking in a deep breath. "The crew does not know. Most of them remember those early days, but none know how… damaged I am from it. I would like to keep it that way."

Jason nodded. "I will not breathe a word of it."

Her head cocked at him. "Are you done with me? You know what you came up here for. I would prefer if you would leave me, now."

His eyebrow arched at her snapped words, but he offered a single nod and stepped from the railing.

He made it past the blanket Chomper was now fully devouring and then stopped, turning to her.

Katalin braced herself. Was that not enough for him? What now?

He walked back toward her, stopping just shy of the railing. His hand reached out, wrapping around the smooth wood, his fingers tracing the grain. He looked to be searching for words.

She waited, face quirked in impatience.

"Captain Kat, I will be honest. I have been walking around with a gaping hole in my chest for two years. A gaping hole that grows wider each day I am far from my homeland. I had begun to wonder if England was a long-lost dream, and that I should just accept the brutality that had become my life on the ocean."

He watched the back of his hand move up and down, palm gently tapping on the railing. "But talking to you the other night…it was something I thought never to experience again. It felt like a little piece of my home, people I once knew, traveled across the ocean and landed on the ship. Gave me hope. I went to sleep thinking it had been a dream, a cruel trick by you, even though I knew it was not."

"So you are homesick?"

He shrugged, his gaze shifting to the vast water. "Beyond. I never knew how much so until I talked to you. It is a hollowness that is unyielding." His eyes moved to hers. "I am humble when

I ask to just sit, Captain. Sit on those crates and talk with you. On whatever topic you see fit. I just want to listen. Just want to remember that my life before the sea was reality. Reality I can get back to."

Ignoring the awkwardness of the silence, Katalin took a long moment to assess his face in the moonlight. She only saw true, raw honesty in his eyes.

"Hell, Jase." She shook her head in slight exasperation. "You request that of me, and I am the devil to deny you."

"So you will sit?"

She sighed, motioning to the row of crates that lined the back edge of the deck. "I am on watch, so up here regardless. Let us sit. I am yours until dawn."

# CHAPTER 4

Katalin wasn't sure how Jason knew when she was up there—she was usually random in taking the night watch depending on how tired she was—but every one of the five nights in the past week that she was on deck, he showed up.

It was something she had begun to look forward to as much as he said he did. As to why she so enjoyed those nights with him under the dark sky, she had figured it out pretty quickly. He had become a friend, and she had never had a friend before.

The crew was always the crew, whether her father was in charge or she was. Her father was her father. Even on her father's island, staff was staff. She had never had anyone to talk to without a gamut of unspoken expectations weighing on her.

But with Jason, there were no expectations. He was not truly part of the crew—just a passenger that was laboring on the ship for passage. The only expectation he had of her was to hear her voice—and that she chuckle at his odd observations of ship life.

Jason was a novelty, she acknowledged that.

But it was starting to play with her mind. Wayward thoughts had begun to seep into her consciousness. Wayward thoughts that she couldn't afford. Not as captain.

She couldn't afford for her eyes to specifically seek him out on the deck during the day. Couldn't afford thinking it was beneath him to have to carry another slop bucket or to swab the decks one more time. Couldn't afford thinking that she needed to search the ship for some boots for him. Couldn't afford watching the sweat that dripped from his brow in the hot sun.

She couldn't afford any of it, and she needed to stop.

No attachments.

Jason was going to be off the ship within a week.

But then the winds died.

Not a breeze. Not a whisper of air that would puff the sails.

Five days passed and the ship only drifted with the waters. Drifted nowhere near land and Katalin found herself counting on those middle-of-the-night hours with Jason to keep her mind even. Her optimism alive. He did that for her—his deep voice soft in the night, steady, easing the constant worry that ate away her days.

On the sixth day, the last morsel of food had been eaten. And they had caught no fish in four days.

And still they sat.

Becalmed in a dead man's sea. No wind. No fish. They should have been in port by now.

Their only saving grace was that their fresh water supplies and—more importantly—the supplies of rum were holding.

The night of the eighth day, Katalin overrode what her good sense was telling her, and came above deck to relieve Fin of the helm. She had been avoiding the night watch the last two nights, truthfully, avoiding Jason. She was now beyond worried, and she hadn't wanted that weakness to surface in front of him. Not as captain.

But she couldn't sleep, no matter how long she lay on her back staring at the moonlight flickering across the dark wood ceiling. The winds had never been so unkind to the Windrunner. Hating to admit it to herself, she had come above deck hoping that Jason would show up. Show up and just talk to her. Take her thoughts off the mind-numbing worry for just a few hours. Calm her, even if he didn't know he would be doing just that.

For the first half hour, she sat on a crate by the starboard railing, foot tapping as she kept her eyes on the white sails, searching the air for the slightest breeze. Eventually, Chomper started to gnaw on the edge of the crate by her nervous foot.

Her mostly whitish coat reflected in the moonlight. Katalin scratched her one black ear. "I know, girl. Is it good? I may just join you and take a nibble myself, I am so hungry."

She patted Chomper's side, her fingers landing on the bones of the goat's protruding ribcage.

Damn, they needed to get to land.

"You need to sleep, Captain Kat."

Katalin looked up to see Jason approaching, his bare feet silent on the planks of wood. He was good at that, moving about silently, not drawing attention to himself. Impressive for his large frame.

"I have been sleeping, Jase."

He pointed to the crate next to her and she nodded. She had told him time and again that permission to sit with her was unnecessary, but he continued to hold onto the small gesture of respect.

He sat, leaning back on the railing and stretching his long legs out in front of him, bare feet flexing.

"I do not wish to start out being contrary, but I am going to do so." Jason looked at her, not a hint of his usual smile on his face. "You have not been sleeping. You have been pacing. I could hear your footsteps all through the past two nights."

"You could? I did not think one could hear sounds from my quarters."

"There is one hammock that affords the proper acoustics. It is also the one under several drips, so it is usually free."

So that was how he knew her nightly whereabouts. Sneaky. She eyed him. "Which means you have not been sleeping either."

He shrugged. "The wind will or will not come no matter if you are asleep or awake, Captain Kat. You cannot make it appear by sheer will."

"True. I cannot. But this is my ship. My crew. Pacing is the one thing that is under my control. So I do it. It is better than sleeping through the slow starvation of the Windrunner."

"Is that where we are headed?"

"As long as the sails are starved for wind, then we are starved for food."

She stood, gripping the railing as she looked at the smooth inky waters. "I have always loved the sea. It is my home. I have never wished to be off it. But now. Right now. This is the first time I have ever longed to be on dry land." She turned, leaning on the railing and staring at the sails again. "My father's island, the Snake Horn, is beautiful, but I have never felt completely comfortable there, even though we have spent more and more time there in recent years."

"Your father owns an island?"

"Yes, as do some of the crew. Do not let their manners or their dress fool you. Not only is my father wealthy, but each of the crew is as well. The years with my father gave them all riches. Although a few have had trouble with coins slipping through their fingers."

"Wine and women?"

She smiled, nodding. "I am sure you can take a guess as to which ones those are. But we all take care of each other—there is plenty to go around. And we only set sail now when it is specifically requested of us. Loyalty to the past. Loyalty to my father. But each of them belongs on the sea, and they know it. It is where they are happiest."

Chomper nudged Jason's knee, and he bent over to scratch under the goat's chin. "But the happiness is waning."

"Yes. Waning fast. We have never experienced this before. A few days of slack sails, but never anything dire." She shook her head. "It is my fault. We should have been further south. I lost the wind."

"Are the winds more sure to the south?"

Katalin shrugged.

"Then you cannot blame yourself, Katalin."

"I am the Captain, Jase. The winds are my responsibility." She sat on the crate. "But I do not wish to talk of the blasted winds. They are all that is in my mind. You. How about you— what will you do once you touch land again?"

Jason leaned back, face to the night sky. "Land. It is hard to imagine after all this time. Two feet on solid ground. I will first probably smell the dirt, and then, as much as it distresses me, I will probably get on a ship, as awful as that sounds. I need to get back to England. I have…unfinished business there that needs attention as soon as possible."

"You have told me of your parents, of your sisters and growing up, but what does it look like, England?"

His eyes came down to her, crinkling with the smile that spread his face. "I have seen the islands in these waters from afar, been to the corners of the continent—but England... England holds a green like no other place on earth. A green that is blanketed in the winter with a layer of snow, which only brings forth spry new green in the spring that shocks one into seeing color again. Hills roll gently. Forests where I grew up are thick, full of wonder and mystery. It is home. A home that were I to never get back to, I would die broken, incomplete."

She smiled in odd wonderment at the sheer joy on Jason's face when he talked of his country. "I have never met someone so loyal to a land—to an ideal, a way of life—as you, Jase. You love your home."

"You have no loyalty?"

"My loyalty is to people. My father. The crew. Not to a place."

"The ship is a place."

"Aye. There, you have me." She patted the railing behind her head. "The ship does warrant the loyalty, the love."

"And your father must have fond memories of England since he had you tutored by Englishmen."

"I honestly do not know what my father thinks of his homeland. We have never talked about it."

"I get the sense that you and your father do not talk of much, aside from the ship and the crew."

"That..." She pointed at him, ready to defend her relationship with her father, but then her finger crooked, deflated. "That is quite close to the truth. He does not like to speak of the past, nor does he like to speak of the future. I know very little of what is in his mind—but that does not mean I do not love him. He is my family, above everything, and he is all I have."

"I meant no disrespect, Katalin."

"Thank you for saying so." Katalin's eye caught slight movement on a sail, and she stood, walking closer to the edge of the quarterdeck to stare at the fabric for a minute. No movement. It must have been her imagination. She walked back to Jason, stopping in front of him. "As I was saying, I cannot condone ill speak of my father, even if it comes from my own mouth."

Jason stood, blocking the direct moonlight to her face. "Have you ever thought of leaving this life, Katalin?"

She looked up at him, trying to read his eyes that were now in the shadows. He had just asked the question she had never dared fully broach in her own mind.

Turning her head, she looked at the waters past the stern. "I cannot leave my father. His eyesight is near gone. His health stoops him—he cannot move without the cane now. He depends on me too much to handle certain…affairs."

"Such as captaining his ship."

"Yes. Among others." Her hand went on her hip, and she looked at his face, noting how dark the stubble along his jaw looked, yet still she could see the white scar that ran the length of his face, from his left temple to his jaw. She would have to ask him about that someday. "The threat on his life is valid, Jase, and I will do what is needed to keep him safe. And the crew. I cannot leave them. I love this ship, love being a captain too much. It is the life that has been ingrained in me since I was a babe. How you feel about England, I feel about the Windrunner."

"But do you not wish to be married, have children?"

"This is who I am, Jase. I cannot be a woman. A real woman with a family and a home—I cannot even imagine that. I am a captain and I cannot be more. If I was more, everyone would see me as a woman. And women are not allowed on ships such as the Windrunner."

"Pirate ships?"

"Privateering ships. And the code is the same whether we are pirates or privateers."

"I do not believe you."

"No?"

"I think you are more, Katalin. Much more, whether you admit to it or not." He took a step closer to her, staring down

at her, deepening the shadow she was under. "You are kind
and witty. You harbor fierce loyalty. You adore your crew. You
are smart. You care about that goat because you have to have
something to nurture. You managed to take me from wishing for
death, to hoping for life again. And just by talking to me. You did
that. As a woman, not as a captain."

Katalin's jaw dropped slightly, and she turned her head from
him, dodging his eyes. She had no words against what he had just
said to her. Nothing. No man had ever talked to her like that.
Ever looked at her like that.

His hand went to her chin, and Katalin almost jumped away
at the shock of his fingers on her. But her feet were lead and
offered no escape.

He gently tugged her chin forward so she had to face him,
even if her eyes could not meet his.

"Do you not wonder, Kat? Do you not dream? In all of our
nights together, I have never touched you—never said anything to
make you uncomfortable. But I am going to now."

His hand dropped from her chin, but he did not back away
from her. "I like you, Kat. I more than like you. At first, I was just
happy to have a friend, to have someone to talk to. But it turns
out that you—you I would like whether we are on this ship or
in a London drawing room. I like your spirit, Kat. And I do not
think I am wrong in saying that in our time together—you are
relaxed, happy—not a captain. Am I wrong?"

Katalin rubbed her forehead, index finger slipping under her
bandana as Jason's words sunk in. Making her entertain thoughts
she had no right to entertain. No attachments.

She found her voice. "I am not stupid, Jase. Of course I
recognize that I am happy. That you make me happy. That I look
forward to talking to you. Being with you. You make me laugh.
You make me feel. Of course I see all of that. But I do not know
what to do with it."

"This. This is what you do with it."

His lips were on hers before she knew what was happening,
before she could sense his intentions. She froze, losing herself to

his lips, soft in the sea of hard, demanding stubble. To his hand sliding behind her neck, tilting her head. To the shiver that ran down her back as he captured her bottom lip, teasing it. To the taste of him slipping into her mouth.

Just as Katalin's eyelids dropped, blacking out her world to only his kiss, Jason pulled away, taking a step backward. Her eyes flew open.

With his face still in shadows, she could not discern his thoughts, but his breath came quick, and his deep baritone went even lower, gruff. "That is what you do with it, Kat."

Before Katalin could blink, he stepped around her, disappearing down the stairs and below deck.

What the hell was she to do with that?

~ ~ ~

Three more days passed with spotless blue skies. Just windless sun.

They were supposed to have been in port by then, and every day that passed, Katalin was finding it harder and harder to keep the morale on the ship even. To keep her own morale even—and that was not helped at all by the fact that she had been completely avoiding Jason since he kissed her.

Every day, Katalin was sure it was to be the day winds would float their sails again. They were still near a small splattering of islands where they could replenish water, gather fruit, and hunt a wild boar or two. They only needed the slightest bit of wind to get there.

But the wind never came.

It was in the middle of windless day twelve when she left her cabin after checking her charts, ignoring the gnawing pain in her empty belly, only to find an empty deck. Not good. She went below deck and was greeted by a ring of her full crew outside of the galley.

Katalin swallowed hard at the sight, steeling herself. They looked desperate. Hungry. Accusing. She forced her right hand to remain casual at her side and not slide to the hilt of her cutlass.

Frog was closest to her, and the one they must have volunteered to speak. Unlike the others, he didn't look accusing, only apologetic. Admirable, for he was one of the burliest of the crew and had to have the worst stomach pains.

"We scraped every bit o' the ship, Cap'n, time and again. We cin find nothing, Cap'n. We cin catch nothin'." He shifted uncomfortably, his hand scratching the back of his head under his greying ponytail. "Nothin' Cap'n. We done everythin' we could, Cap'n Kat. We even waited. Days. But we can't no more, Cap'n. We only have one thing left aboard, Cap'n."

His eyes flickered down to Chomper standing next to her leg. The goat had wandered out of her cabin, following Katalin like always.

She stopped her hand from flickering to Chomper's black ear. She had known it for days. Chomper's milk had dried up a week ago, as had her usefulness on a ship. But Katalin had still held onto hope, still held onto the possibility of the slightest breeze sending them on their way.

But no breeze had come. No waves had rolled.

Her gaze swept over her crew, meeting each and every one of their eyes.

They weren't going to force her, she could see that. But they were judging her. Judging what her choice would be.

Chomper was no longer her goat. Chomper was now the last food they had. The last way they could survive.

She nodded.

A collective sigh hit the crowd.

"I cin take him to Cook, Cap'n," Frog said, stepping towards her.

"No. I do it." She looked down at the top of Chomper's head. The goat was busy nibbling on the bottom seam of Katalin's shirt. Katalin didn't push her away, as she usually would have done. Chomper could have her damn shirt if she wanted it.

Katalin's finger slid along the wiry hair at the back of Chomper's neck. She knew she didn't need to guide the goat, that Chomper would follow her regardless, but she needed her fingers on Chomper while the goat was still living and breathing.

One last time.

Chomper nudged the back of her leg as they started forward. The crowd split, and Katalin and Chomper moved forward into the galley.

Katalin closed the small arched door behind her.

She stood in the middle of the empty galley for minutes, hand still in the warmth of Chomper's fur, staring at the pots and knives.

There was no food in her belly, but that didn't stop the dry heaves she had to swallow at the thought of what she was to do. Her father's sudden voice echoed in her head.

No attachments.

Everything on board must serve the ship.

Serving the ship is the only thing that matters.

Katalin pulled the short knife, her father's knife, from the scabbard at her waist.

Serve the ship.

~ ~ ~

Jason stood in the back of the crowd. He could only catch glimpses of Katalin through the jostling men in front of him. He was taller than most of the men, but she was shorter than most, and the angle afforded him only brief snippets of her face through the bandanas and braids in his way.

But then the crowd split, and Katalin silently walked through the men, hand on Chomper's neck, and into the galley. The door closed softly behind her.

Jason's stomach rolled. Was he the only one that saw Katalin's face crumble at the mention of Chomper?

Sure, they were hungry. Days past hungry. But they could last a few days more. How could the crew not see that?

Minutes passed. Jason had never heard the crew as silent, as still, as they were in those moments.

The galley door swung open.

Katalin stepped from the galley, grimacing smile on her face. She lifted her bloody knife high above her head and thrust the tip of the steel into the wood along the door, leaving it protruding. "We eat, me hearties. We eat." Her voice was loud—too loud.

The crew bellowed their approval, and Katalin slipped by their fists raised in excitement, their hands slapping her shoulders in approval. By the time she moved through the crew and passed by Jason, he could see that her hard smile had started to fade.

The rest of the crew surged forward, dispersing, some into the galley, some above deck. But Jason turned, watching Katalin retreat up the stairs to her cabin, her head fallen.

Allowing distance, he followed her, only to see her hand slip twice on the latch to the door before she caught a solid hold on it and opened it, disappearing into its confines.

Jason backed down the stairs, watching the continued celebration in front of him, but could not stop his eyes from swinging back to the stairs up to the captain's quarters. Silently, he slipped from the crowd.

Stopping at the captain's door, he paused. A pause that only lasted a second before he rapped on the door. No answer. His knuckles hit the wood again.

"Aye. Come in." Katalin's voice sounded strained.

Jason opened the door, slipping in and closing it behind him.

Katalin stood, hands on her hips, chin tilted down even as she stared up at him, daggers in her red-rimmed eyes. "Yes? Your business?"

He took another step inward, closing the distance between the two of them in the cramped space. "Are you sound?"

"Of course. Why would I not be?"

His head cocked at the harsh snap in her voice. "It is acceptable to love something, Captain Kat. To care about others, even if the other is a goat."

She cackled a forced laugh, spinning from him, arms crossed atop her belly. "Captains do not love, Jase. It is an emotion that does not serve the ship. My father made sure I respected that fact long ago. Anyone—anything—can come and go from this vessel, and I am to care naught except for what they can contribute to the ship. How they can serve the ship. It was simply that goat's time to serve the ship. I do not care, beyond the bellies it can fill."

"No, Captain. I disagree. You care about your crew. You cared about Chomper."

She looked over her shoulder at him. "You do not get to disagree, Jase. You do not get an opinion. You have not lived this life. You do not know what you speak of. No attachments. Death is too easy on these waters. It rewards no one to love. No one."

She turned completely away from him as her hand jerked up to her face, and Jason could see her wiping her cheeks.

"What do I care of a stupid goat?" Her arm went down, tightening the hold she had across her stomach. A hold that was only partially successful at holding in the shaking her body was determined to do.

Jason silently shuffled forward, gently setting both of his hands on her shoulders. She twitched at the touch, but did not jerk out from the hold. "You work so hard not to be vulnerable, Katalin. But you are." He set his lips closer to her ear. "I see it. For all the blindness the others have for you, I see it."

She shook her head. "The others learned long ago to see nothing in me but my father. The lines he drew amongst his crew. He was harsh, but they knew exactly what was and what was not expected of them. They respect that. They do not look for cracks in me. They do not want to see them. Not like you seem to be intent on doing."

"I see the obvious in front of me. You hurting." His hands slipped down her arms, following the grip she had on herself. He pulled her back to his chest, tightening his hold. "Am I to turn away from your pain because there is some archaic code on your ship? Turn away when I can slip my arms around you? Help shoulder the burden on your heart?"

Her head went down. For a moment, her body shook uncontrolled. Uncontrolled except for her fingers which had gripped his forearms. Gripped them like a lifeline.

But then she took a deep breath.

And with the exhale of that deep breath, she growled, jerking away as she spun to him, her palm up between them. "Do not, Jase. I do not need this. I will have no attachments. Whatever game you play with me, it will not work."

"The only game I play is honest sympathy, Katalin."

"It is Captain." Her hands went back to her hips. "And I do not wish your sympathy, nor is it welcome aboard this vessel, boy."

Jason blinked at Katalin's sudden flash of rage, and his hands went up, palms to her. "I know you are under unyielding pressure, Captain, but not from me. I only want to help, I only want—"

"You do not understand a thing, boy," she said, venom in her voice. "There is no way you can. The only thing you can do for me now is leave."

Jason opened his mouth to counter, but then stopped when he saw her eyes—pain and rage and confusion brewing a dark storm in the blue—and instead gave a slight incline of his head. "As you wish."

He took a step backward to the door, grasping the handle behind him. "I assume you will not be eating?"

She shook her head, mouth tight.

"I will abstain as well, then." He opened the door, taking a step out.

"You gain no favors from me by starving, Jase," she said, her voice low, near breaking.

He stopped, eyes pinning hers. "I do it out of respect. Loyal goats are hard to come by, and yours deserved more than its end."

He moved out of the cabin, clicking the door closed after him.

# CHAPTER 5

The sails filled early in the morning three days later. Within eight hours, they were dropping anchors in a small cove at one of a chain of small, uninhabited islands.

The least important on the ship, Jason rode the last trip of the longboat into land, and by the time he set foot in the shallow blue waters, Cook already had a roaring fire near the beach and was dismantling a wild boar.

Barefoot, Jason stood in the shallows of the water, gentle waves rolling over his feet.

Land.

It was the first time he touched dry land in more than two years. He swayed, having a hard time not falling to his knees in gratitude. It was not land he could stay on, but it was land. A gift.

He afforded himself a moment to bend down, grabbing sand in his hands, clutching it to make sure it was real. Once fully assured of reality, he looked around. Green trees and jungle vines growing unhampered lined the beach, the ocean and wind the only thing saving the sand from the thick brush. Above the line of trees in front of him, Jason could see the island rose above, reaching a tall peak a good distance inland.

Already, the crew was milling about, the rum flowing freely and the worry of the windless days long forgotten. A tight group surrounded Cook, drool slipping down their chins as they watched the boar meat get spiked above the coals pulled from the roaring bonfire.

Jason caught sight of Katalin down the beach with another six of the crew, laughing as Poe sliced through a guava on a rock and handed her a slice. She bit into it, juice running down her chin.

She had refused to speak to Jason since the day of Chomper.
Avoided him at every turn. Would not meet his eyes. And refused
to leave her cabin at night.

Jason forced his eyes away from her.

No attachments. She demanded no attachments.

Her choice. Not his.

Jason set off with several of the crew to collect more guavas
and papayas, eating his fair share as he piled them high near
Cook.

Hours later, fat with fruit and boar meat, and having already
replenished countless water casks, Jason found himself picking his
way through the thick island foliage up the rocky mountainside.
Swearing at the hidden rocks tearing his bare feet, Jason's eyes
were on the ground when he stumbled into a clearing.

He had been near the stream following the sound of the
waterfall and knew it was close, but he was unprepared for the
scene before him when he looked up.

Water tumbled over a sheer rock ledge, dropping at least
triple the height of the Windrunner's main mast into a pool of
deep blue waters. The whole of it was framed by the lush greenery
of trees, vines, and flowers.

Utopia. Utopia with a naked woman swimming in the
middle of it.

Or what he assumed was a naked woman. A naked Katalin.

She wore no shirt—that he could tell as she stroked through
the water, her bare back glistening above the surface. And with
a quick scan along the edge of the pool, he spied her shirt, vest,
breeches, and bandana wet and lying flat, drying on a rock in the
sun's fading rays. Naked, indeed.

He watched her silently for minutes, knowing he should
make himself be known to her, yet resisting that very thing. Her
hair was free from its braids, and it was the first time Jason could
see its actual color. A wild mix of strawberry and light blond hair
flowed behind her.

Water splashed as she stopped her stroke, straightening
herself in the water. With a quick breath, she dove forward and

under. Her backside broke free of the water, her skin smooth and strong with lean muscle, before her legs followed suit—thighs, calves, heels, toes—kicking as she descended into the depths of the pool.

Moments passed with her deep in the water, only air bubbles to give her location, and Jason suddenly had to rearrange his member under his ragged slops. Land wasn't the only thing he hadn't touched in two years.

She broke free of the water with a gasp, and after a quick swipe of her face, she opened her eyes.

Opened them right at Jason.

The squeal that escaped her was not captain-like at all.

Jason stumbled as he tried to whip away, avoiding her eyes. There was no hiding the fact that he had just been gawking at her naked body like a twelve-year-old boy. After nearly bumbling to his knees, he found his footing and tilted his head, blatantly staring up at the vines growing over the tree in front of him.

"Do you not have your dry legs about you yet?"

"Dry legs, Captain?" Jason said into the thick air, not turning around.

"Versus sea legs, Jase," she said, and he could hear the humor in her voice.

"I guess I do not, Captain." He coughed, his gaze not leaving the trees. "I apologize. I did not mean to interrupt. I was sent up to find you. Everyone else is drunk and lazy with food and did not want to climb the mountain."

"I am needed?"

"Not really. The water casks are all replenished and the crew just wanted to know about the plan for moving on back out to the ship or setting up camp."

"You can turn around, Jase. Only my head is above water."

He turned slowly, head tilted downward as he tried to maintain the slightest bit of decorum. But he could still see her. She was treading water, hair wet and framing her face.

Hell. How could he not be attached?

She was beautiful. He had only seen her up close in moon- or lamp-light, and rarely without the bandana covering her head down to her eyebrows. He knew she was pretty, but this—even at this distance he could see he had grossly underestimated her features.

How had he never realized she possessed that much naked beauty?

He already liked her immensely. Admired her. Was enamored with her. Even if she wanted no attachments.

And now she looked like that.

The only thing he had wanted for the past two years was to get home. One goal. And now he was suddenly lusting after the damn captain of the ship he was trapped on.

"How deep are they into their cups?" Her voice rode along the water, loud, but smooth over the rush of the waterfall.

"Swimming."

Katalin rolled her eyes and swam closer. "Blimey. It sounds like they already made the decision for me. And they rightly know that."

"Do you need to get down there?"

"No." Her hand flipped out of the water, waving them off. "Since I am sure they are almost to a one drinking until fully passing out, I think they will be fine without me for the immediate future."

"You know your crew." Jason chuckled. "Half are already face-down in the sand. The tide was coming up, so I already dragged a couple up from the beach."

She laughed. "Be sure they thank you for it come the morrow."

"I do not think they realized how beautiful it was up here, or I would not have been sent." Even as he said it, Jason wasn't quite sure if he meant the raw nature or if he meant Katalin.

"Their loss. Every one of them could use a bath." Katalin's arms rolled back and forth, creating ripples as she treaded water. "Feel free to come in. I guard it well, but I will share my bar of soap." She pointed to the shore by her clothes. "You will end up smelling like tangerines, but there are worse things. And I do promise to not return the ogling that you did not have the good sense to disguise."

"I did not hide it well?"

"No, Jase. No, you did not."

"I apologize."

"It is forgiven." The smile on her face gave evidence that she was not nearly as upset as she had right to be, and that her anger at him from days earlier had dissipated.

Jason made sure his eyes stayed on hers and didn't veer downward. "Is it deep?"

"Deep?" She took a deep breath and threw her arms above her head, disappearing below the water. After a moment her head popped up. "Not too deep. Maybe another length of me. Why?"

"I do not swim."

Water sputtered in front of her mouth.

"What? Jase? You do not swim? Why on god's good earth not? You have been floating on a bloody ocean for years." She stroked through the water closer to him.

He crossed his arms over his chest, shaking his head. "I never learned. I can make it across shallow rivers and the like, as long as I can bounce off the bottom. And I can flounder about to keep my head above water, but not for very long. I tend to sink. I did not grow up near any deep or large bodies of water, so I never needed to learn, nor thought to."

"But the longboat—you went in the water—you saved me."

He shrugged. "That was necessary."

A splash flew up as she hit the water with a fist. "Any one of those bilge-sucking idiots could have jumped in and gotten me out, but they sent down the one that cannot swim." She shook her head, eyes to the blue sky. "I am thoroughly disgusted at my crew."

"I am fortunate it was me."

Her dark blue eyes flew to him. "You are? Why?"

"You talked to me because of it. Beyond that first night, you talked to me." Jason's posture eased, his arms falling to his sides. "I do not think you would have done so without my actions."

"I do not know if that is true."

"No? I watched you for a week never so much as look in my direction."

"You were watching me?"

"I was."

"Trying to figure out the oddity of me?"

"Yes. And also just watching you. Your mastery of the ship. The men. Of navigation. You are efficient, the men listen to you, and you are very good as captain. So much so that it is the only reason I can understand how a man might begin to not see you as a woman. That is what I saw that first week."

"Even with that, even with the last few weeks, you still see a woman, Jase, don't you?"

"I do. That is honestly what shines brightest in you. At least as far as I can see."

She nodded, grim, her head turning as her eyes washed over the thick greenery surrounding the pool. After a moment her gaze shifted back to him. "Be that as it may, you are to remove your clothes this instant. You are getting in this water and learning to swim."

Jason coughed, eyebrows arched. "My clothes? I would rather not."

"Why?"

"The crew is already suspicious of me, no matter that I have done everything and more than what is asked of me. I will not be found in a compromising situation with you."

"And I will not have a sailor on my crew that cannot swim." She started to stroke closer to him. "So strip down and get into the water. That you see me as a woman is your problem, not mine, Jase. That you cannot swim is my problem." She paused in her strokes to point. "There is a sandy shallow area by those three big rocks over there. That is where we will start. Captain's orders."

Jason sighed. "Captain's orders?"

"Captain's orders."

"Fine. But I will leave my trousers on."

She was already moving to the shallows and chuckled. "If it will help your sensibilities, Jase, then by all means, do so. But my clothes are drying right now and I do not get clean water very often, so I will be remaining as God gave me to this earth."

Jason walked over to the few boulders, stripping off his shirt as he eyed Katalin in the water. She had reached a point where she could stand and was waiting patiently, smirking. Thank the heavens she was still in water up to her neck.

With a shake of his head, Jason waded into the warm pool. His trousers immediately became waterlogged, dragging on his waist. But he wasn't about to admit that to Katalin. He needed to keep his slops on if he was to escape this whole debacle without compromising his captain.

He stopped a few arm lengths away from her, standing, the water up to his lower chest.

"What now?"

"You are going to have to come deeper. I want to see how you float, first."

He took a few more steps into the deeper water, still maintaining distance between them.

"Good. Now lean forward, kick your legs out, and float."

Jason leaned forward, kicking his legs, but they didn't rise to the surface. They stayed down, heavy weights against his float.

"Did you really just try?"

He rolled his eyes. "Yes."

"Hmmm." She moved forward, stopping right next to his arm. "Not very coordinated. You are a sinker. Try again, and I am going to push up on your stomach."

Jason's eyes focused upward on the tops of the trees. She was bloody naked and only a damn hair away from him.

At his side, her arm moved, searching in the water until her hand found his belly. Her palm went flat on the expanse.

"You have seen me stroke. Once you are horizontal, floating, start stroking and kicking. You need movement to keep afloat.

Take a deep breath for extra buoyancy, fill your lungs, and lean forward again."

If only to end the torture, Jason took a deep breath, leaning forward. Her hand pressed up on his belly, bringing his lower torso and legs in line with the water's break.

"Good. Now smooth stokes. Rhythm. That is all you need."

His arms lifted out of the water, stroking, and he was moving forward in short order.

"Good God, Jase." Katalin's sudden outburst echoed in the clearing and her hand jerked from his belly.

Jason immediately stopped movement, his feet sinking to the pool floor. On guard, he searched her face. "What? What is it?"

Her hands went on his arm, and she twisted herself around him in the water until she was facing his back.

"Your back, Jase. Good God."

Jason drew tall in the water, his face turning stony, mouth tight.

He had forgotten to hide his back.

"Jase, I had no idea—you mentioned the cat-o'-nine-tails—but this. I know the scar on your face, but this—this is beyond reason. What did they do to you?"

Her fingertips ran lightly over the ravaged skin, the ragged lines of raised scars on his mangled back. She trailed one particularly long line from above to below the water, straight down his back.

A statue, Jason did not move away from her, even though every muscle in him begged to. He stood, accepting her fingers on his skin. If only so she did not see him as weak. See the scars control him. He would not allow that. That pain would never control him again.

"Jase?"

He cleared his throat, body still frozen in place, but he did glance over his shoulder at her. She was staring slack-jawed at his back.

"I am sorry, Kat. I did not mean for your eyes to have to see the horror that is my back."

Her eyes whipped to his, fire burning in them. "Your back is not horror, Jase. Whoever did this to you—that is where the horror lies. That is where the demon exists. Not here." Her fingers slid along a line near his shoulder. "Not on you."

She shook her head, eyes closed. "How? Why? Why would anyone do this?"

"I did not always listen well on a ship where basic human respect lacked. But I was lucky. I survived. Many I knew along the way did not. I have watched men die in slow agony from the very same thing."

Head still shaking, she drew her hand away, circling his body until she stopped in front of him. "I would not consider that luck, Jason. That is beyond what anyone should have to endure."

His eyebrow arched at her use of his full name. "I have my life, Kat. I landed on your ship. There is luck in the unlucky."

"I do not understand how you cannot be bitter."

"I am. But I have had no time to wallow in it. It serves no purpose. Not now."

"Because your purpose is now what?"

His cheek with the scar flew up in a half-smile. "Serve the ship. Serve my captain."

She laughed—thick and warm and easy. "Is that so?"

"I am in the water, half-naked with a naked woman per my captain's orders. I would not be doing this on my own accord. My honor would not allow it."

"I do enjoy when you talk of honor, Jase. You have lived a very different life than I." She pushed off of the pool bottom, floating backward into deeper waters. "And speaking of the reason we are in the water, you also need to learn how to tread water."

She reached sufficient depth, and her arms began to move back and forth in smooth rhythm, keeping her afloat. "Come out here and mirror what I am doing."

Jason moved closer to her, following her lead and rolling his arms evenly through the water.

She smiled at him. "Perfect. Your head is barely bobbing. It is easy, is it not?"

"Yes." He nodded. "More than easy."

Her head cocked at him, eyes squinting. "You are not…"

She suddenly dove toward him, disappearing under the water. A moment passed, and then her head broke the surface right next to him.

Her hand was already in motion, sending a tall wave of water splashing into his face. "Bamboozler—you can still touch ground."

Jason laughed, hands up to block the onslaught of water she continued to send his way. He let her have her way for a few seconds. "Truce. Truce."

Several more splashes hit his cheeks before she halted, shaking her head in amused disgust at him. "Lying to your captain puts you on deck swabbing duty fairly quickly, Jase."

"I can imagine."

Both of her hands swung wide, starting another round of splashing.

Chuckling at the latest barrage, Jason moved forward into the wall of water, grabbing both of her forearms, stopping her.

Her laughter as she looked up was well worth the price of water on his face.

Loath to remove his fingers, he gripped her, shaking his head, a smile still lining his lips. "You do not have the slightest inclination of what you are doing, do you, Kat?"

"What?" Her nose crinkled. "I take offense. I know how to swim perfectly well."

"No. Doing to me."

Her eyes went wide. "What?"

His hands dropped from her arms. "Hell, Kat. You are naked. Touching me. Laughing. Beautiful. This is more than any man should be forced to bear."

She blinked hard at his words, her face turning serious. Her breath turning hot. "I did not know…"

"How can you not know what you do to me, Kat? How is it not more obvious than the ocean that has surrounded us for weeks?"

"If it is the same thing you do to me, Jase. To my stomach, to my chest, to my mind, then…then I know." She closed her eyes, dragging in a deep breath, water beading off her chest. "I know. But it has to be hidden. Denied. The crew…"

"Right now. Right here, Kat. The crew is absent. There is no one. Nothing to hide. Nothing to deny. Just us."

She opened her eyes, slowly nodding. "Just us."

His right forefinger went to a wet lock of hair at her temple, twisting it around his finger to his knuckle. "How has no man ever touched at you? Looked at you like a woman?"

"They know my father." Her eyes locked in his. "No man has ever dared to touch me."

He leaned in, his lips brushing the wet hair behind her ear. But not her skin. He didn't dare touch her skin. Not yet. "I do not know your father."

"I hope you never do," she said, her voice a whisper.

He pulled back, meeting her eyes. The blue in them had gone dark, smoky. "Tell me you want this, Kat."

"I…I do…but my father—"

"Hell, Kat, your father or not—life, limb—I do not give a damn." His hands went to her jawline, cupping her face, thumbs tracing her cheekbones. "Once I touch you, once my lips meet yours, I will not be able to stop. Ever. I will want you again and again. Your body. Your mind. That I know. Do not allow me to touch you, Katalin, if you ever intend to make me stop."

Her breath went rapid, her chest rising and falling out of the water. He could see her wavering, deciding. She closed her eyes, giving the slightest shake to her head.

Jason froze.

And then her eyes opened—the heat in them unmistakable. "I will not make you stop. I want this. I want you, Jason. I know nothing of this—I have no experience, even if I have heard everything an imaginative sailor could ever say on the act. But I know down to my soul that I want whatever you are going to do to me, Jason."

He refused to move for a very long second. Letting her words hang. Letting himself believe the words she spoke.

She didn't waver. Didn't take the words back. It was real.

Jason didn't waste another second before he encased her, finding her mouth, his hands going under her hair, down her back to press her body against his.

She met him, her lips delicate as she explored his touch, his mouth. He nudged her lips apart, surprised she followed his lead so completely, submitting to him. Submitting to what he was going to do to her.

She was captain on the ship. But here in this moment, she had willingly fallen under his control. He explored her mouth, plunging in, licking her teeth, her lips. Damn, she tasted good, the guava she had been eating earlier still sweet in her mouth.

Her hands went up, surrounding his neck, fingernails digging into the muscles on his shoulders. Without his guidance, her legs came up in the water, instinct sending them around his waist.

Straining against the cloth of his trousers, Jason shifted himself as she tightened her legs around him. Hell—so perfect. He was already nestled in the crux of her, her hips circling, matching the movement of his mouth on hers.

He pulled back, tugging her hair to expose her neck to his lips, his tongue. Her skin wet and slick, he moved up and down her neck, holding himself gentle, holding himself back from the ravaging he truly wanted to do.

His hands went down to her hips, setting her movements in an even wider circle until he could take no more.

Bringing his arms up, he wrapped her body as he started to walk to the shore. Stopping at the edge of the water, her legs still wrapped tightly about him, Jason went to his knees and laid her on the scrub of sand.

On top of her, he kissed her thoroughly before he untwined her legs and pulled up straight, ripping at the rope tied around his waist. His trousers dropped, but he didn't give it a thought for he was too engrossed in gazing at Katalin's nude body.

Her arms tanned from the sun, her skin eased into flawless creamy whiteness. Her breasts, solid, bigger than his hands, but not by too much. Both her arms and legs were lined with lean muscle, setting ridges that he had only seen on men into her skin. Beautiful in the power they held.

He shook his head, exhaling as his eyes ran up and down her body. "God, Katalin, you are gorgeous. Gorgeous everywhere. Your body. Your mind. Your heart."

She smiled, wicked as she looked up at him. "You are fascinating to look at as well, Jason." Her eyes flickered down to his crotch. The smile went wider.

Balanced on his knees, he nudged her legs apart as he move forward through the shallow water. His fingers entwined into her honey-red hair. "You do want this? Truly?"

"Truly." There wasn't a glimmer of doubt in her eyes as she looked at him. "I trust you, Jason. I want you—I want you taking care of me."

Growling, he bent over her, attacking her neck as his hand teased and tempted her body, moving downward, landing at her core. He sent two fingers into her folds, plying, awakening.

Her hips answered him before her low groan, thrusting upward at his touch, her body arching, begging him to continue the assault.

"Blimey, Jase—that—blimey—"

"Touch, me Kat. Hands on me." He hovered over her eyes, voice commanding as he watched the pleasure wash over her face. He was more than ready for her, but he needed her to touch him, to feel him straining, pulsating—to know exactly how much he wanted her.

Her hand was tentative as it moved from his waist, along the line of muscle on his belly, to the line of hair. Eyes wide, her fingers flipped, skimming along his skin, along his throbbing ridges. Gentle. Too gentle.

"Tight, Kat. Full."

She smiled, looking suddenly aware that she had just as much power over his pleasure, as he did on hers. Her hand slid fully around him, clamping as she ran her palm, her fingers, up and down.

"Hell, yes." The guttural mutter barely came out as Jason buried his face in her neck.

His tongue slipped out, tasting her skin once more as he moved along her jaw, landing on her mouth. She was pitching against him now, his fingers working her nubbin hard, then soft. Rhythmic.

She started to gasp against his mouth, arching away from him, hands moving to claw at his backside, and Jason took the moment. With a swift thrust, he slid into her, pushing through the thin membrane.

Her body cringed around him at the intrusion, gasping, and Jason slid partway out, allowing enough room for his fingers to invade her folds again, proving the pleasure could outweigh the pain.

"Jason—this—this—"

"Just let me do this, Kat. Just let it come."

She went silent, desperate, clawing at his back, writhing against him as she demanded her body reach what it thirsted for.

He slid deep into her again, thrusting against her pitching body as he nudged her folds into submission, into freeing the eruption they held fast to.

Screaming—swearing—Katalin jerked up from the water, both pushing and pulling Jason as her body went into spasms.

With shallow breath, Jason continued his onslaught, her body tightening around him in waves of contractions, gripping him tight, giving him no quarter. Water flew, and he could not slow himself.

He wanted to wait, to enjoy it, but he was no match for her screams, for her wet body tight to his, and he came, cursing the fates as the explosion commanded every muscle in his body.

Cursing the fates because he knew it for certain, in that instant, down to his soul.

He would give up anything to be with this woman.

Anything.

# CHAPTER 6

Her head snug on Jason's chest, Katalin watched the last rays of the day's sun dance along the tree-tops, rubbery green leaves rustling in the wind. The sky had already turned into a deep purple, giving way to the approaching grey of darkness.

Happiness. Such an odd emotion, she almost didn't recognize it. She was happy. Light.

She had never given much thought to the emotion—her life was what it was and she wasn't unhappy. She knew how to laugh, smile, but she had never, until this moment, realized what happiness truly could be.

A day ago she had been in the deepest despair, and now, now she was, of all things, happy.

Jason had done that, given her that, and she was loath to return to a world before it. So she had insisted they move out of the water and onto the small sandy patch near the edge of the pool, but no farther. She wanted to lie there, putting off for as long as possible going down the mountainside to join the others.

She knew the majority of the crew would already be passed out, and if they truly needed her, they would send someone up to get her.

Jason's fingers threaded through her hair, twisting and untwisting the locks. Listening to the steady thud of his heart in his chest, Katalin's lungs tightened. She hadn't wanted this, hadn't expected it, yet by the grace of the fates, this man fell into her life, and wanted her. Wanted her for her—not to captain a ship, not to be the dutiful daughter—wanted her because he liked her voice, liked what she did, liked who she was. A friend.

A friend that had become so much more.

"I am sorry, Kat."

"For what?"

"I did not wish to turn you into a fallen woman."

Katalin laughed, popping her head up so she could see his face. "Oh, you are serious."

"Yes. I behaved in an atrocious manner, seducing you. I was the furthest thing from honorable."

Katalin settled her cheek back on his chest, her fingers sliding low along the muscles lining his stomach. "Are you sure you were the one seducing, Jase?"

"What? You cannot mean..."

She smirked into his chest at the shock in his voice. "I did not intend for this to happen—far from it. But the second you appeared from the jungle—let us just say I did not mind your presence one bit. I knew full well what could happen, and I did nothing to veer the course of things."

"But you were an innocent and I ruined you."

Katalin chuckled. "An innocent? Ruined me? Hardly, Jase. What you did was far from ruining me. You forget that we come from very different worlds. I am the captain of a ship—do you truly think I, or anyone around me, save for my father, cares if I am ruined?"

"I care."

"You are the only one, Jase. The only one. I wanted—no—I needed every second of what you just did to me after the last fortnight." She tapped his chest. "Every second. I needed to not be a captain, just for a little spell. So you can let your honor rest for a moment."

"I do not think it can, but for your sake, Kat, I will try."

She hid her smile, keeping her mouth closed, and turned her head to kiss his chest.

"What truly is the color of your hair?" His voice, low, vibrating under her cheek, interrupted the quiet after a few minutes. "It was darker when it was wet, but now that it is dry—now I see it is complete randomness between honey and red-blond."

"It is odd. But has there been anything about me that you have not found odd?"

His hand slipped down her back, fingers finding her nude bottom and cupping it. The touch instantly sent shivers along her thighs into her core.

"I did not find your reaction to me when I was deep inside you at all odd. That was exactly as it should have been, Kat. You arching, begging, screaming. Perfectly correct in every way."

Katalin jabbed her fingers into his ribs, tickling. She was rewarded with a slight squirm from him.

"I am glad there was at least one thing you have not questioned about me."

"I only question because I want to understand," Jason said. "To know you. You are only odd to me because I have never experienced one such as you. And I find odd irresistible."

"You do realize I find you just as odd, Jase? You must remember I have been surrounded by sailors my whole life. They are all I have ever known, and they live with their own peculiarities."

"Then it is a good thing fate blew the winds the way it did. I do believe my life would have never been complete, had I not met you."

She retightened her hold on his torso. "My hair is darker right now because I have been at sea for several months and keep it covered. Usually it is lighter, almost all honey blond, because it is under the sun." She picked up a tendril draped on Jason's chest, looking at it. "But right now the red is showing itself."

"Whatever color it is, it is unique. Unique and beautiful, just like you."

She didn't lift her head from his chest, but did tilt her face so she could see him. "I am afraid I do not know what to say when you tell me such things, Jase. I have never had a friend, much less a man…"

"Telling you that you are beautiful?"

She nodded.

He smiled. "You do not need to say anything, Kat. Accept the compliment and thank your mother and father they produced the loveliness in you."

"My father told me once I look very much like my mother. There is very little in me that looks like him. He is a brute of a man."

"Well, then, he had the good sense not to pass any of his looks on to you. You are the furthest thing from a brute."

"Thank you for that, I think."

The sun rays disappeared completely, and she went silent. Jason followed, his hand still working through her hair, untangling snarls as he went.

Long, calm minutes passed as stars appeared above them.

His fingers working her hair stopped, cupping the back of her head before his low words slipped into the thick night air. "Heaven help me, Kat, I know you wanted no attachments. But I will be honest when I tell you I am damn well attached to you. Even if you want—demand—it to not be so. I do not know how you can ask me to not be attached to you."

Katalin shifted up, propping herself on her elbows so she could see his face. Even in the moonlight, she recognized the hurt, the bruised pride in his eyes.

"This is about what I said in my cabin?"

He nodded.

"What I said, what I did, Jase...those days adrift with no hope." She shook her head at the memory. "It is why I demanded no attachments. I did not do it to hurt you. If the winds had not caught sail…"

"What? What if they had not caught sail?"

She swallowed hard. "I have heard many tales of near end from starvation on ships. It is not kind. By all accounts it is a horrible, awful affair. The worst in humanity surfaces—let your imagination run. As captain, I would have taken the brunt of it."

Her palm went on his chest, fingers wide. "I needed you to not be attached to me. Chomper was attached to me, and you saw how that ended. That was about so much more than the hunger of the crew. That was about me as captain. Me sacrificing for the crew. And my fate was to be sealed with the fortune of the winds—yours was not. I could not take the chance of your survival, if there was to be a chance. After all you have been through, you are too close to returning to your beloved home. I could not take that from you. I could not put you in the jeopardy that was mine."

Jason sat up, moving Katalin with him, and then settled her in a straddle on his lap. His hands rested on her shoulders, fingers settling on her neck as he captured her eyes. "Do you not realize that—for some gut reason I cannot even define—I want so desperately to protect you that it hurts—physically hurts—in my chest when I cannot? That I cannot hold you, shelter you from all of the pressure the ship, the crew puts upon you."

"I am not a lady in need of protection, Jase."

"You are." His hands moved up to her face. "You are to me, and I will be damned if I am forced to deny that. Forced to deny what you mean to me. Forced to watch you burdened, even if that is what you choose."

She stiffened. "I choose no burdens I cannot handle, Jason."

"It is not a matter of whether or not you can handle the pressure, Kat. Of course you can. I have seen that with my very eyes. It is a matter of me not wanting to see you scared, or sad, or frustrated, or in danger. It is a matter of me wanting to see you safe. Happy. Smiling. Secure."

Her heart caught in her throat. No one had ever wanted to ease her burdens, ease her responsibilities. Not even her father.

It was foreign, and she couldn't stop the rush of emotion that manifested at Jason's words. She had never even acknowledged the pressures put upon her, much less thought of easing them, of sharing the burden.

Her chest tightened. What he wanted of her and what she was obligated to do were very different things. "I am still captain, Jase. I cannot remove myself from that responsibility. Not now. You have to understand that."

"I do. You are captain. But not here. Not in this moment. Here in front of me you are just Katalin. Just the woman that I would move heaven and earth for."

Her head swung back and forth, flummoxed. "I do not know how you did it, Jase, but you have made me want things I never dreamed existed. I was content in what my life was. But you have made me think about other possibilities of life."

"Is that bad?"

"It is terrifying."

"No. Do not be terrified. Not now." He moved forward, lips on hers as he spoke, the grizzled hairs on his chin rubbing her skin. "Right now, be happy. Feel everything I want for you. Feel how I want you."

He slid a hand down to the small of her back, pressing her hips tight to him. She could feel him pulsating and hard once more.

"You can save terrified for tomorrow, Kat. We can both save thinking for tomorrow. For the last two years I have been living in one moment, never knowing if I would make it to the next. I wasted too much energy worrying, and it never changed the next moment. Never. Never saved me from pain. Never saved me from humiliation. Life came as it saw fit, and I was just lucky to survive it."

He pulled back from her slightly, finding her eyes. "It is why these hours with you, these minutes, are the most precious. It is why I just want to hold you, be with you in this moment, Kat. No worrying on the morrow. Just be with me in this moment."

She opened her mouth to him, and in all honesty, her soul to his words. To his need to just be. Leaning forward, her lips met his, and everything slipped from her mind with ease. Her responsibilities. Her worries.

~ ~ ~

Worry reappeared early the next morning.

Even though Jason had bristled at the deception, he agreed with Katalin that anything between them had to be kept secret from the crew. That he had been willing to proudly announce them to the world had warmed Katalin's heart, but she had no idea how the crew would react to the lowest sailor on the ship sleeping with the captain.

She guessed it would not be good.

Especially because of their loyalty to her father. They would all protect her, life and limb, and if they saw Jason as the slightest threat to her, he would pay dearly.

By the time the crew gathered the fresh water, guavas, papayas, and a few boars, and transported it all back to the ship, dark clouds had already surrounded them. They set sail, hoping to make north of the storm, but another bank of clouds converged, trapping them in the middle of a wicked squall.

Late evening appeared before the roll of the ocean went smooth.

Except to bark orders his way, Katalin had to ignore Jason all day. That is, when she wasn't holding a petrified breath as her eyes flew across the ship, searching for his sopping form after every wave that crashed the deck.

Those moments, she refused to ignore him. Those moments made it all too real.

He meant too damn much to her.

But now she had him right where she needed him most, lying naked, belly down on her bed. He had slipped into her cabin unseen, exhausted, beaten by the ocean. But that had not deterred him from stripping off her clothes the moment the cabin door locked.

Katalin allowed herself this one change in habit—she almost always left the cabin door ajar, even while sleeping. But after the harshness of the day, she figured none of the crew would question her need for solitude and sleep.

Not that she had slept yet. Jason made sure of that. He had also made sure to silence—either with his hand or mouth—her screams. He didn't want himself to be found naked in her cabin any more than she did.

He swallowed the small soft rectangle of her bed, so rather than wedge herself in between him and the wall of the cabin, Katalin draped herself over his back. Her chin only coming up to

Jason's shoulder blades, she took a deep breath, inhaling the scent of his skin. Still salty from the waves crashing the deck.

Her forefinger traced the three lines of scars that were under her nose, slowly running across the ragged edges where smooth skin made way to raised pink damage. "These scars. I hate them and I adore them."

She shifted her head to kiss the closest scar, the low light from the lamp flickering shadows across his back.

Jason tightened under her, the hard muscles in his back straightening against her nude body. But he did not move his head or open his eyes.

"I do not know how you could possibly utter the word 'adore' in the same breath as 'scars.'"

Her hand slid up along his ribcage to his shoulder, where her fingers traced a slow dance along his jaw. "They brought you to me. So while I hate that you had pain. Despise that someone delivered these atrocities upon your body. They brought you to me. They made you take up arms against your captors. And that made me notice you. Bring you aboard. How can I do anything but adore them?"

His eyes finally opened to her, and he spun in the bed, lifting her up and resettling her on his chest. "I am going to have to reassess my opinion of them."

She hovered over him, her face above his. "You had to live through their creation, so you keep your opinions on them. But I—I get to adore them. Give them the honor they deserve. They are a part of you."

"Speaking of honor, my dear Kat." A smile played on his lips.

"Yes?"

"You need to stop calling me 'boy' when you are mad at me. I am at least five years your senior."

She thwapped his shoulder. "I only do it when you deserve it. And today you deserved it. Of course I was mad. You put yourself too damn close to the port railing at least six times today when we were pitching. You did not keep an eye on the ocean. I have seen too many men swept to sea to not be mad at where you were. You deserved every lashing of my tongue today. Especially now that I know you cannot swim."

"You taught me how to swim."

"You are a sinker. You proved it. I will not have you swept overboard, and if I have to call you 'boy' to make that happen, I will do just that."

"I was where I was needed on the ship." He fingered a tendril of her hair that had escaped the front of her braid. "Serve the ship, Captain Kat. Your rule."

"No. No Captain." Her head nudged back and forth as her lips landed on his chin. "Not when I am naked atop you. If anything, you are captain in these moments, Jase. It is already proven I will do anything you order me to."

"It is? Anything?"

She worked down along his jaw, her tongue tasting his neck. "Have I denied you any of your demands?"

He laughed. "No, not yet. But that must be because I have not been imaginative enough." His hand slipped under the back of her braid, half undone, and he ran his finger down the back center of her neck. A motion he knew sent shivers down her spine. "I need more time when I am not beaten and weary from the ocean. How long do we have?"

"Today slowed us down," Katalin said. "It will take a day, maybe longer, before the tear the main sail suffered today will be repaired. We will not be to top speed until then. Beyond that, it will be four days if the sails are full before we reach port."

Katalin watched as Jason's eyes went hooded, his smile disappearing.

"I meant until I had to disappear back below deck," he said, voice stilted. "Five days, Kat?"

"No. I see your face, Jase. No. Do not." She pushed herself up off of him, swinging her legs to hang along the side of the bed as she turned from him.

"We cannot ignore it, Kat. We will reach port and then what?" He sat up, hand on her shoulder. His voice had turned soft. "I have thought of nothing else since the waterfall."

"No."

He reached out, grasping her chin, gently turning her face to his. "I refuse to give you up, Katalin. I can imagine no other course."

"You need to return to your home, Jase. You will not be whole again until you do."

"Yes, yes, I do need to return home. But you make me whole, Kat. You. It has shocked me how completely and without mercy you have invaded my being."

"But your home."

He shook his head. "I do not know how I can trade one for the other, Kat. I need to return home, but I need you with me. Please, Kat, please come with me. At least consider it."

His words—the possibility—sank into her mind. She wanted to tell him. Tell him that she was terrified, deep in her chest, at the thought.

She had never lived in his world, only her father's. On the ship. On the island. Surrounded by the crew. It was what she knew—all she had ever known—and she was good at it. A loyal daughter. A fair captain.

What was she except a sailor? And once they were in Jason's world, what then? He hadn't been with his own people in years. What if all of this, their time together, would pale once his feet were back on solid land?

He wanted her now, she knew that, but in England? Would he still want her then, after he regained all that had been lost?

And what would happen to her father if she left? The crew?

The thought of leaving them. Terrifying.

She wanted to tell him all of that but could only manage meager words. "I do not think I can. I cannot abandon my father. The crew."

"Kat, please—"

She shook herself as she grabbed his wrist, bringing it to her lap. She looked down at his arm, staring at the light of the lantern flickering across his tanned skin. "Jason, I do not want to figure this out right now. I want to enjoy you. Enjoy us." She looked up, meeting his green eyes, the dark flecks in them smoky. "I know, deep down, you need to go back to England. And that is not where I can be. Not with who I am. What I have done." Her words choked off.

"I do not ask you to be anything you are not, Kat. I want you exactly as you are before me."

Her fingers went over his mouth, silencing his words. "Let me have this, Jase. These moments. Without talk of the future. Without worry of the future. I cannot enjoy this moment if I am consumed with the next. You were the one that told me we could do this. Leave worry for the future. Enjoy the moment. Please, just give me this, Jase."

He opened his mouth against her fingers, and Katalin could feel his breath exhale, ready to argue.

But then he stopped, closing his mouth to whatever he was about to say. He nodded, grabbing her hand, clutching it—a lifeline to a man who couldn't swim.

# CHAPTER 7

Two days passed, and Jason came to her every night, yet left before dawn for a hammock below. He spoke no more of her accompanying him to England.

It was in those dark, empty moments after he left—empty bed, empty cabin—that Katalin had begun to face the very real prospect of a life without Jason.

She didn't like how it felt.

Damn him for sneaking into her life, her mind, her heart. She had been content before him. But now she hadn't been content since he had touched her by the waterfall.

Her mind was consumed by him during the hours she had to deny his existence. And when she was with him, she was consumed with making the seconds last as long as possible. None of it brought contentment. None of it brought peace. Only a mad, wildly happy heart when they were to together, and conversely, a gnawing, raw heart when apart.

She ached for him during the day, sternly keeping her eyes off of him, and when he came to her, it was another world. A world of passion and acceptance and moments where she felt more herself than she ever had.

On the third night after he had left her cabin, it had only taken minutes before the walls of the room became suffocating. Looking to escape the sleeplessness, she escaped up to the quarterdeck and the darkness of the night.

Pup Joe was manning the wheel, eyes on the inky seas around them. The crew still called him "Pup" because he was the youngest of them. But he was still at least ten years her senior, so she had always just used his name. She stepped up next to him. "Ye can head below, Joe. I will take watch."

Joe jumped. She was quiet on the decks, and he wasn't the first she had surprised in the middle of the night.

"Ye sure, Cap'n? Me eyes be bare able to open it be so still an' quiet up 'ere, but I cin 'andle it."

"I be sure, Joe. Below deck fer ye."

He nodded, dragging his feet as he moved down from the quarterdeck, and disappeared below the main deck.

Katalin set the wheel and stepped away, reaching the starboard railing. She placed one forearm long across the wood, leaning forward as her eyes scanned the gentle swells closest to the ship. The tips of the waves glittered in the slim light from the lantern Joe had lit. The skies were still spotty in their overcast, several thick lines of clouds blocking most of the moonlight on the waters. To the east, though, Katalin could see a slew of stars shining, free from the cloud cover.

A pang of sadness hit her. As lonely as it was to be in her cabin without Jason, being up here without him—without his soft, deep voice filling her night, without his curiosity, without the way he looked at her—this was even worse. The night was black. Empty. The magic of a confidante, a friend, gone.

She shouldn't have sent Joe below deck so soon.

"I could not sleep, Kat."

His low voice reached her, both startling and tightening her chest. She could not turn around right away, instead, had to draw a deep breath to settle her body and mind.

Control regained, she drew straight and spun to him. He stood at the edge of the quarterdeck, shirtless, his rope-tied slops casual about his hips. Barefoot as usual, even though she had procured boots for him days ago.

Arms along his sides, his right hand clenched and unclenched. In the low light he looked unsure of approaching her. Ridiculous, for the things he had done to her body just hours ago.

"You are not alone," she said, and swore at herself that her voice wasn't as strong as it should have been.

He took a hesitant step toward her. Stopped. Then shook his head, swiftly closing the distance between them. He halted just before her, his arms still at his sides.

He looked down at her, eyes searching hers. Serious eyes. Eyes that were trying to invade her soul.

"Marry me, Kat. Marry me. I want you as my wife. You are already mine. Mine where it matters." Eyes not leaving hers, he reached out and grabbed her left hand, bringing it up to spread her palm across his heart. "But that is not enough. I want you as my wife. Before God and man."

Katalin blinked hard, trying not to sway as she took in his words. She had not expected this. "What?"

"I believe I made a grievous error days ago. I do not think I was direct in my intentions when I asked you to be with me. That was my mistake. It was what I was thinking, marriage, but I was not direct in my words. I was still coming to terms with it myself."

His left hand came up, settling along her neck. "Make no mistake, Katalin, marriage is what I intended when I asked to be with you. I need you as my wife. And I also never want anyone to give you less than all of the respect you deserve."

Her breath held deep in her chest, Katalin could barely form words. But her hand tightened on his chest. "Jason, it was never about marriage. It is about my father, the ship."

"Captain any damn ship you want to, Kat, I refuse to leave your side. And if that means I do not return to England immediately—I will do it. Someday I will convince you to accompany me there, but until then, I will only be by your side. I will not lose you to your father or the ship for my own selfish reasons—just because I wish to return to my land."

Her head shook. "I do not want to trap you, Jason. In all honesty, you have not seen a woman in two years. I have been rather convenient. You may feel very different once we reach port."

A slow smile, heated, spread across his face. "The only thing that has been convenient about you, Kat, is how our bodies fit so perfectly together. And I will be brutally honest—I sure as hell want to trap you. I want—need—you close to my heart, my body. On land. On sea. I have come to the conclusion that it does not matter where. It only matters that my soul knows we are to be one. That will never change."

She could not turn from him, but her head tilted back, eyes to the night sky. Clouds cleared, stars now twinkled above them. Consistent stars—always the same, always her guide.

But what purpose was a guide if she never needed it? If everything remained the same? If she stayed on these waters she knew for the rest of her life, what purpose did that guide serve? What would happen to her if she didn't take this chance, this happiness that was hers when she was with Jason?

All she had to do was accept it.

Her eyes dropped to his. "I cannot keep you from the land you love, Jase. I refuse to. It is part of who you are. It is engrained so deeply within you it would be a sin to keep you from it."

"But Kat—"

Her right hand joined her left on his chest, both palms flattening over his heart. "Yes. Yes I will marry you, Jason. I love you, and I will not keep you from your home."

"You will come with me?"

"Yes. I will go to your home with you, your land. I need to see, feel why it is so important to you."

His arms clamped around her, steel against her softness, and he lifted her. Arms wedged in front of her, Katalin couldn't move, couldn't even look up at him he had her so completely buried.

But it was perfect. All she wanted was to keep her cheek on his bare chest, breathing in his essence. His essence giving her strength against the future. Whatever the future would hold.

He spun, letting his hold loosen as he set her feet on the deck. He leaned back against the railing, legs spreading as he kept her snuggled close to him.

The smile on his face, and everything she saw in his eyes— gratefulness, love, passion, awe—took away any last doubts she had.

Jason cleared his throat. "Now that I can breathe, I do have to disclose, so it does not come back to haunt me—when I said you are perfect as you are—I meant it—except for one thing."

Her eyebrow cocked. "Which is?"

"You will, unfortunately, need to be out of breeches and in a proper dress, you realize? Once we get to England, that is. Society's rules, not mine. I would love to have you always in breeches."

She laughed, then gave a dramatic sigh. "Yes, I had considered it, and I must admit it almost broke the deal."

Groaning, he squeezed her, producing a shriek. But in the next motion he made up for it, pulling her onto him and kissing her soft and slow, like he had all day just to adore her lips.

When they broke, it took moments and deep breaths to gain control against the fire in her core, begging for him to take her. The sun would be rising too soon to get that in.

"There is an island we will be passing tomorrow," she said. "It is slightly out of the way, but I can make an excuse for a stop there, even though the crew is desperate to get to port. We have friends there, including a man of God—self-proclaimed, though I doubt that matters. He has known me and my father since we arrived in these waters. He has always been good to me. He can marry us. I do not wish to have to convince my father of our plan to marry—he will put up too many barriers. And it is not his choice. It is mine. But if we do not marry before we reach Snakehorn, he will make it his choice."

Jason's jaw took on a hard line. "I am not afraid of your father, Katalin. I would prefer to have his blessing. It is the honorable way."

"As would I. But he is much more likely to bless it if it is already done. I do not want to give him a chance to give me an ultimatum between choosing you or him. Please, Jase, just let it be this way."

After a moment of thought, of watching her face, he nodded. "Your desire is my command, Captain."

She smiled. "Thank you, my captain."

~~~

Katalin stepped from the small room in the back of the adobe church. She smoothed down the skirt of the fine silk dress, hued in the lightest peach. It was a nervous motion, she knew, but Jason had never seen her in a dress. Naked, yes, but never in a dress.

Jules, the ever-fussing wife of Pastor Robert, had dragged Katalin to the back room the moment she realized what was about to happen. She wasn't about to allow Katalin to wed in her ship clothes.

Jules had bustled through a short rack of dresses hanging in the back room before pulling one and holding it up to Katalin's body to size it. Not allowing Katalin to protest, Jules had her in the dress and was freeing her hair from their braids before Katalin knew what was happening. She wondered with curiosity whether Jules kept the selection of gowns there for just the purpose of hasty weddings.

Stepping from the back room into the small church, Katalin saw it was empty save for the sack of booty they had brought with them for Pastor Robert and the needy. The booty had been her excuse to stop at the island, and once she had made it to shore with half the crew and asked for brawn to carry it, the crew had happily volunteered Jason for the job, as she guessed they would. None of them wanted to hike up the side of a hot mountain to the church. They all liked sitting and drinking too much, now that they were so close to home.

Katalin walked to the main door, finding Jason and Pastor Robert chatting in the sunlight beating down on the front of the orange-clay church. Jason's rugged handsomeness stood up to the bright sunlight, and he looked as proper as proper could be with only the rogue clothes she could find on the ship. Though tight in the arms and shoulders, the dark blue jacket she procured fit him well enough over his white linen shirt, still wide open at his chest. He had on the boots she had found for him days ago, the black leather stretching up over his calves, giving a sense of polish over the bare feet she always saw him in.

Handsome. Handsome and hers.

She stepped forward to join them, and Jason turned to her.

She watched as his eyes lit up upon seeing her, and then his jaw slowly slid downward as he scanned her body. She had left her braids half-in, her hair pulled off her face, the braids crowning her head until the locks loosened and fell in waves down her back. She smoothed her skirts again, but her nervousness had dissipated. Jason's reaction told her he found her pleasing in a dress. So much so, that he looked as though he wanted to tear the gown from her body—in a good way. A very, very good way.

"Kat…" he said.

"Yes?"

Pastor Robert stepped away from them, disappearing into the church and giving them a moment together.

Jason grabbed her hands. "I knew you were beautiful, Kat, but this…this is beyond."

"The dress fits well enough?"

"More than." His hand came up, swiping his knuckles gently from her temple to her chin. "If I did not know better, Katalin, I would pin you as a proper English lady."

She smiled. "I can be a lot of things, Jase. But right now, I only want to be one thing."

"What? Whatever you want, I will make it happen."

"Make me your wife."

His beaming smile came easy. "Done."

Pastor Robert stepped back into the open air. "Jules is ready. I am ready." He looked directly to Katalin. "Dear child, are you ready?"

"Yes. Thank you, Pastor Robert."

With a nod, the pastor turned, walking into the small church and to the altar as he muttered loud enough for Katalin to hear. "May your father forgive me for doing this without his blessing."

Before they had arrived at the church, Jason had urged her to not necessarily lie, but to at least avoid the topic with the pastor of her father being unaware of the wedding. But that was the first question Pastor Robert asked of her, and Katalin fessed to the truth immediately. She wasn't about to lie to a man of God. Especially on her wedding day.

Jason leaned down to whisper in her ear as they followed the pastor. "I was mourning what will be the absence of your breeches in the future, but now, seeing you like this, I do not believe I will ever miss them again."

"No?" she whispered back.

"No. Aside from the fact that you are gorgeous and the gown only exaggerates that fact, there is much easier access for me under your skirts."

She hid a laugh as she swatted him.

They halted, arm in arm, hand in hand at the altar.

Within moments, they were married.

~ ~ ~

The most agonizing part of the wedding was keeping it a secret from the crew.

They had decided to hide their vows until they reached her father's island. After every voyage, her father and the crew feasted together, before everyone dispersed to their respective homes. Some lived on her father's island, some had settled on islands nearby.

It had been that way since she was a little girl and her father had purchased his island. A feast, a celebration of victory, and then on to the settling of life between voyages. There would be no better time to tell everyone about the marriage.

Besides, Katalin hoped that the more crew that were gathered around, the better her father—all of them—would take the news.

So it was late into the darkness before Jason could join Katalin on their wedding night. It had been an agonizing day after they had rejoined the crew following the wedding, as Jason and Katalin had had to maintain more than enough distance from one another.

And it was killing Katalin.

Deep in the darkness, when Jason finally entered her cabin, locking the door behind him, she could tell it was killing him as well.

She was naked, waiting for him, and flew to her feet the moment he stepped foot through the door.

To her in two strides, he seized her, without word, one arm pulling her upward to his mouth, the other hand thick in her hair she had let down.

He already pulsated hard on her belly, ready and straining for her as his mouth captured hers, ravaging her lips. He pushed her backward, setting her on the navigation table and her sexton clattered to the floor as he pulled the rope loose from his waist.

Katalin shoved up on his shirt as his trousers dropped, and he joined her, skin on skin, his mouth hungry on her neck.

Her legs wide and already straddling him, she pulled on his hips, driving him close to her, her body arching in its need for him. But he stopped, the tip of him nudging the vastness that needed to be filled. He drew up, grabbing her face, searching for her eyes.

A slow smile formed across his face, the languidness of it fighting the shaking muscles, the urgent strain Katalin could feel in his body. His control of himself, of her, made her breath catch.

His voice rough, eyes searching her soul, his thumb dragged along her lower lip. "My wife."

Katalin took a deep breath, battling against her own tremors. "My husband."

It was all he needed.

With a growl, he pushed forward, deep into her as his mouth covered hers. His hands went under her backside, holding her solid against his hard thrusts, until it was too much, and he lifted her fully from the table.

Gripping her hips, he brought her up and down on his shaft, sliding her slowly along him until her nails were deep into his shoulders, her teeth biting the skin on his neck in effort to not scream.

Their bodies tight together, Katalin swiveled her hips in agony, trying to take some control back, but instead, only driving herself into a wicked pace. A pace that had her gasping for breath until she could take no more. Her core swelled and then pitched into spasms, her muscles contracting with the hot release encapsulating her body.

Jason held on, admirably, but was far from unaffected, and could only give her seconds before he lifted her hips until he was almost free of her. And then he pounded himself deeper into her core, again and again, until a raw growl escaped as his body clenched, filling her.

He stood solid as their bodies throbbed together, Katalin's limbs wrapped around him. Her chin hanging over his shoulder, hot skin sticking on hot skin, Katalin fought to catch her breath.

Jase turned his head, whispering into the hair at her neck. "I do not think I can hide this—us—for another hour, much less two more days, Kat. All I want to do is touch you. Lock us in a room for a week. Even though I do not think a week would sate me. Maybe two."

She captured enough breath to speak, turning her head to rest on the muscle at the end of his shoulder. Her hand curled up along the back of his head. "Two days, Jase. Only two. We can make it. Two days is not so long."

"Two days is an eternity. We can make it, but the need to shout from the crow's nest that you are mine, that I am the happiest man alive, threatens my very sanity. By the grace of the fates, you are my wife, finally, and I want the whole damn world to know it."

"That enthusiasm will do you well when we are in front of my father. You are as tall as he, but not nearly as wide—I do not wish the scene to come to blows."

Jason bristled. "I am not afraid of your father, Kat."

"I know. I love that about you. Aside from me, you are the only other person I know that is not afraid of him. Of course, you do not know him."

"All I need to know of him is that he produced you." He peeled her arm off his shoulder, setting her onto the table and leaning back to let air flow between their chests. He cupped her face. "The most beautiful, smart, kind, witty—all words that do not do you justice—woman I have ever met. It is something I will forever be indebted to him for."

Katalin smirked. "If you turn that charm on him, he is sure to cut your throat. But I like it."

"Believe me when I tell you, announcing to your father that we are married will be fine. All will be well. There is no other course of action. We would not be together now were that not to be so. Fate would not be so cruel." He kissed her, logic secure, and then pulled up. "Two days? Two days and you are all mine, Kat?"

Katalin nodded, beaming. "Two days. That is all. It is almost here."

# CHAPTER 8

Fate did, indeed, possess that cruelty.

Cruelty that came in the form of a clipper ripping through the waves early the next morning, fast in pursuit, its guns at the ready.

By the time Clegg had spotted the ship from the crow's nest, it was already clipping along at a speed double the leisurely pace the Windrunner was maintaining. A pace that Katalin scrambled the crew to match, but it did little good. The Windrunner could not fill sails fast enough.

It only took an hour for the ship to catch them.

Spanish flag flying high, its intent became clear with the first cannonball.

Jason was below deck when the call for all-hands on deck came. But before he could make it to the scramble happening above deck, Poe pulled him back below.

"We be needin' yer brawn below, matey. The balls be heavy."

Dammit. Fist hard in his thigh, Jason followed Poe. All he needed to do was get to Katalin, but if he could help drive the Spaniards off before they even reached the Windrunner, he had to do it.

Swearing under his breath, Jason went down and started hauling cannonballs. He hauled and loaded and lit fuses for what seemed an eternity. Until—even through the smoke stinging his eyes and the ringing in his ears—he could hear the second the Spaniards breached the ship.

Just before gunshots started echoing below deck, he heard Katalin booming, loud and clear. "No surrender, mateys. No surrender."

His gut dropped.

Clashing metal, shots, and screams filled the air seconds later.

Jason dropped the cannonball he held and raced up to the top deck.

Through the smoke of gunpowder and bodies clashing, he found Katalin within seconds. Alone on the quarterdeck, she held the wheel, still turning hard against the pull of the ropes attached to the Spanish ship.

Jason saw the man flying through the air on a loose rope from the enemy ship before Katalin did, and it set his feet in motion. He broke into a run, dodging swinging cutlasses as he made his way aft.

Eyes not veering from his wife, his heart stopped as Katalin spun, off-guard, right before the man kicked her with a full swing straight in the chest.

She went flying.

Landing on her side, she pulled her cutlass as she absorbed the impact.

Lucky. The brute landed flat on his back and he was gasping for breath after knocking his own wind out.

Up the steps to the quarterdeck, Jason flashed past Katalin before she popped to her feet.

In an instant, he kicked the brute's sword out of hand and then picked him up at the scruff, dragging him to the back rail. With a heave, he shoved the man over the railing, plunging him into the ocean.

Jason spun to Katalin, grabbing the sword he had kicked from the man as he advanced on her. "Dammit, Kat, get somewhere safe."

"We are on a bloody ship, Jase. There is nowhere safe."

"Then get me a damn barrel to stuff you in," he growled, stopping in front of her, heaving a scowl at her.

"This is not my first time in battle, Jase." She took his scowl and glared up at him, her toes touching his, not moving from his anger. "I know what I am doing. You have seen it yourself. I am good."

He grabbed her upper arm. "Dammit, Kat, I could give a bloody damn if you are good or not. I need you safe."

A pistol shot whizzed past them, tearing up wood on the deck next to Katalin's feet.

Her head whipped down, then back up just as quickly. "I am safest fighting, Jase. That, I can control." She ripped her arm from his grasp and took a step away from him. "I refuse to be dead weight, or God-forbid, something to protect. I am the damn captain of this ship and I will not cower."

Backing from him, she stopped at the top step down from the quarterdeck. She had to shout to be heard over the clash of the battle. "So use that steel and join me, or stay out of my way, Jase. Either way, they are not going to take us."

She jumped to the main deck, not bothering with the stairs, landing and attacking the first Spaniard in front of her.

"Bloody fucking hell, Kat," Jason swore after her, but his voice was lost to the battle din.

He burst down to the main deck, and immediately a sword flew at his head. He blocked it with the steel in his hand, and was grateful the cutlass didn't crumble. Good Spanish steel.

The attacker swung the dagger in his other hand, and Jason jumped back, running into the side of the wall below the quarterdeck. It gave him the stability he needed as the Windrunner rocked into the Spanish ship, and he sprung, leg kicking the stomach of the man in front of him.

The man dropped, losing both weapons, and Jason straddled him, punching him out before he could crawl to the blades.

Jason looked up, needing to find Katalin, searching the scene in front of him.

Seconds slowed as he took it in. Arms and limbs and steel and guns were flying fast in the haze of exploding gunpowder blanketing the ship.

The Spaniards had swarmed the deck, the front line of the Windrunner crew only managing to slice away five rope lines from the Spanish ship before they were engaged in battle.

Blood splattered wide, and Jason realized the Spaniards overpowered them three to one. The Windrunner crew battled with more brawn and bravery than he had ever seen on the seas.

And with Katalin's full crew, maybe...maybe they would have stood a chance.

But this. This was to be a massacre.

And then he found Katalin.

She fired a pistol at one Spaniard just before swinging wide with her cutlass at another. There was a third coming at her back.

Ducking a dagger swinging at his head, Jason tore across the deck, shoving bodies as he went.

But the steel sliced through her arm before he could reach her.

The force of the swipe sent her crashing to the deck, her cutlass flying out of her reach.

Jason was over her, his legs straddling her in two steps.

"Throw down your arms, mateys, we surrender." His deep baritone thundered over the clashes of steel, guns and screams.

Jason solidified his stance over her, sword in-hand, even as he was surrounded. His eyes flickered to each of the three around him. Surrender or not, they would have to kill him to get to Katalin again.

But then the men in battle closest to him stilled.

"We surrender," he yelled again, his voice reaching all those still engaged. "We surrender, and ask for quarter."

"No, we fight, Jase. We fight." Katalin hit his leg, her tone still holding authority.

He could feel her scrambling under him, but there was nowhere for her to go. They were surrounded by sharp tips of steel.

"Do not do this, Jase. No surrender."

Jason heard her, but he refused to look down at her.

"We surrender, mateys. The Windrunner surrenders." His voice left no possibility to be unheard or denied.

The deck went silent.

One by one, steel clattered to the deck.

"No, Jase. No. Do not do this," her voice hissed as she pushed herself to sitting, grabbing her bleeding arm.

He dared a look down at her, nothing but raw power and full command on his face. "Silence, wench."

She recoiled as if he had struck her. It was what Jason intended, and it worked. She had to be quiet.

His eyes on hers, he watched as she swayed, her eyes going glassy as the blood from her arm ran through her fingers holding the wound. Thick red streams trailed down her wrist, down her forearm until the blood pooled at the edge of her white linen shirt.

It churned his stomach.

He wanted nothing more than to bend to her. Hold her. Take her pain.

But he could not.

He took his eyes off her, moving a step to block the sightline to Katalin from the Spaniard closest to her.

He could let no one know she was captain. Let no one know she was the most valuable thing on this ship.

Drawing all attention, he bellowed, "Where be your captain?"

It took seconds before bodies started to move, making way for a stout man bustling through the crowd. The Spaniard sheathed his thick cutlass, crossing his arms as he stopped in front of Jason.

"Ye be the one to call surrender?"

Jason could only discern this was the captain before him. He nodded, tossing his sword to the deck. "I am."

"Ye be the captain of the Windrunner?"

Jason did not hesitate. "I am."

The man chuckled. "Well then, we be havin' both quarter, and the kiss o' the gunner's daughter fer ye, ye blaggard."

# CHAPTER 9

The coughing woke Katalin up. She had vague snippets in her mind of being with the crew in the hold of a ship, of being tossed into a dank cell, but she knew she hadn't been truly lucid for days. The last thing she fully remembered was Jason above her, surrendering the Windrunner.

She had lost too much blood to maintain consciousness, even though she recalled Frog, desperate above her, trying to quell the blood flow soon after she passed out the first time.

She cracked her eyes open. The rough cough filtered through the wet stone wall in front of her nose.

Pushing herself up, she propped her forehead on the bumpy grey stone, closing her eyes.

The cough came once more.

Her eyes flew open. "Ja…Jason?" She banged on the stone, bruising her palm as her voice came back to her. "Jason? Jason?"

Breath held, she pressed her ear to the stone. Seconds passed.

"Kat? Katalin—is that you?" His voice was muffled. Muffled, but she could hear it.

"Jase? Truly it is you? I thought…I thought…" She couldn't force her worst fear into actual words.

"I know, Kat."

His words stopped. Her hand flew up to the wall, fingernails curling against the rock. "Jase?"

"I am here, Kat…I feared—hell—I feared the same with you. Your arm—has the bleeding stopped? Are you injured elsewhere?"

"The blood?" She looked down at her bare upper left arm, where the sleeve had long since been ripped away. In the ray of light from a small open rectangle in the stone cell she was in, she found the wound, her fingers slipping along the dried blood, following the long gash in her skin. "It is scabbed. No more flowing blood."

The numbness of sleep was wearing off, and the small movements sent every bruised muscle in Katalin's body into screaming pain. She leaned against the stone for support. "Jase... Jase, I do not know what they did to me. I just awoke. My entire body, it is in pain."

"Can you move? Is anything broken?"

Katalin took assessment of her limbs, fighting every breath that sent a sharp pain into her side. "I think I am fine—my rib." She eased air into her lungs, trying not to move her chest. It helped. "It is nothing I will not survive."

She could hear him swear.

"Jason, you...did they...did they..." She stopped, the horror she was thinking stealing her words.

"Yes."

His one word said volumes, and Katalin gasped. The deep breath sliced a sharp pain into her side. But it was nothing against the pain Jason must be in.

His back.

Shredded skin upon what was already there.

She fought the sudden nausea that hit her.

"How many did we lose, Kat? The crew? I have not seen any of them. They kept me away from them—from you."

It took her a moment to collect herself enough to answer. All she could see in her mind were images of Jason's bloody back. Of a whip cracking his skin.

She shook the chill from her spine.

"I have been in and out. I do not remember much. I know Clegg and Joe and Red did not survive. But that is all I know."

"I tried, Kat. I tried to stop it before...God rest their souls. I tried."

"No. It is not your fault, Jason. I did it. I should have..." She cut herself off, searching for what, she wasn't sure. "There were not enough of us. I should have known. I should have..."

"You did what you needed to, Kat. Do not question it."

She nodded, eyes closed. She failed the ship. Failed the crew. Failed Jason. Failed herself.

"Kat?"

Hand on her forehead, she cleared her throat. "I am here."

"Kat, there is a hole in this stone toward the outside wall."

Katalin propped herself against the wall, crawling painfully along the dripping stone, knees squishing on muck she'd rather not think about. Fingers running over the rock, she searched in the dim light. She stopped when she saw the hole. Only a finger's width wide.

"Yes. I see it."

She stuck her right pointer finger through the hole.

Within a moment, she could feel Jason's fingertip touch hers.

Overwhelmed at the slightest flicker of his touch, her heart crumbled.

Tears slid down her face as she froze for the longest moment, closing her eyes and taking every ounce of the strength that vibrated from his skin to hers.

"Forgive me, Kat. I failed you. One bloody day as my wife, and I did not protect you. I will never forgive myself."

"No. I would not let you protect me, Jase. The fault is not yours. You saved me."

"The moment you do not let me protect you is the exact moment when I should be protecting you the most, Kat."

Katalin fell silent. She couldn't make this better for him. She couldn't make it better for her. They were stuck.

Prisoners. Apart.

She let all this happen. If she hadn't given Roland the Rosewater and part of the crew, they could have defended themselves. If she had spied the Spanish ship earlier, they would have outrun it. If she hadn't stopped on the island to marry Jason, they would be in safe waters by now.

The tip of her finger moved against his. "What is going to happen to us, Jase?"

"I do not know, Kat. I do not know. I have never been captured for piracy before."

She could hear how heavy his voice was. "Nor have I."

"They did not dispose of us right away, they threw us in here," he said. "So I suspect we are to be tried for piracy."

"I was only awake for a few minutes here and there with the crew, Jason. But they know the code. I made them swear it. And all will abide by it. None will give you up as captain. Especially because you are not. We all go down before we let one fall for all."

He did not respond, not that she expected him to. Weighing what was to be certain death curtailed both of their words.

His voice, low, raw, cut into her thoughts. "I will wait, Kat."

"Wait?"

"Here on earth. This life or in the next life. I will wait for you. You will join me eventually, and we will be together again. Do not lose faith in that."

She thought her body too weak to produce more tears, to produce sobs, but they ravished her chest, unyielding at his words.

She shoved her finger tighter into the hole, the stone cutting into the delicate skin between her fingers.

"Kat?"

She swallowed a sob, trying to find words for him. It took long moments. "I will keep faith, Jase. I promise. I will keep faith."

For twenty-nine days, every day, Jason made that vow to her.

He would wait. In the morning. In the afternoon. In the evening. The vow.

He would wait. Until the next life.

～～～

The door creaking loudly woke him, and for a moment, Jason thought it was the door to his cell. For four weeks, he had sat alone in this filthy box, the only comfort being able to touch Katalin's finger through the hole in the stone. Hear her voice.

Jason sat up from the matted hay, groggy, his eyes immediately going to the small line between his cell and Katalin's.

It wasn't until he heard the screams that he realized his wooden cell door was still closed and that the screams came from the cell next to him.

Katalin.

His heart dropped, seizing his breath.

No. Not Katalin.

"Jason—no, no—Jason—no, no, no—please no!" Her voice screeched in terror. Pure terror. "Jason! Jason! Jason!"

Flesh hitting flesh. Grunts. She was fighting. Fighting hard. Fighting even as she screamed for him.

He ran to his door, roaring for Katalin, pounding on the wood. Pounding until blood from his fists flew, splattering the stone walls, disappearing into the dark wood grain of the door.

Her screams stopped.

"Katalin!"

No sound.

"Katalin!"

Silence.

Then, in the silence, he could hear the soft thud of a cell door close.

He collapsed against the wood, all hope—his love—lost.

~ ~ ~

He had cared nothing, seen nothing, heard nothing, since the moment Katalin was dragged from her cell.

It had been a day, maybe more, and then he had been hauled from his cell into a room large enough for a small crowd. The heat of the people intensified the steam in the building, even with a row of windows propped open along one wall. The windows only partly caught the breeze from the sparkling bay of water Jason could see from where the building was situated.

Set on a chair up to a wooden table, pistol at his back, Jason faced a thin old man in military regalia and full white wig, sitting behind his own table atop a slightly elevated stage.

A trial. Or at least the farce of one.

For the next two days, Jason sat for hours, not listening, not speaking, only searching the windows for signs of Katalin.

One by one on those two days, each of the Windrunner crew that survived the battle was brought forth, plopped onto a chair next the judge, and each was questioned.

And one by one, they answered every question according to a code Jason only partly understood. Katalin was right in her confidence of the men. Every answer, every syllable each of them gave had been rehearsed at some point and was exactly the same as the last man's. Words that were riddled and gave the judge exactly no information.

The last question every man was asked as the judge pointed to Jason, "Is that man your captain?"

"Nay," each would answer. "That man is not me captain. I am me captain."

The code.

Far into the second day, it suddenly occurred to Jason that the judge was growing increasingly agitated at the lack of evidence against him. Sweat slid down the judge's brow as his questioning became more pointed, more bitter, more leading.

The code was beating whatever this farce of a trial was. A trial that Jason had already figured would end in his own hanging.

It was when Frog left the stand after answers mirroring the rest, that Jason had to run back through his mind who had been on the stand.

Names and faces flipped through his mind. His head cocked as he realized that past the three that had fallen, Frog was the last crewman from the Windrunner. The last to speak.

Hope sparked.

With sudden interest, Jason looked at the judge. The man's face was pinched, sweat even heavier on his brow as he glared at Jason.

If no one named him as captain—everyone was their own captain—what would happen? It was obviously what this judge wanted to hear—someone from the crew to name Jason as captain.

The spark expanded into the smallest flame.

But then the judge smirked.

"Bring the last one in," the judge ordered over the whispers from the crowd behind Jason.

The whispers grew louder.

A side door by the judge opened, and two large men dragged a squirming body into the room.

It wasn't until they set her on the seat by the judge that Jason realized who they held.

Katalin.

His wife alive. Moving. Still fighting. Relief so raw flooded Jason that he had to lean forward, hands on his knees to steady himself.

The men flanked her, each holding a shoulder down as she continued to squirm.

The judge waited until the crowd quieted before addressing her.

"I will not question you like the rest, miss."

Katalin avoided everything, keeping her face down as far as her chin hitting her chest allowed. She still wore her ship clothes, now tattered—breeches, boots, vest—but her white linen shirt was new, its sleeves down to her wrists. Her head had long since lost its handkerchief, her braids askew and half apart. Even at this angle, Jason could see her eyes closed so tightly her forehead wrinkled.

"I only have one thing for you to answer, miss." The judge pointed at Jason. "That man. Is he your captain?"

Silence.

Face red, the judge got up from his chair, stalking over to Katalin. He grabbed her chin, forcing her head up.

She fought him, twisting, but was no match for the man's strength. Not with two others holding her down.

"Open your eyes, woman. Is that your captain?"

Tears streamed down her face as she shook her head, trying to crawl back into herself.

"You know the consequences, woman. Open your eyes. Is that man your captain?"

Complete, cold silence took over the room.

Ever so slowly, Katalin cracked her eyes, tears running even thicker. She met Jason's eyes.

Pain unlike anything he had ever imagined shone in her eyes.

Her mouth opened, voice shaking. "Aye. That man is my captain."

Before Jason could blink, before he could react, the two men picked Katalin up, dragging her out the door.

A death sentence.

A death sentence by his very own wife.

# CHAPTER 10

Numb, Katalin sat in the longboat, the rocking of the low waves pitching her body back and forth. Within minutes, she was standing in the middle of the main deck on one of her father's ships, holding herself at the waist, vaguely wondering how she got there.

Her father, tall and thick, strode in front of her, feet and cane thundering on the wood planks.

"We set sail." The command echoed across the ship, not to be taken lightly, and the frenzy of the crew that surrounded Katalin quickened.

Katalin looked around at all the faces. She spun three times, horror overtaking her as she noted every man.

Her father stalked by. Katalin grabbed his arm, stumbling as he pulled her along, not breaking stride. Panic flooded her voice. "The whole crew is here, Father. Here. Not on land. You promised to get Jase out. You promised. You swore the crew would get him out of there if I did that."

Her father stopped, looking down at her with his one good eye as he shook her arm free. He glanced up over her head. "Bring her below deck, Vince."

A thick hand clamped onto her shoulder as her father moved off. Katalin ducked, losing Vince's hand, and ran after her father.

"Father—you promised," she screeched, grabbing his forearm with both hands, yanking him to a stop. "You swore to me you would get him out."

He grabbed her face with one hand, thumb and fingers digging hard into her cheeks. "He is gone, Katalin. It is done. Someone had to hang for the Rosewater. He was it. That was the deal I made for you, for the crew."

"What? No, no—you swore to me." She shoved off of him. Turning, desperate, she found Fin and grabbed his shirt. "Fin, Fin, go back with me—we can get him out. There is still a chance. Help me. We can still free Jase."

Still, silent, Fin looked at her. She instantly recognized the pity in his eyes.

She moved to Frog, standing next to him. "Frog?"

He stayed silent as well.

She whipped back to her father.

"They are not your crew any longer, Katalin. They are mine." His eyes went to Vince. "Lock her in my cabin."

Katalin looked to the shore. They were on the outer edge of the bay. But she could make it.

She could make it.

Before a hand could stop her, she ran to the side of the ship. One leg made it over the railing before she was grabbed and yanked back, sprawling to the deck.

Her father stood above her, hands on his hips, his cane on the ground next to him. Seething, his face had gone red, matching his bushy beard.

Katalin went to her toes, moving again in a desperate clamber to the side. Before she could even grab the railing, her father slapped her hard, knocking her to the deck.

Stunned, she tried to find her feet, but dizziness held her and her boots only slipped on the wood.

"He is already dead, Katalin. They did it quickly."

"No." Her head shook. "No, I would feel it. I would know. I would know. I need to go back." She tried to scramble upward.

"Take her below." Her father's voice was deadly. "Tie her to the ship, lest she think she can swim back to shore for a dead man."

It took three of her crew—her father's crew—to carry her below. One on each arm. One carrying her legs. Even at that, she fought, scratching and screaming. Drawing blood the entire way.

It did no good.

~ ~ ~

On his back, Jason stared at the one star he could see out of the tiny rectangle hole high on the wall of his cell. He was to hang, early the next morning, and as such, he figured he didn't need any sleep.

May as well stay awake while he was still alive.

Not that the current state of his dead soul was much to be alive for.

What should one think about when they only had a night to live? He had pondered it for hours.

Jason tried to force his mind to his family once more. To his mother, father, sisters. To his land. The land he loved. To take stock of his life in some measure. What he had accomplished. Where he had failed. He knew all of that was what should consume his final hours.

But instead, all he saw in his mind was emptiness. Vast, gaping, emptiness. The shattering of his soul had done that. The betrayal.

Katalin's betrayal.

He had almost been a free man, or at the very least, there had been a chance he wouldn't hang. But Katalin had made sure to pound the nail in his coffin. She had looked right into his eyes, and offered a death sentence.

He had been a fool.

Especially because, even with the ultimate betrayal, he still loved her. Loved who she was—who she had been. He could not stop it. Not hate her in these final hours. As much as he wanted to, he could not. He had seen the fear in her eyes. Watched her tears. And yet, even after her words, he still wanted to protect her. Still wanted to believe she wouldn't do that to him.

A complete and utter fool.

Jason adjusted the hand he had propped under his head on the cool stone. One leg bent, the other stretched long, he tried once more to imagine his homeland. Rolling green hills. Flying free and fast on his favorite stallion, Black Star. Cook's bread pudding. Simple things that he had rarely noticed in everyday life. Simple things that now meant the world.

Simple things like Katalin's nose settling into the divot on his shoulder. The smell of citrus when she unbraided her hair. The earlobe he adored having between his teeth.

He grimaced, shaking his head.

Home. He needed to think of home.

The smell hit him before the explosion. The specific scent of burning nitrate on a fuse. And then he heard the distinct sizzle of sparks consuming a wick.

He rolled to the closest stone wall, covering his head, taking the chance that the explosion was on the outside of his cell, and not inside the building where he dove.

He guessed right.

Stone and rock and dust covered him. The explosion taking his hearing, he pushed up through the rubble, only seeing glowing embers lighting the cloud of what remained of his cell.

Just as he shoved the last big rock off his leg, a hand came out of the dust, grabbing his arm. Searching, he could see no face.

The hand pulled him, dragging him through the opening. Jason didn't care who or what it was. He only knew that this was his only chance at escaping death. So he forced his bruised legs into motion, following with haste the best he could.

Running through the dark, he ignored the yelling behind him, moving fast and far up the hill behind the cells. Cresting the ridge, the man in front of Jason finally let go of his arm, but didn't stop his fast pace. Jason heaved, running behind him, desperate to keep up.

Up and down three more hills, thick with vegetation, the man in front of him eventually pulled up, waiting for Jason to close the last few steps between them.

His feet barely solid under him, Jason doubled over, hands on his knees, gasping for breath.

"We be far 'nough we be walkin' from 'ere."

Jason looked up. Dappled moonlight shone through the thick trees above, and he could finally make out the figure before him. A sailor, definitely, but he did not recognize the thick man. "Who?"

"Roland, matey. Cap'n Kat be rewardin' me with Rosewater—that be the ship ye came from, no?"

Jason nodded, the long-past memory racing into his mind. "Yes."

"I carried ye 'board the Windrunner before I gots me ship."

"You were part of Captain Kat's crew?"

"Aye, matey. Ye ain't be thinkin' we leave a mate to the rope, are ye?"

Jason shook his head. "No...yes...I do not know what to think. Where did you come from?"

"I be hearin' they be hangin' a pirate here. Come to see and found it be yer arse. Easy 'nough to get ye out. Plus, easy pickin' now we be here."

Jason looked over his shoulder past the hills they had crested. Putrid rising smoke was thick behind them. "Is the town burning?"

Roland shrugged. "Cap'n weren't used to pillaging, but I don't be havin' no reservations on it. Me crew be join' us soon. But I be getting you to an English outpost. It be where ye headin' to, ain't ye, boy?"

"Yes. But Captain Kat." He cringed at his own words coming off his tongue. But he could not leave her. He had vowed to protect her, and dammit, he was going to keep that vow.

"We have to go back for her, Roland, they have her." Jason stood, starting back through the jungle. "I cannot leave her. I have to go back for her."

Roland grabbed his arm before he took three steps. "She be gone, boy. Gone with her father. Ye be the last one to get."

"No. She would not leave me, Roland."

"That she did, boy. She threw ye to the wolves to save her skin. She left and the lass did not look back. I seen her meself on the cap'n's ship."

"No."

"It be the truth, matey." Roland shrugged. "Ye can go back and look. But ye be findin' no Cap'n Kat in these parts. And we be leavin'—with or without ye."

Jason eyed him. Seconds passed. And then Jason nodded.

They moved onward, and Jason refused to look back at the rising smoke.

# CHAPTER 11

The power of the wealth and titles gathered in the Primrose drawing room at Curplan Hall was impressive.

The Duke and Duchess of Dunway sat next to each other on a mauve settee, while the Marquess of Southfork poured two brandies. The Marchioness of Southfork stood from a side chair for the third time in five minutes, pacing to the window that faced the graveled drive to the estate.

Concentrated power, yet none of them knew why they had been gathered so.

The duchess watched her friend stop at the window. "Your aunt did not give the slightest indication for our gathering, Reanna? I am beyond curious. When she left England after your wedding, I had thought never to see her again. Beyond you, she said there was no other reason to set foot on English soil again."

"It saddened me, of course," Reanna said, turning from the window. "But I also gathered her memories of London were not necessarily good ones. The viscount only lived for two years after their marriage—there was such an extreme disparity between their ages—and there were no children. I guess I could not expect her to stay here on my account, but I do miss her presence. There is no one I would rather face a full drawing room with, than her."

The duchess nodded. "She is the epitome of grace and propriety. I know I step lightly around her. The slightest glance from her and I always sat a bit straighter, spoke with perfect cadence. Which makes this even stranger. Pulling us together on such late notice borders on rudeness. She gave no indication why we are here?"

"Still, no." Reanna shook her head, attention going back to the drive. "My aunt arrived in London, made the request for this meeting here at Curplan, and that was the extent of our conversation. I do believe she knows she is being mysterious, but was not willing to let the slightest clue slide. She did say she would be down within minutes."

At that, the marchioness's Aunt Maureen, Lady Pentworth, walked into the drawing room. The woman's mere presence commanded the room, not only because of her statuesque bearing, but also because her personality demanded it. She stood in the middle of the room, perfectly coifed, and bypassed all pleasantries.

"Please, sit, Lord Southfork, Reanna."

The marquess shifted a quick glance at his wife, his cheek rising in amusement. He was not one to be ordered about in his own home. But he was also one to give his wife anything she desired, and right now, she desired to help her aunt. Killian was not about to spoil that. He picked up the two full glasses of brandy, handing one off to the duke as he passed him.

Killian sat on a wingback chair and Reanna joined him, sitting on the edge of the matching chair next to him.

"First, I thank you for your kindness in my sudden and abrupt request for you to gather, and to extend the invitation to his grace and her grace." Maureen inclined her head at the duke and duchess. "I appreciate everyone's willingness to attend. Thank you, Reanna, for bringing this impressive group together."

"You are welcome, Aunt."

Reanna's aunt paused, her right hand landing flat over her stomach, smoothing the crisp silk cloth. "Second, I must apologize for my lack of earlier details, but before I continue, I must ask each of you for your utmost discretion. I do not wish to offend, but I must be assured of absolute silence beyond this room on what I am about to speak of."

Both the duchess and Reanna leaned forward, eyes wide at Maureen. The duke caught Killian's eye above their heads. Killian shrugged at him.

"It is agreed?" Maureen asked, eyebrow arched.

Four heads nodded.

"Thank you. I will be blunt as to why we are gathered here." Maureen turned her attention to her niece. "Reanna, you have a cousin."

"I what?" Reanna's head jerked back, shock evident. "I have a cousin? But how…"

Maureen stared at her, silent in her patience.

"But, Aunt Maureen, you are my only relation." Reanna's mouth dropped open. "That could only mean…"

The duchess began to stand, grabbing her husband's hand. "These are private matters, we should excuse—"

"Please, your grace, stay," Maureen said, stopping the duchess in place. "I apologize for the unseemliness of the situation, but it is imperative that all of you have the knowledge that I am to share. I have a crucial favor to implore of the set of you, but the history must come before the request. At this point in my life, I have little to hide, and what I have to tell you causes me no shame. It should, but it does not."

The duchess slipped down to her seat. Silence covered the group.

Reanna pulled herself from her shock. "So you have a child, Aunt?"

"Yes. I have a child. A child I had believed to be dead."

"The viscount's?" Reanna asked.

"No."

Reanna nodded, eyes growing wider. "How? Why?"

"A year after I married the viscount, I had an affair with a sailor, a first mate on a ship that had come to port in London. I was young and disillusioned with what marriage entailed. How the man and I came to meet and what we did bears no interest upon this situation. What does, is that I became pregnant. The viscount had refused to touch me after our wedding night, so it was evident the babe was not his."

She paused, taking a breath, and then continued on, her voice a staccato in the concise tale. "I left London for an extended stay with my sister to hide the pregnancy." Her eyes went to Reanna. "Your father agreed to keep the pregnancy a secret and then find the babe a good home. I was frightened, and it was the best solution, so I agreed. But as my pregnancy progressed, I changed my mind. I could not give up the babe. My lover, Reginald Dewitt, was near your father's estate. He had followed me to Suffolk. I had decided to run off with him, leave England, my husband, and start a new life with Mr. Dewitt and our baby."

Maureen's eyes veered out the window, and for the slightest second, she looked grave. She cleared her throat, but her voice refused to yield to emotion. "But it was not to be. I do not know how your father knew what I was going to do, but he did. Soon after my baby was born, he took her. It was a hard labor, and I was near delirium. Hours later, he returned. He told me my baby had died. Stopped breathing. I was sure he had murdered my baby."

Reanna's hand went over her mouth, her skin blanching. Killian's fingers instantly went to the back of her neck, rubbing.

Eyes on her good friend, the duchess cleared her throat. She looked to Maureen. "But he did not?"

Maureen shook her head, sadness twitching the outer corners of her eyelids. "No. No he did not. It was a baby girl, and she lived. Reanna's father brought her to Mr. Dewitt and told him the baby was his to do with as he pleased. Told him I wanted nothing more to do with him or the baby."

"A lie?" the duchess asked.

She gave a crisp nod, elbows out as she clasped her hands in front of her belly. "One that destroyed me. Mr. Dewitt left England with the baby, and I never knew what happened to him. When I went to the house where he was staying while I was pregnant, to tell him our baby had died, he was gone. I assumed he had changed his mind about me and left. I never imagined what had actually transpired."

"Aunt, how do you know all this?" Reanna found her voice, but leaned noticeably into Killian's hand.

"It is precisely why you are all gathered. I have only just learned that my daughter lived. Mr. Dewitt contacted me. He named her Katalin and took her to the Caribbean. They have lived there all these years. But they are now journeying here as we speak."

"You have never met her?" Killian asked.

"No. This will be the first time since I held her in my arms as a newborn."

"Why now? Why did he contact you?" Killian's eyes narrowed.

Maureen took a moment to look at each of the four individually before she spoke. "This is when I must ask a prodigious favor from the four of you."

"Whatever you wish, Lady Pentworth," Killian said. "You are the one true relation to Reanna. So anything we can assist with, it is yours."

"Thank you, Lord Southfork, that is kind. Now that you have heard the past, I must please, once more, be assured of the utmost in discretion from all in this room."

Killian glance about at his wife and friends. "You have it."

"I appreciate your blind willingness, Lord Southfork, so I will get right to the point. My daughter, by way of her father, has lived an unusual life. She grew up on the ship her father captained, the Windrunner. In the past several years, she had taken over as captain of the Windrunner, since Mr. Dewitt's health has deteriorated."

"A captain? A woman?" An awed half-smile crossed the duchess's face.

"What sort of a ship did she captain?" Killian's look of concern was obvious.

"It is debatable—privateering or pirating—I am not assured either way."

Reanna coughed. "She is a pirate?"

"Was. It is past. Two years, past." Maureen waved her hand. "And she was a captain, not necessarily a pirate. The Windrunner sailed with various letters of marque, I am told. Regardless, privateering or pirating, I do not know that it matters. It does not to me. What does matter is that there is a very specific threat upon her. There are some that know she captained the Windrunner, and those same intend to harm her with that knowledge. They intend to accuse and bring her to trial for piracy."

Killian gave a low whistle.

"You understand the danger. I intend to save her from that."

"So Mr. Dewitt and Miss Dewitt are the additional guests you had mentioned that would be joining us here?" Reanna asked.

"Yes. I could not save my daughter when she was born, but I intend to do so now."

"How?" The duchess was teetering on the edge of her seat, the pink flush on her cheeks showing her obvious excitement.

"Quite simply, I intend to marry her to the highest ranking peer I can find," Maureen said. "It is crass, but being a peer affords one the privilege of peerage—certain protections both legally and socially. She has already agreed to the plan. While I do not aspire to a love match, I do aspire for a man that will regard my daughter enough to defend her against such damning allegations as piracy. Beyond that, I only wish a man that will, at the very least, be kind to her."

"And that is where, I presume, the four of us come in," Killian said.

"Indeed. She, first, needs to be polished into a lady I can present to society. I have hopes for the upcoming little season. I am told she has adequate looks and she is smart. That will help. Subsequently, she will need to be introduced to the right eligible bachelors. I am assured that between the four of you, you will be able to discern not only appropriate gentlemen, but also ones that have characters above reproach. I want her untouchable."

Killian stood, his hand not leaving Reanna. "Your candor is appreciated, Lady Pentworth. We will do whatever we can to help." He glanced down at the duke and duchess.

Aggie nodded with enthusiasm. Devin gave him a crisp incline of his head.

He turned to Maureen. "When shall we be expecting Miss Dewitt and her father?"

"Tomorrow."

~ ~ ~

Katalin took a deep breath, staring at the ragged edges of her fingernails, pulling at the frayed edges to smooth them. She looked at the thick double doors in front of her. They had arrived at this place, Curplan Hall, an hour ago, and she was still disconcerted.

The oppressiveness of London—she had never been in a city such as it. The frenzied busy. The smells. The squalor they passed along the docks. The people yelling and hawking.

Then there was the long carriage ride. She had never ridden in a coach for any length of time. Ships were the transportation she was accustomed to, and she walked everywhere on the island. As plush as the carriage was, it was jarring traveling on these roads. Not to mention that the small space of the coach was suffocating.

And then they had arrived at this beautiful castle. Beautiful and intimidating.

Katalin and her father were shown to their rooms, which were just as impressive as the exterior. She was sure her mouth had been agape since she had arrived.

As if she wasn't nervous enough.

So now she stood just steps away from meeting the mother she never knew she had.

"You will do fine, lass," her father bent to whisper in her ear. "Remember what is at stake, and you will do fine. Remember that all of this is a veneer. A veneer that we need. Do not forget what is at stake, daughter."

Katalin nodded, her eyes not leaving the dark grain of the wood before her.

The wood moved and her father ushered Katalin into the drawing room.

Four steps in, the one person in the room turned to them. Katalin froze.

Her breath stopped as she stared at a face that mirrored her own. Her face, but with the lines only years of living could add.

Her mother.

For a split second, Katalin saw a wave of emotion cross the woman's face. So much so, Katalin was afraid her mother would faint.

But the moment fleeted, and in the next instant, her mother straightened to an impossibly correct posture and approached Katalin, her face nothing but a mask of assessment.

Silent, not hiding her inspection, her mother stepped close to Katalin, her deep blue gown swishing. She was as tall as Katalin, had dark glossy hair with a splattering of grey coifed into a perfect chignon. Stopping in front of Katalin, her mother's eyes ran up and down Katalin's body.

Katalin forced herself not to fidget from the oddity of it. This was her mother—a mother that never knew Katalin existed.

Shouldn't she be happy to be reunited with Katalin?

Shouldn't she be hugging her? Smiling?

Instead, her mother's face was blank, slightly pinched. Katalin immediately discerned this woman would allow no emotion to creep onto her face.

Her mother gave a crisp nod. "You are me, save for your father's hair. It is just unique enough—the mix of red and blond—for it to create interest."

She slowly walked around Katalin, her eyes continuing the assessment. Katalin became acutely aware she was being inspected like a cow on the selling block.

"But our similarities are too strong," her mother said. "I will have to invent a branch of the family to explain the resemblance."

She stopped in front of Katalin, leaning in to inspect her face closely. Satisfied, she straightened and then reached up with both hands to cup Katalin's breasts, weighing them through the grey muslin dress Katalin wore.

Shocked, Katalin jumped backward, curving inward as her arms flew up, covering herself.

Unaffected, her mother dropped her hands. "Fortunate. You are larger than I in that area. We will have to use them to our advantage. That dress does little to accent them, nor is it in fashion. The dressmaker will arrive tomorrow to remedy that issue. And the scar on your arm is unfortunate, so the dressmaker will also have to be inventive on covering it."

She gave another quick glance up and down. "You are also trim. We will have some work to do, between your wardrobe and hair, but garnering initial glances by suitors should prove advantageous to our goal."

Katalin's mother finally acknowledged the other person in the room, looking to Katalin's father. "Her skin is not as light as I would like, but it is acceptable, Mr. Dewitt. You did well by keeping her out of the sun. All things considered, her appearance will do us favor in attracting courters. But I will reserve raising my low expectations until I see her before others. You did say she was smart? A quick learner?"

"Maureen—"

"Time is of the essence, Mr. Dewitt." She cut him off before his word was fully out. "We cannot afford nonessential conversations. Is the girl a quick learner?"

"Aye," Katalin's father answered, irritation bristling his face.

Her mother tapped her own chin, her eyes falling back on Katalin. "We shall see. Katalin, you named her?"

"Aye."

"Also odd. But curious. That may also do us well. Mystery." She cleared her throat, taking a step away from Katalin. "I have arranged for an early dinner with our hosts, Lord and Lady Southfork. Lady Southfork is your cousin, Katalin—my sister's daughter. You will also meet the Duke and Duchess of Dunway. They have also graciously agreed to help us. All have been apprised of the situation and your history, and all have promised the utmost discretion."

She moved to the double doors of the drawing room. "Let us dine. I need to assess your base knowledge of manners and polite conversation."

Katalin turned, staring at the back of the tight, dark chignon in front of her as her mother moved out of the room.

She glanced at her father, her eyes wide.

He shrugged. This was as bizarre to him, as it was to her.

Katalin moved forward, and he followed, his cane hitting the floor harder than usual as he leaned to her ear. "Chin up, lass. This will get better."

Katalin could only give a weak smile, holding back tears that threatened.

She hadn't known what to expect when meeting her mother for the very first time, but clearly, it wasn't this.

What had she wanted? A hug? Tears? A hello?

At the very least, the smallest modicum of emotion from this woman that was clearly her mother. She had to admit that she had expected that.

Katalin took a deep breath, keeping her steps even as she tried to drain back tears that threatened. She already knew the slightest drop slipping down her face would not be looked upon kindly.

She suffered through the dinner. Blindly answering questions that were asked of her by her cousin, the duke, the duchess, and the marquess. None from her mother.

All were more than pleasant, but Katalin was acutely aware the entire time of her mother's eyes constantly on her. Silently judging every word she spoke. Every bite she took.

Exhausting. Utterly exhausting.

She needed air.

# CHAPTER 12

Nightfall quickly approached, and Jason pushed his horse, stepping up the pace. He had gotten a late start from London, but still hoped to arrive at Curplan before darkness. He needed to confer with Devin and Killian while he still had the memory of the night before fresh in his mind.

He had been at the tables next to Lord Walton at the Horn's Rooster. Lord Walton had been deep in his cups, so deep, he had been bragging about a merchant ship that had, with some encouragement, conveniently sunk while traveling through one of the main shipping lanes in the Caribbean.

Convenient, because the merchant ship was one in direct competition with Lord Walton's shipping company. But the ship that had sunk was one in the fleet of the D&S Shipping Company. The company Jason had quite a large stake in, and not as important as the fact that it was the Duke of Dunway's company—and the duke was his brother-in-law.

Walton must not have noticed Jason, or, if he did, must have thought Jason too drunk to understand what was happening around him.

Granted, Jason was near to it, close to passing out—but he had held onto Lord Walton's words until they had made sense in the morning. And once Jason had assured himself he had heard right, he had cleaned himself up and headed straight to Curplan to talk to the duke and Southfork.

Jason also had a niggling fear that, drunk, he had been loose-lipped in the past about shipping schedules and cargo around Lord Walton, and that he was the direct cause of the latest mishap with the ship.

But that, he would have to handle later.

With a quick glance at the setting sun, Jason veered his horse off the main road into the woods, taking a direct cut-through trail to the main hall of Curplan.

A half mile from the hall, Jason left the woods, slowing as he entered the manicured area of the estate. He followed the tree line in the direction of the main stables, but then, to his left, movement caught his eye.

A woman walked down the slight hill to Curplan's small pond, lined by willow trees. He could only see the back of her.

Light hued hair, it was hard to tell the exact color in the dimming light. Her sleeveless, grey dress was far too thin for the current September chill.

Even though it was only the back of her, there was something oddly familiar. Something in the way her body moved. Her gait.

Familiar.

Too familiar.

Heart suddenly thundering, Jason stopped his horse, tossing the reins over a low branch and loosely tying them.

He slipped into the woods, stalking through the forest to the far end of the pond. Hidden, he was still too far away, couldn't clearly see her as she stood behind a wrought iron bench at the edge of the water, hands gripping the top back of the seat, her head down.

Jason rounded the pond in the cover of the willow trees, quietly slipping through the low-hanging branches.

The second he was close enough to see her clearly, even in the fading light, he froze.

He stood, mesmerized, not believing his own eyes.

Katalin.

Her hair, still long, half piled on her head, half draping down her back, was darker, but still multi-colored, the red giving way to blond. Her skin was lighter, less tan than on the ship, and Jason could see her arms, her body, still held lean muscle that identified her as more than a simple lady, even though she was dressed as one.

She moved around the bench and sat, kicking a rock in front of her into the water. It disrupted the calm, sending water rings across the surface, rolling into the swans that squawked by the far edge. She watched the water until the rings disappeared and then sat back on the bench, her eyes scanning the trees.

Her eyes passed over him, pausing for a moment as she looked through the willow branches. Jason was sure she saw him.

But in the next instant, her head bowed, and Jason could see her shoulders shaking. Shaking violently.

He made no movement toward her.

Her head whipped up, and for a long while, her eyes stayed closed, tears streaming.

She cracked her eyes slowly, and the moment she saw him again, she crumbled.

If Jason had any doubt it was truly her, it vanished the instant he heard her voice.

"Just go. Go, Jase. Please. Please go. I cannot continue to see you everywhere I look." Her voice cracked with a sob. "You cannot continue to do this to me. Not now. Not when I have to go through this. Please—please just leave me alone. Go."

She closed her eyes, dropping her head again. She stayed this way, tears dripping from her face for minutes until Jason saw her chest rise and fall with several deep breaths.

And still he stood, unable to move.

Lifting her head, she opened her eyes to him once more. Her head began to shake before the words came.

"No. No. No. This is not fair, Jason. Not when I open my damn eyes. You already have my damn dreams. You cannot do this to me. You cannot continue this torture."

She stood, fists at her sides as her yell escalated in his direction. "Damn you, Jase. You cannot haunt me like this. No. Not here. I cannot do this now. Not now. Not after her. You have followed me for years and I cannot undo the past. I cannot. I would…I would give anything—everything—to undo it."

A sudden gasp jolted her body, and she doubled over as though struck, hand over mouth, as she staggered back, hitting the bench. Her head shook. "No, not that. Not that. Not that."

Her words faded as she crumpled in half, collapsing onto the bench. Sobs racked her body as she buried her face in her hands.

Breath held, Jason slipped backward, removing himself from her view.

He moved to far end of the pond again, hiding in the whispering trees, watching her.

For at least an hour, from fading light to darkness, she sobbed, rocking herself. Until, with what looked like immense effort, she finally pushed herself to standing and started to trudge up the hill to the main hall.

Jason watched her until she was out of view, heart still pounding in his chest.

What the hell was Katalin doing at Curplan?

And what the hell had happened to her?

~ ~ ~

Katalin stood through six hours of the dressmaker draping and poking. Six hours of listening to her mother run through lists and rules.

Lists of the peerage. How the hierarchy worked. Whom to address when. Proper topics of discussion. How not to slight a dowager duchess. The correct posture on a settee. How to politely exit from a handsy dance partner. The optimum depth of a curtsy.

It went on and on.

Katalin retained as much of it as she could, but was secretly grateful for the dressmaker forcing her into one position. It gave her a reason to not have her eyes on her mother the entire day, pretending interest in every nuance Katalin would ever need to survive in this ridiculous world of London society.

The duchess and Katalin's cousin popped in and out through the day, and Katalin found each of them a welcome relief from her mother's judging hawk eyes. Katalin could already tell that she wanted to know more about both of them—they struck her as interesting women. As Katalin's life had always been mostly barren of women her age, she found them intriguing novelties.

But conversation in front of her mother was impossible. Impossible because her mother had only one mission—make Katalin presentable for society. Even if it was what Katalin needed for survival, she hadn't anticipated it would be this hard, or that the confidence she had always had in abundance would desert her so quickly under her mother's scrutinizing eyes.

If only her life didn't depend on it. All she really wanted was to go back to her father's island, to have her family back.

At least she hadn't seen Jason's ghost today. Small favor. Since arriving in England, he had visited her constantly in her dreams, but that was to be expected—this was the land he loved. The land he had needed to get back to.

But aside from yesterday, and the moment at the docks where she saw his ghost, he hadn't visited her while she was awake since she left her father's island.

She saw him often on Snakehorn.

Walking on a beach. Sometimes on a ship stopping for haven. She had been comfortable with the sightings of Jason. She knew he wasn't real and didn't really care whether he was a true ghost or just an aberration her overactive imagination conjured. Either way, she had always been comforted by seeing him.

Especially when she was sad or lonely or tired. She missed him so much. And seeing him always lifted her soul.

Until last night.

Last night he looked so real. So breathing. So vivid. And he was dressed so differently. Dapper in a gentleman's coat. He had never come to her like that, and she had never imagined him like that.

It scared her.

She knew she was here to move on with life—she had to, or she could very well be hanged. But seeing him like that—it terrified her. Terrified her because she didn't want to lose her memories of him, and if he appeared to her like that, it only meant she was losing memory of him.

She needed to move on. But she couldn't lose him. Lose his memory. She couldn't.

A pin jabbed her shoulder, and Katalin twitched. The dressmaker was as tired as she was, and had long since stopped apologizing for rogue pins.

Katalin shifted off of her left foot that had fallen asleep as her mother moved in front of her.

She looked Katalin up and down. "That shall do for today. Your first set of dresses will give them enough to work on for several days," she said with a quick clap of her hands. "We have a short break before dinner is to be called. Please freshen yourself and be dressed within the hour. I do believe Reanna had several gowns of hers moved to your room. They should fit fairly well."

"Yes, thank you." Katalin nodded as her mother turned and exited the room.

Katalin waited patiently as the blue silk wrapping her body was carefully removed, pins dragging across her skin.

~ ~ ~

Katalin stepped into the drawing room next to the dining hall. Pre-dinner wine looked to be in the hands of everyone. Her father and mother were in deep discussion in the corner. Her father did not look pleased, and her mother had the usual pinched look on her face.

Katalin needed to avoid whatever that was.

She scanned the room for escape, and it came in the form of her cousin spying her and coming forth to grab her elbow.

"Katalin, I am so pleased—that dress is wonderful on you. While turquoise does me well, forest green has never been my color, though I do keep trying it in hopes that it will somehow work with my hair and coloring." Lady Southfork smiled, leaning toward Katalin as she steered her into the room. "I am always dreadfully disappointed, so I am delighted this gown has found a much happier home on your body. It is truly quite perfect with your lighter hair, and it does not make you look at all yellow, which is my problem."

"Thank you." Katalin smiled, somewhat flummoxed at the conversation. She did not usually regard clothes—save for keeping private things hidden in an appropriate manner—much less talk about them in conversation. Females were so very different to be around.

"We will be dining in a few minutes. Would you like some madeira?"

"Please, Lady Southfork."

The warmest smile came from her cousin. "While I appreciate the effort in politeness—no doubt a direct result of my aunt's haranguing—you are my cousin, and I hope, soon to be friend, and I would be offended if you did not call me Reanna."

"Of course, but only if you call me Katalin. My mother has been stressing the importance of titles, and I did not want to offend you."

"It does take quite a bit to offend me." Reanna winked at her. "So you are in safe waters with me."

Katalin smiled, grateful for the genuine kindness her cousin extended. Looking about the room as Reanna retrieved her a glass of madeira, Katalin found the rest of the party, the duke and duchess, the marquess, and a man she did not know, standing in animated conversation in the middle of the room. She looked curiously at the back of the man. All eyes in the little group were on the newcomer, and the duke and the marquess did not look pleased. They looked, in fact, murderous.

The duchess leaned forward, her hand touching the man's arm. She was agitated, but not nearly as lethal as the others.

Reanna's eyes followed Katalin's as she handed her a wine glass. She gave a deep sigh. "That appears to need interruption. My husband looks as though he is going to hit something, or someone." She slipped her hand under Katalin's elbow. "Come, you are the perfect diversion. I can introduce you to the duchess's brother."

Reanna stepped into the group, blatantly cutting the low voices into silence. With a sweet smile, she tugged Katalin closer.

"Lord Clapinshire, I would—"

At that moment, Katalin saw whom she was to be introduced to, and her glass dropped, the shatter echoing in the room.

Silence throbbed around them.

Silence Katalin did not notice as she walked forward, both hands outstretched. She stopped in front of the man—Lord Clapinshire—shock moving her limbs without conscious thought.

Her hands went onto his face, moving from his cheeks to his eyes to his nose to his chin to the scar that lined the length of his face. Over and over his skin they ran.

He did not step away, did not flinch or avoid her hands. He only stared at her.

With not so much as a gasp, Katalin passed out, dropping like a cannon ball.

~ ~ ~

Jason caught her before her head hit the floor, lifting her fully into his arms.

"Do you have her, Clapinshire?" Killian asked.

"I do," Jason said, refusing to let his eyes go down to her face. It was bad enough his arms were all over her. Touching her—letting her touch him—his anger at her multiplied tenfold.

"Is she addled, Mr. Dewitt?" Lady Pentworth asked, her eyes sharp on Katalin. "You did not tell me of this."

"No. The girl has a stronger spine than, dare I say, yours, Maureen. I have never seen her even close to the debacle I just witnessed, much less dropping to blackness like that." He drained his glass of wine.

Jason turned to his sister and the marchioness. "Aggie, Lady Southfork, this lady does not appear to be awakening, perhaps you two can show me where to deposit her?"

"Yes, yes, of course. I apologize for her actions, Lord Clapinshire. I have no explanation for what she just did." Lady

Southfork set her wine glass down on the nearest table and gathered her skirts, hurrying to the door. "You are very kind to be so patient with her. Come, let us bring her up to her room."

Lady Southfork hurried out of the room, his sister at her heels. Jason followed, shifting his arms under Katalin for a better grip.

In the hallway, away from all gawking eyes, Jason lost the fight against the exact thing he was trying to avoid, and he glanced down at Katalin's face.

Long lashes closed, her face had softened, losing the shock of seeing him. Her mouth, cheeks, forehead, relaxed, peaceful—just as she had always been when sleeping on top of him. She still smelled of tangerines. Nearly two years of trying to kill her memory, and the mere smell of her brought back every moment they had together.

Perfect. She was still damn perfect.

Jason's jaw flexed against her beauty. Still perfect—and still the woman that had condemned him to hang.

His eyes left her face, concentrating on the swishing skirts going up the stairs in front of him.

Katalin was here for a reason. He just had to find out what that reason was and then make sure he was far, far away from it, and from her.

Touching her body, it was already obvious his hands would have a hard time overriding his own good sense. Good sense that told him to make sure Katalin never entered his life again.

He had trusted her once.

He was not about to make that mistake twice.

# CHAPTER 13

Katalin shot straight upward the second consciousness hit. Gasping, it took her a moment to realize she was in a bed in the room she was staying in at Curplan.

"Good, you are awake."

Katalin's head swiveled to find her cousin sitting by the bed, a lamp shining light on the book open on her lap.

"How long have I been out? I fainted?"

"Yes, you did. And you have not been asleep for too long. A few hours," Reanna said. "I did not wish you to wake up alone, if you did not remember passing out. It is disconcerting."

Katalin rubbed her forehead, trying to clear the fog in her mind. "You say that as if you know exactly what passing out feels like."

"I have blacked out once or twice." Reanna shrugged. "Mine were from cracks on the head, though. Much different. And mine were also not preceded by some of the oddest behavior I have ever witnessed."

"Odd?" Dread flooded Katalin.

"Do you not remember?"

"I...I..."

"You fondled the face of the duchess's brother."

"I did? That was real?" Katalin covered her eyes, mortification setting in. "Yes. I know. I did."

"So I must ask—why would you do such a thing? Is it a custom where you grew up? Or a sailor's custom? It was very strange."

"Custom? No. Nothing like that." Katalin's hands dropped from her face. "I know my mother told you about my past—you are very curious about my life, Reanna, are you not?"

"As a cat." Enthusiasm flooded Reanna's eyes. "Aggie and I have been entirely anxious to get you alone away from your mother, truth told."

Katalin chuckled. "I must admit to the same thing. You both seem delightful, and I have never had friends."

"Never?"

Katalin's mind shot to Jason. She quickly shook her head. "No. Never any female friends."

Finger slipping into the book to hold her place, Reanna leaned forward, patting Katalin's knee. "We will have to remedy that in the days to come."

She sat back, eyeing Katalin. "But that does not answer for your odd behavior. Do you know Lord Clapinshire?"

"Who? Lord Clapinshire?"

"Yes, the man you fondled. Oh, I suppose you did not catch his name when you were introduced?"

"No. I suppose I did not. I do not know the man." Katalin answered too quickly, and she knew it. She slowed her words. "Lord Clapinshire, you say? You said he is the duchess's brother? What is he doing here? Does he know anything about me or why I am here?"

"No, not to worry on that. He knows nothing about you, nor will any of us share the privileged information about your history," Reanna said. "Lord Clapinshire is merely here because he needed to talk to my husband and the duke about their shipping company. I do not know what it was about. An emergency of some sort, I imagine. He did hold up admirably under your… hands, though."

"Thank you. That does put my mind at ease," Katalin said.

"I must ask, Katalin, why would you fondle him so? I do not wish to continue to pry, but if something like this were to happen at a ball or a dinner, it would be disastrous for you. I would just like to make sure we know what is going through your mind to avoid such a thing in the future."

Katalin groaned inwardly. She had no excuse. None that she could actually share. And she could tell Reanna was thinking she was slightly daft.

"I do apologize," Katalin said. "I did not wish to ruin the evening. I have no explanation for my actions. I have been overwhelmed since I arrived, and I thought I knew the man. The stress of this. It is all so much. So very much. My mother is…"

"Hard?"

Katalin nodded, eyes pensive. "Hard…Yes, that is a good word for her. I mean no disrespect."

"None is taken," Reanna said. "I know her. And I both understand her—understand how she is—yet at the same time, I do not understand why she is like she is." Reanna leaned forward, squeezing Katalin's hand. "She can be crusty, very hard to know, to talk to. But believe me when I tell you she is also the most generous person I have ever known. She does care—deeply—but she seems to have no way to show it outwardly. But that does not mean the kindness and the caring is not in there."

"I had always been told she was dead." Katalin frowned. "And then I found out she was alive, and was willing to help my father and me—and I guess I just had imagined her differently. Hoped for different."

Reanna gave her a sympathetic smile. "I can imagine. But just be patient. I know my aunt can be much more than what she has shown these last few days. This is probably overwhelming not only for you. It probably is for her as well."

Katalin nodded. She hoped so. She truly did.

~ ~ ~

Reanna left her once she was assured Katalin was well. Claiming she was going straight to sleep, Katalin instead jumped out of the bed the second the door closed after Reanna.

Throwing a robe over her chemise, she waited a few minutes before she cracked open her door to find the long hallway empty and dark—perfect.

Creeping through the shadows of the enormous home, Katalin eventually found what she was searching for—the sounds of male voices. She followed the voices, slipping into a dark room next to where they came from. She assumed the men were in the study but couldn't be sure. She had mostly just been ushered from place to place in Curplan.

She found a spot along a dark wall in what appeared to be another drawing room. She needed to be able to hide in case someone entered, and the tall draperies next to her would do nicely in that situation. Most importantly, she could hear the male voices in that spot, though they were muddled and she could not make out words—but she could definitely make out Jason's deep baritone.

Then she waited.

And waited.

It was hours before the voices quieted, and Katalin heard the door to the study open and close. Footsteps thudded on the wood floors. One…two…three sets of footsteps. Katalin moved into the shadows in the hallway, trailing the men up the stairs.

At the top of the steps, the marquess split from group, going left while the other two went right. From her spot low on the stairs, Katalin waited until the marquess entered his room before she slid up into the opposite hallway.

The duke was just entering a room as she peeked around the corner down the long hall. And that left only Jason.

He walked down the hallway, past her mother's room, her father's, and her own. Three doors past hers, he stopped and disappeared into a room.

Heart wild, Katalin stood in the shadows, gaining courage. She needed desperately to go into his room to see him, but at the very same time, was terrified what would happen once she did.

Her husband.

Her dead husband. Alive and well and here.

And not acknowledging her.

Katalin inhaled deeply for fortitude and set her bare feet forward.

She opened his door and stepped into the room, silently closing the door behind her.

A lit fireplace crackled light into the room, and Jason stood, back to her. He had already removed his jacket, cravat, vest, and boots. And for an instant, Katalin could imagine him on the Windrunner, bare feet, white shirt, slops hung low with a rope belt.

"You are real." It was the merest whisper from her lips.

He spun, facing her, his white linen shirt open wide on his chest. And not the slightest bit surprised by her presence. "Yes."

"Not dead?"

"No."

She gasped, her hand at her throat. She had seen him hours earlier, she knew that, but the shock was just as raw as it had been hours before.

He took a step to her, his eyes guarded. "Do not faint on me again."

"Do not ask it of me." Katalin tried, but could not get air into her lungs. She started to sway.

Jason grabbed the nearest chair and slid it behind her, pushing her shoulder down until she was seated.

He stood, arms across his chest, staring at her while she fought for air and consciousness. All she could do was stare at his bare feet.

Minutes passed, and Katalin's breathing finally calmed, her eyes able to focus.

"Tell me when you have regained your sensibilities."

Her head jerked up. "Can I touch your face again? I see things…I fear…"

"I am real, Kat. As real as I was the other day at the willow tree."

Her mouth dropped. "That was you?"

"It was."

She flew up, slapping him hard across the face. "Bastard."

Feet not moving, his hand went to his cheek, rubbing the skin with nonchalance. "So your sensibilities are back."

She shoved his chest with two fists, mostly because he deserved it, but also to prove he was alive and breathing and right in front of her. It sent him back a few steps, yet still, the cool detachment was all she saw.

She swallowed the steps between them, setting herself only a breath away from him. "Damn you, Jase. Why? Why didn't you come to me? I thought you were a ghost. Why didn't you come to me? Oh my God."

Her hand flew over her mouth and she staggered backward at his silence. "You were alive. Alive. Why did you not come to me before this? Why not on the island? Why did you not find me, Jason? Why?"

"Why did I not find you?" His eyebrows arched as his arms re-crossed over his chest. "Why? You delivered a death sentence to me at that trial, Captain. And then you left me there to die. And you dare to ask me why I did not find you?"

"Oh, God, no. No." Her breath sped out of control, her head spinning. "No—you don't understand—my father—he promised me he would save you. All I had to do was say what I did at the trial, and he promised me he would save you. And then he brought me out to the ship. He told me it was too late, that you were already dead. But I didn't believe him. I refused it. I would have felt it. I would have felt you die. I tried to get back to land."

"You did not try too hard." His voice was venom.

"No."

Loud. Too loud.

Jason's hand whipped forward, clamping across her mouth.

She grabbed his wrist, ripping his hand away, but her voice was in check, low and hissing. "My father had to tie me to a damn bed so I would not jump overboard to swim back to the island to you. I was not leaving without proof. Not until I saw for myself. He cocked me over the head and not only tied me up, he had to lock me below to stop me."

"And after that, Captain?" Fists cracking his own knuckles, his own voice pitched louder. "Days, months, and you could not find a way to me? Find out the truth? Roland got me out of there. How could you not know that?"

"What? He did? No. My father lied? I have seen Roland—he lied to me?" Her head flew back and forth as her voice lost all bitterness, falling to a whisper. "But I started seeing you. In my dreams. Walking on the shore. Sitting across from me at dinner. You came to me. Your ghost."

She looked up, tears brimming as the enormity of all that happened hit her. "You were in my dreams, Jason—everywhere I looked. And I started to believe you had died. That was the only explanation. That was the only reason I would see your ghost everywhere. And I could not...could not stand..."

"Could not stand that you killed me?"

She crumpled in half, her arms tight around her belly, her chest clamping short all breath, all heartbeat.

He said the words.

The words she heard in her own mind—the words that had haunted her in every minute of every day for the past two years.

She killed him.

Reeling, she stumbled to the door, unable to look at him.

Her hand on the doorknob, she stopped, looking through her tears at the door in front of her.

"Lady Southfork asked me if I knew you." She took a gulp of air so she could force words, but could not bear to look back at him. "Do I know you, Jason? Do I?"

"No."

She closed her eyes, fighting the one word. After a silent moment, she opened her eyes, hands wiping the wetness from her cheeks as she attempted to stand straight.

"Good." She nodded. "That should make this easier, as that is what I told her."

# CHAPTER 14

Another day of fittings, but Reanna did manage to arrange a short reprieve for Katalin. Her cousin had snatched Katalin's mother to oversee some of the trim work the dressmaker had gotten to. Reanna knew her aunt would want to control that, down to the stitch, so it gave the perfect reason for Reanna, the duchess, and Katalin to take a stroll through the gardens.

The duchess pushed her baby, Andrew, in an elaborately carved baby carriage on the gravel pathway, humming a tune to him. The crunching of the gravel, along with Aggie's hum, prompted his eyelids to start drooping, but he fought the sleep, trying to keep his eyes open on Katalin.

Katalin watched his chubby cheeks, his tiny mouth smacking, entranced. "How old is he, your grace?"

"Four months, plus a few weeks." Balancing the bar of the carriage with her wrists, the duchess took off her short white gloves, reaching down to caress his cheek with the back of her bare knuckles. Baby Andrew's head turned, nuzzling into the touch. "Four months that are beyond words—I cannot even describe how much I adore this little being."

"I can imagine," Katalin said. "He is a wonder. I do not think I have heard him cry once since we arrived."

The duchess chuckled. "How I wish that were true. I will have to tell the nanny she is doing a spectacular job at whisking him away at the right moments."

The baby's eyes closed, peace relaxing his face, and seeing it, sudden tears brimmed on Katalin's lower lashes.

She forced her gaze away, trying to blank out her mind by concentrating on a tall wall of sculpted evergreens lining the outer edge of the garden. Inhaling deeply, she drank in fresh air, the smell of hydrangeas sweet in the soft breeze.

The day had turned unusually warm for September, with humidity reminiscent of a hot August day. The warmth brightened Katalin's spirits, as it reminded her of what a cool winter's day on her father's island felt like.

Reanna paused along the long border of a raised plant bed, bending over to pluck a rogue weed from the flowers. A long root came up. "The gardener hates it when I pick his weeds, he thinks I am judging his skill, so we need to walk to the woods so I can toss this without him knowing."

"Gladly, the longer I am outside, the better," Katalin said. "I have never spent so much time indoors."

"Your life on the island—you must have spent most of your time outside?" the duchess asked.

"Yes. Father's house is positioned for the breeze, but it is always more comfortable outside. There are numerous shaded verandas and porticos. But that has been difficult, keeping me out of the sun to lighten my skin. Father said it was necessary, but the lack of activity has made me soft."

"Soft?" The duchess laughed. "You forget that I have seen your arms, not to mention your whole body, coming in and out of the fitting room. You have muscles I have only seen on my husband."

"Am I too manly?" Katalin asked, suddenly worried. "My mother did not mention it, but maybe she was being polite?"

"Polite? My aunt knows no bounds when it comes to molding the finest young ladies of the ton," Reanna said. "She presented me as well, so I know exactly what you are going through. Tell me, have her hands been all over your breasts?"

"What?" Katalin sputtered a cough. "Yes. How did you know?"

Reanna shrugged. "She did it to me as well. She is particularly obsessed with getting the exact right height of neckline on the gowns—showing enough to entice but not too much to be crass. She finds it an art form. Up, down, squeezed, separated—she spent hours getting my breasts just right above the trim of the gowns."

Katalin's mouth dropped. "Thank goodness. I was beginning to think it quite strange."

"You will get used to it." Reanna stopped, shaking her head. "No, that is a lie. One never gets used to that much fondling. It is incredibly humbling. And she has cold hands. But if you can smile at least inwardly at the absurdity of it, you will be able to suffer through."

Katalin chuckled. "I will have to try that—the inward smile, lest she think I am enjoying it."

They continued on down the path, three wide, Katalin in the middle. But the moment there was silence, Katalin's mind wandered to Jason. She shook herself. She couldn't think of him. Not now. Not yet. She had spent most of last night in a sobbing heap on her bed, and she could not crumble in front of her cousin and the duchess.

"Please, talk to me of something other than social mores, and gowns, and titles. Anything." Katalin's eyes pinned Reanna. "You. Tell me of those times you have been knocked out. You did not say it, but it sounded like there was quite a tale behind those words."

Reanna laughed. "I do love your directness, Katalin. And you are right, there is a tale—but if you want to hear about excitement, you should ask the duchess how she met her husband."

Katalin's head swiveled to Jason's sister. "Your grace?"

"Please, call me Aggie." Her hand left the carriage to squeeze Katalin's forearm. "And if you truly want to hear it, I will tell you. I must warn you, though, you are not the only one with a past that needs to remain discrete. But since you have entrusted us with the secret of your past, I see no reason why you cannot keep mine."

"You have my complete, and may I say, very piqued attention, Aggie," Katalin said, eyes wide.

Reanna laughed, pointing at Aggie. "Your interest, Katalin, is more than warranted for what has happened to this one."

Aggie smiled, their steps quickening. "Has anyone ever told you about the east side of London?"

~ ~ ~

Katalin was immensely grateful for the full day. Between her long afternoon with Reanna and Aggie, and the poking and prodding of the dressmaker under her mother's eyes, it had kept her mind off the one thing she didn't dare to think about.

Jason.

Dinner could have been extremely painful, and she had been dreading it all day, but thankfully, Jason did not attend. She wasn't sure if he had left Curplan or was choosing not to dine with the rest. Either way, she didn't dare ask.

It was in the silence of her own room, in bed late that night, when her thoughts took on a mind of their own. As much as she tried to shove Jason out of her mind, she could not.

Down to a thin chemise, Katalin rippled the fabric at her chest, trying to puff air onto her skin. The heat of the day had not dissipated. No breeze graced the open window, and the thick warmth did nothing to help her fall asleep. She flopped onto her back in her bed, forearm covering her face.

Jason was alive—alive. A miracle.

But within that miracle, he did not claim her as his wife. He saw her. Talked to her. Yet did not claim her. And it was clear he had no intention of doing so.

Hell. She wasn't even sure if their marriage was legitimate with English law to begin with. Could a self-proclaimed man of God on an island in the middle of nowhere really marry them? Maybe Jason knew that. Plus, everyone called him Clapinshire. Was Jason Christopherson even his true name? But that was the name he married her under. A false name? A rogue pastor? Were they ever really married?

She took a deep breath, trying to quell tears before they started again. The truth was that it didn't matter if their marriage

was legal or not. It was real to Katalin. She was his wife. He was
her husband. Painfully real.

And that brutal truth was the cruelest part of him being
alive.

That he was alive was a gift in itself. She would rather have
him alive than dead, even if he did not want her.

But it meant losing him all over again. Shards of the
destruction that had been her life after she thought he died hit
her. Could she really go through that again?

An errant thought popped into her head. Maybe this had
been Jason's plan all along. Use her while he was on her ship and
then dispose of her once he went back to his land. Maybe.

Katalin jerked upright in bed, staring at the shadows on the
walls. Her eyes veered to the open window. The moon was bright.

She needed to get out of here.

Not bothering to put on a dress, Katalin shrugged into a
light robe and slipped barefoot through the dark house. She heard
nothing, so could only assume all were asleep.

Making her way outside, her feet carried her without thought
down the sloping hill to the pond where she had first seen Jason,
thinking he was a ghost.

She stopped at the bench, sitting, staring at the willow tree
branches she had seen him in. She was a fool. She had railed at
him like an idiot. A fool. Maybe he thought she was crazy. Maybe
that was why he denied her.

Standing, she walked over to the weeping willow, stepping
into the shadows of the hanging leaves. Her fingers wrapped
along a long hanging branch, mindlessly plucking free the tear-
drop leaves.

"What are you doing here, Kat?"

She jumped as his voice, low and rumbling like she always
remembered it, cut through the thick air behind her. She expected
to be alone out here, but he had always known where she was on
the ship—time had passed, but why would he be any different?

Turning, she faced him, fingers still entwined in the branch.
The white linen shirt he had on glowed in the moonlight, tucked

into buckskin breeches cut off at the knees by tall black boots. Her breath caught. He looked like he could be on her ship. Cleaned up, but on her ship.

"I could not sleep."

"No, Katalin. Here at Curplan. All my sister would tell me is that you and your father are Southfork's guests. Why are you here?"

"Oh. I…" What could she tell him? She needed to find a husband with a title to protect her from hanging for piracy? No.

She took a deep breath, fingers tightening on the malleable branch. "Lady Pentworth is my mother."

"Your what?"

"My mother. She is alive. I just found out months ago. I am illegitimate. It is why we are here—to meet. Lady Southfork is her niece, my cousin, and Lord Southfork agreed to host us here."

Even in the shadows, she could see his eyes narrow at her. "You could have met her anywhere. Why bring Southfork and his wife into it? My sister and the duke? Why are you really here, Kat?"

"A vicious twist of fate?" Her head tilted back, and she had to hold in a delirious laugh as she stared at the bright moon through the willow leaves. She looked at him. "I had no idea the duchess was your sister, Jason. My cousin asked them to come, to help."

"Help with what?"

Katalin bit the inside of her cheek, exhaling. She could not hide this truth, and he would find out soon enough. "My father and mother both wish to see me married. Give me a respectable life. My mother cannot claim me, but this—this she can do. Make me acceptable to society."

He paused, his head jerking away to the pond before looking back to her. "So you are here for a husband?"

She stared at him, unable to answer. He had denied her last night. All she had wanted was for him to grab her. Hold her. Call her his wife again.

But he did not.

And she could see right now, he still had no intention of doing so.

She nodded.

He rushed her, willow branches flying as he thundered to her. Stopping, his chest almost touched her, his breathing harsh.

But he said nothing as he glared down at her. Made no movement to touch her.

Katalin's heart constricted. He still was not going to claim her.

Tell him. Her mind screamed. Tell him.

Instead, she spun away, unable to take his heat that close to her body. Crossing her arms over her stomach, she took a few steps from him, her back toward him. "Who are you, Jason? Why do they call you Lord Clapinshire?"

"I am an earl, Katalin."

Her chin went over her shoulder to look at him. "An earl? And you never thought to mention that fact to me?"

"I was not an earl at the time we met. My father was still alive when I was thrown onto the first ship. He died in the years I was away."

"Jason." She turned back to him, stepping close as she grabbed his arm. "I am...I am so sorry. I remember that he was very dear to you."

He shrugged her hand off his arm. "Yes, well, it is years past at this point."

"Oh. Of course." Her hand fell back to her side. "I am sorry, Jason. I am still trying to come to terms with the fact that you are alive. Alive and here. But not acknowledging—I do not know the right things to do—to say."

"I do not think there is anything to do or say."

"What?" She rubbed her forehead, anger starting to flush her limbs. "Then why in the hell are you out here, Jase? It is the middle of the night. Why the hell are you torturing me like this?"

"And what you did to me was not torture, Kat?"

"Me?" She stepped in, finger poking his chest. "You told me you would wait, Jase. This life or the next, you said. You promised. Day after day. Well, here we are. Together. The next life. A miracle we both survived what we did. That I…"

She cut off her words, turning from him, head shaking. "And you do not care. You did not wait for me. It was a lie. All of it. You were a lie."

"I never lied to you, Katalin."

"No?" She dragged her palm across her cheeks, wiping away frustrated tears. "Everything we had was a lie, if this is what you would do to me now. Treat me like this. It meant nothing to you. I meant nothing to you." She whipped back to him, fists hard in her thighs. "And I would have died for you, Jason. Died for you."

"But you did not. You chose to have me hanged instead."

Her gasp sent her staggering backward, away from his cold words. "No. I told you. You cannot think—I was stupid, Jase. I trusted my father and I should not have. I believed to my core I was saving you. And I have had to live with the torment of my own stupidity for years. You do not know what it is like, waking up every day, knowing what I caused. That I killed you."

Her words had no effect. If anything, Jason looked even colder.

"Pretend you never saw me, Kat. Pretend I am still dead. You were clearly doing well before I showed up."

He spun, starting to leave.

She lunged, grabbing his arm, stopping him as she rounded his body to plant herself in front of him. "No. This is vicious, Jason. You cannot be alive. Alive and in front of me. And then you ask me to give up on you. Give up on us. I cannot do it. I love you. I have never stopped loving you."

"There is no us, Katalin."

Her grip tightened on his arm. And then the possible reality that he had moved on from her hit her.

Her soul would be forever wrapped up in this man, and he could have forgotten her. Hell. He could have married another for all she knew.

Her throat closing, she forced words out before the ability left her. "You no longer love me?"

"Kat, I do not know—I never expected to see your eyes again."

He tried to move away, but she snatched his other arm, not letting him move. She couldn't speak, could only stare up at him, demanding he look at her. Answer her.

"Blast it." He sighed, shaking his head. His eyes met hers. "Of course I do, Kat. Why the hell do you think I am out here? But you left me to die. You. You made that choice—you tied the noose and abandoned me. What am I to do with that? I need to let you go, Kat, but I am having a damned time doing so."

Katalin's legs went weak, and she almost dropped, but in the next instant, his hand went fully over her mouth, and he spun her, grabbing her around the waist. He lifted her, dragging her deep into the cover of the willow. On the dark side of the tree trunk, he set her down on her feet, but didn't remove his hand from her mouth or his arm from its solid hold around her waist.

It took several seconds for Katalin to figure out why they were suddenly hiding. She heard the laughter before she saw them. And then into moonlit view, the marquess and Reanna moved down the hillside to the water, his arm tight around her shoulder.

Katalin could hear the marquess talking in a low whisper but could not hear what he said. Reanna laughed again. Within a minute, they were at the water's edge by the wrought iron bench.

A dried twig dug deep into her bare foot, and Katalin shifted. Jason's hand dropped from her mouth. With the movement, Katalin became acutely aware that her entire backside was molded into Jason, their breathing in unison. If anything, his hold around her waist had tightened since her cousin and Lord Southfork had appeared.

Her hands went to the bark of the trunk in front of her, closing her eyes as she tried to steady herself against the feel of him. The scent of him.

But then the laughter by the pond made her eyes open, and all of her attention went to the scene before her.

Already shirtless, the marquess was quickly losing his trousers. His wife was already naked.

Blast it.

Trapped. Utterly trapped, and this in front of them. Blast it.

Both laughing, the marquess snatched his wife, lifting her up and carrying her into the water. With abandon and a wicked chuckle, he plunged both of them deep into the water. Her squeals surfaced when their heads broke free of the water. Squeals that were quickly squelched by the marquess as he attacked his wife, kissing her into silence.

Captivated, Katalin slowly shook her head. "We should not be watching this," she whispered.

"No. We should not." Jason's breath was hot on her ear.

Focus not leaving the water, she stole a glance at his face out of the corner of her eye. "You are not averting your eyes."

"Neither are you."

"How can I? She is beautiful. Him as well."

Jason grunted next to her. For a moment, she thought it was in anger, but then his arm on her belly tightened, and she could feel him growing hard against her lower back. No, not angry. Not angry at all.

Guilt over watching the entirely too-intimate moment was starting to war with Katalin's guttural need to have Jason's hands on her. To feel his heartbeat, listen to his breath, curl into his body—his body that she had missed for so long.

And then the marquess and Reanna clearly started making love, her body rising up and down in the water, his hands lifting her, roaming her skin, mouth moving from one breast to the other.

Katalin swallowed hard, frozen. "We are not moving."

"We are stuck. It would make noise." With his whisper, she could feel his chest vibrate with the words. Feel his lips next to her head. His attention was clearly no longer on the pond. It was on her. Fully on her.

His free hand slipped up slowly along the side of her body, moving inward to curve around her breast. But it was not enough for him, and he slid his fingers under the thin fabric of her robe, pushing down her loose chemise to get to her skin, her nipple.

Katalin closed her eyes, head arching back to his shoulder. The thought of stopping him didn't even enter her head. Her thighs tightened at his touch, her core already throbbing. It had been far too long. Hating her or not, he still knew what to do to her body.

His head came down, lips on the base of her neck. "Hell. You feel the same, Kat. Your body on mine. Your flesh still fits to my hands."

She pulled her left hand from the bark to grab the back of his head, holding him to her bare skin.

"God, Kat, I cannot be near you like this. Not without touching you."

"So touch me."

His groan was low, soft, but it held every intention in its soft rumble. His hand around her waist dropped, his forearm sliding between her legs as he worked the chemise up, his fingers eventually finding her bare leg, prickling her skin as he ran his hand up her inner thigh. Katalin doubled forward when his fingers, warm and thick, slid into her folds.

She would have screamed, but his other hand came up, covering her mouth, smothering the noise. He pulled her back into him, straightening her against his body, his hand still over her open mouth.

She rode his hand for minutes, trying to catch both air and her senses, and when she did, she realized Jason pulsated even harder into her lower back.

Mouth still open, she slid one of his fingers between her teeth, capturing, sucking at the exact moment she wedged both hands behind her, grabbing him. It took a moment to gain access past the fall front of his breeches, but once she set him free, he strained large into her hands, raw and demanding.

She took the opportunity, her fingertips flowing up and down his smooth skin, exploring each and every ridge of him, until his breath at her ear turned just as ragged as her own.

Katalin went to her toes, stroking him hard, trying to pull him under all the fabric of her chemise and robe. Trying to make contact.

"Jason, please." Her voice was a begging whisper. "Please, Jase, I need you in me. In me deep. Your body in mine."

He didn't shift to move the fabric between them, instead answering with his hand, his fingers plunging into her, her thumb circling harder.

"Jase, please." She pulled on him hard, unable to stop her own hand from mirroring his deep finger strokes. He only quickened his pace, refusing to enter her.

His growl came, reverberating in her ear as she could feel him shudder behind her, the sudden wetness on her hand. The contractions under her fingers.

But she was already too close to her own edge to pull away, and she could only grind down on Jason's hand in her as her fingertips went to the rough bark in front of her, tearing the wood.

Jason teased and prodded, pushing her until she spasmed hard, trying to control her scream.

The hand over her mouth told her she wasn't successful. She didn't give a damn.

When she was no longer in danger of sound, his hand dropped from her mouth and he let her night rail fall to her feet.

"I am still yours, Jase." She got out between ragged breaths, her chin on her own chest. "Do not deny yourself from me."

"No." The word was instantly in her ear. "There is no us. I am no fool, Katalin. I will not fall under your spell again."

His hands left her body as he stepped away, sudden cold spots where his heat had been.

Support gone, Katalin struggled to find footing on her weak legs, fingernails digging into the wood of the willow as she propped her forehead on the rough trunk. Her eyelids closed tight, attempting to squeeze in the tears determined to fall.

Her mind started to work again before her body did.

He had just used her. Used her and left her.

A hot flush ran up her neck, flooding her face.

Humiliation.

Humiliation only made more bitter by the heated laughter from the pond.

# CHAPTER 15

Four miserable days went by. Poking by the dressmaker, scolding by her mother, and agonizing dinners where she had to watch Jason, drunk, avoid her like the plague.

He never looked at her, never acknowledged her in conversation, never gave the slightest hint he thought there was anything but empty air where she was.

What he was still doing at Curplan was beyond her. It was obvious his reasons had nothing to do with her—or maybe it was to make sure she told no one of their past.

On day five, Katalin was sitting in the Primrose drawing room, sketching out both the procession into the dining room and the proper seating arrangement at a dinner party that included a viscount, two barons, the wives of each, a dowager duchess, the son of a count, the granddaughter of an earl, and the second daughter of a marquess. Her mother's watchful eye hovered over her placements, offering only the slightest grunt of approval when she placed them in the appropriate order.

Her mother did not afford Katalin the tiniest, "well done," even though Katalin had not made a mistake in days about the hierarchy of the peers.

Katalin stifled a sigh. What was she even doing in this country? A country that clearly did not like her. Her mother only tolerated her presence, and Jason hated her. She truly did not think she could undergo this torture for much longer, her heart hurting at every turn.

She used to be in charge of her life. Not at the mercy of others. Not at the mercy of people judging her—Jason, her mother—and they were only the start. The whole of society would soon be judging her, she had been told again and again. And she was not sure she could stand up to the scrutiny—already she was beginning to buckle under her mother's judgments. Jason's judgments. Beginning to question her own worth.

Katalin would have to talk to her father tonight. There had to be another way to ensure her safety—something other than this elaborate scheme to win her a title. Her father had resisted her pleas thus far. But she was not giving up on getting out of here.

Then a sliver of salvation walked through the door of the drawing room.

Reanna, in a smart royal blue riding habit, moved to the table Katalin was seated at, looking down at the paper in front of Katalin. She chuckled. "That is a tricky one. But it looks perfect. No noses to be bent out of shape." She looked over at her aunt. "Aunt Maureen, you would not believe what the dressmaker has done now. The latest set of gowns has been delivered—you must see them. The details of the lace—dreadful. I do not think you will be pleased."

"Where are they?" Katalin's mother asked, a deep frown already set on her face.

"In the main drawing room. I think this may take you hours to correct. I would have done so myself, but you are the expert. Perhaps I should gather the duchess and we will take Katalin for a while? Do not fret, we will make sure we are productive with Katalin's time."

Already walking to the door, ready for battle, Katalin's mother nodded. "Yes. Please do so. She would do well to learn some common French phrases, since I cannot expect her to learn the entire language in days."

"Of course, Aunt." Reanna smiled, waiting until her aunt left the room. She turned to Katalin. "You look dreadful."

"I do?"

"Yes. You look like a lost puppy that just got kicked. You have for days." With a wicked smile on her lips, she grabbed Katalin's wrist and pulled her to standing, dragging her out of the room. "So Aggie and I have some fun planned."

"You do?"

"Yes, but we need to escape quickly. I do not want my aunt to interrupt our plans." Reanna didn't let go of Katalin's wrist, instead, leading her through the maze of hallways and out a side door that led into the east gardens.

She dropped Katalin's wrist, pointing to the woods in sight. "We just have to take the trail a bit of a way into the woods." Looking down at Katalin's feet, she frowned. "Do you have delicate feet? I do not know that the slippers will do in the forest."

"I will be fine," Katalin said, just grateful she was escaping. "Where are we going?"

"That is a surprise. Come, let us get to the woods before Aunt Maureen spies us out a window."

Reanna took off, skirting through the low maze of the raised flower beds that lined this side of the main hall. Within minutes, they were deep into the woods on a winding trail.

When Reanna veered, leading them into a wide grass clearing, Katalin saw Aggie across the open ground, fiddling with something on top of a stump.

At the sound of their footsteps crunching on dried twigs, Aggie stood, turning around. "Excellent. You are here."

She walked toward Katalin and Reanna, leaving several champagne flutes balanced on top of the flat-topped tree stump.

"We are." Katalin looked from one to the other. "So what is the surprise?"

Aggie pointed to a thick tree near the trail. "That is why we are here."

Katalin looked and chortled. "That? That is why we are here? Swords? Bows and arrows? Are those pistols?"

"Yes, yes, and yes," Aggie said, glee on her face. "I thought it would be the perfect distraction for you, as you have appeared so down these past days. I know the whole situation must be stressful for you, so I thought a little bit of destroying things might do you good."

"Aggie does not believe in letting angst fester in one's chest." Reanna tucked her hand under Katalin's elbow, bringing her over to the weaponry. "I thought her silly when she first mentioned it to me, but then she began teaching me how to use a bow and arrow, and I have learned that it does wonders for my disposition. Although Killian still refuses to let Aggie teach me how to shoot a pistol—he said he would teach me, if anyone would. Though he has been curiously lax on doing so, the bugger."

The three of them stopped at the tree, looking down at the pile of arms.

"Forgive me, I did not know which one you liked using the most, so I brought them all," Aggie said. "I imagined with your past, you would be familiar with all of them?"

Mouth slightly agape in disbelief, Katalin eyed the two ladies. Women like this actually existed?

Reanna picked up a bow. "I may change my mind once I actually learn to fire a pistol, but I think I will always prefer the bow—I find it stealthy. Even if Aggie can out-aim me by far." She leaned toward Katalin, her voice in a loud smirking whisper. "But I can squash her at chess, so we get along grandly."

Aggie laughed. "It is true."

Katalin watched Reanna rummage through the pile of arrows. "I must admit, I have never used a bow. But the sword, the pistol..." Katalin's fingernails curled, itching her own palms. "It has been far too long. Too long, but exactly what I need."

Aggie jumped, laughing with unbound enthusiasm. "Excellent. I can already see a smile creeping onto your face. What first? Swords? Pistols?"

Katalin eyed the open wooden pistol case on the ground. The silver of the matching dueling pistols gleamed. "Pistols. I am accustomed to shooting at objects in close range, so if we are to be aiming at the champagne glasses," she pointed at the stump, "then this should be a delightful challenge."

"Good choice, I will ready them." Aggie picked up the pistol case, bringing it over to another stump several steps away. She set right to work, pulling out of the case the powder flask and lead bullets and setting them on the stump.

As Aggie readied the pistols, Katalin picked up the longsword with the thinner blade, checking the heft of it in her hand.

Stepping a distance away from Reanna, Katalin cut figure eights with the blade, loosening her wrist. Nostalgia panged her—how she missed the security of a strong blade strapped to her waist.

The sword was longer than the cutlasses she was accustomed to, but once she could gauge the weight in her hand, she spun, sword high, swinging the blade deep into the bark of the next tree over. It felt good.

"Beautiful—you have light feet, Katalin," Reanna said over the now-squawking birds above. "That was elegant in its ferocity. Brutal—almost like you wished someone's neck was in the line of your sword, instead of that poor tree."

Katalin shrugged, yanking the blade from the tree. She avoided looking at Reanna.

"My aunt?" Reanna asked.

"I wish her no ill will," Katalin said, choosing her words carefully. She recognized she was still the new one and didn't wish to seem the cad. "I am grateful that she offered to help me, offered a way to keep my head attached to my body."

"But?"

Katalin caught Reanna's gaze and saw only genuine concern in her eyes. Katalin sighed. "I am wondering if my lifelong imaginations of what I dreamed a mother—my mother—would be, are better than the reality before me."

"What did you imagine?"

"I imagined her to be warm. Loving. Smiling—at least on occasion." Katalin thrust downward with the sword, burying the tip into the dirt. "I always pictured her, if she lived with us on the island—as running on the beach, laughing, splashing her feet in the water with me. It was an image I created long ago as a little girl, and I guess I never lost it. It was how I always saw her."

"So you are disappointed?" Reanna asked. "I was hoping the past few days would ease her stern demeanor."

Katalin traced the curved golden hilt of the sword with her forefinger, pondering the question. "I do not know what I am. Yes. Partly. But I have a mother. A living, breathing mother. It was always a hole in me. A hole that is now filled. But this was not what I imagined. She is not what I imagined."

"Maybe with patience? I do believe the emotion is in her—she is more than what she is currently showing."

"Maybe, but she looks at me like a project, a task. Not as a human being with feelings. I had hoped after we met, after she got to know me, she would warm. But she has not. And I cannot make her like me."

Aggie stepped next to Reanna, pistol in hand. "You may be making the assumption that she does not like you. I do think Lady Pentworth likes many more things than she would ever let on. It is true that she is currently very driven to get you ready. That may be overshadowing what her true feelings are." Aggie waved her free hand. "But regardless of what she thinks, there is the fact that you have two people right here in front of you that like you very much."

Aggie stepped to her, holding the butt end of the pistol to her. "And I cannot wait to see your shot."

"First one to break three glasses wins?" Katalin smirked, checking the line on the elegant silver pistol.

Aggie laughed. "Yes. Yes I do like you extremely well, Katalin."

~ ~ ~

Breaking in new horses on the estate, they were far into the south woods when the shot echoed through the forest. At the sound, the duke pulled up hard on his horse, blocking Southfork and Jason.

"Did you hear that?"

"Yes." Killian gripped his reins, already turning his stallion into the direction of the main hall. "But I only heard one."

Another shot rang out.

"Bloody hell," the duke yelled at Southfork's back, deadly fury firing his words. "Where are they?"

"The hall, last I knew."

Jason turned his horse, following the two in a breakneck race down the twisted path.

More shots echoed in the trees.

If Jason ever had any doubts about his brother-in-law and his unfailing devotion to his sister, they were instantly dismissed. The man could not get to his wife fast enough. The same was obvious for Southfork and his wife.

The continued blasts offered the men a trail to follow, and within ten minutes, the three thundered into a small clearing in the east woods.

The duke was the first off his horse.

"Bloody hell, Aggie—what do you think you are doing?" He stalked over to his wife, glowering down at her. "You bloody well know you should not be doing this. You scared me to my grave."

Jason watched as his sister gave a flip of her wrist, pistol in hand, sweet smile on her face. Jason knew that smile. He had grown up watching it. She was in trouble and she knew it, and she was going to try to get out of it. "There is no danger, Devin. Miss Dewitt has just had a few difficult days, so we thought some fun might be in order."

"Fun is shooting pistols?" The duke grabbed her wrist, ripping the pistol from her hand. He stepped away from her, fully cocking it, and fired it at the ground by a nearby oak. The shot echoed through the forest as the duke set the pistol on a nearby stump. His movements jerking in rage, Jason wondered for a second if he was going to throttle something. The stump. A tree. His sister.

Lady Southfork stepped up next to Aggie. "Truly, there is no reason to be angry at Aggie. It was my idea. We were talking about marksmanship and how Aggie is teaching me to shoot with a bow and arrow. And then that naturally led into talk about pistols, which led into talk about swords."

Southfork grabbed his wife's arm, pulling her from Aggie. "Which what, led into you three coming out here to play war? Dammit, Reanna, you said you would not touch a pistol until I showed you."

"I did not touch a pistol, Killian. I know what I promised."

"And the sword?" Killian pointed to the set of swords leaning against the trunk of a nearby tree.

Still on his horse, Jason almost laughed out loud when he saw Lady Southfork's face go to sweet innocence, mimicking his sister's face. She shrugged at her husband, not admitting to anything.

Jason tried to resist, but then allowed himself a quick glance at Katalin. She was a step back from the other two, eyes wide as she watched the scene.

Not judging, not laughing, just fascinated.

Jason surveyed the weaponry behind the skirts of the three females. Several pistols, gun powder, and bows and arrows, were scattered around the three swords. Champagne flutes were set on a far off stump, shattered glass lining the ground around it.

Damn Katalin. Jason knew immediately this was her fault.

"Truly, Devin, we only came out here to ease Katalin's stress," Aggie said. "I would think you would be more gracious in letting me help a friend through a tumultuous time. This was only to provide a fun diversion for the mind."

"Diversion? Do not even try to pin this on anything other than your own insatiable need for excitement," the duke seethed. "Dammit, Aggie, we talked about this. Andrew is not even five months old."

"Correction." Aggie's voice turned irksome. "You talked about it. You lectured me on it. But you most definitely did not listen to what I had to say about it."

Jason could see exactly where his sister's temper was going to lead her discussion with Devin. And the way Southfork was looking at his wife, he guessed they were not far behind.

He coughed.

No response from any of the four, each insistently glaring at their spouse.

He coughed louder.

Aggie's head popped past Devin's shoulder to look at him. "What, Jason? Now you have something to say?"

He hid his smirk, shrugging. "No. The slightest bit of discretion may be in order, that is all."

She groaned a sigh. "Fine."

Aggie started walking away from the group, aimed at the trail that led off deeper into the woods.

With his own groan, Devin had no choice but to grab the reins of his horse and stomp after her. Southfork was already walking off with his own wife in the opposite direction.

Loud voices trailed behind both couples.

Jason waited a moment before looking down at Katalin. She had already gathered the swords, bundling them in her arms, and started walking toward the main hall.

Jason waited until the other two couples were both out of sight, deep into their respective arguments. He nudged his horse forward, quickly catching up to Katalin on the wide path to the hall.

She refused to acknowledge the horse at her side and continued an even pace with head high and eyes forward.

"Kat."

She kept walking.

Jason jumped from the horse. "Katalin, stop."

"No, thank you."

He growled, tossing the reins of the horse onto the nearest branch. A few long strides and he reached her, grabbing her arm and spinning her toward him. The swords clattered to the ground.

"What did you tell them, Kat? What do they know?"

Her eyes went to the heavens, her head shaking with an exaggerated sigh. "What did I tell them? That is what is foremost in your mind?"

"That is what is in front of me, yes. You were out shooting and playing with damn swords with them. So, yes—hell, yes, that is what is foremost on my mind. What did you tell my sister and your cousin about who you are?"

Slowly, she reached up and pulled back his fingers on her bare arm, removing his hand. "They know I have captained a privateering ship."

Hell. Jason shook his head. "You did not. You could not be that stupid."

She spun, walking away from him again, leaving the swords and not hiding her muttered blasphemies.

He fell in line beside her, and he could see that only irked her more.

She gave him a quick glance, not hiding the venom in her eyes. "Stupid, Jason? Pray tell me that you did not just call me stupid. And yes, they know. They know who I am. Who my mother is. Who my father is. What I used to do. That I can be condemned for piracy. That I have only known a life on the seas. That I can shoot. That I have been in battles. They know it all. Why do you think they have been helping me?"

A harsh laugh stopped her, and she turned to him. "But that is not what you are talking about, is it?" She started moving again, her walk turning into a stomp as she waved him off. "Do not worry, Jase. The one thing they do not know about is us. That I have kept hidden. Hidden well."

Jason stood, rooted, running through her flying words once more. And then he hit upon the thing that was most alarming. So alarming it sent his gut dropping.

He ran after her, grabbing her forearm.

"Wait, Kat. Condemned for piracy? What are you talking about?"

"No. You do not need to know."

She tried to jerk her arm free, but he wasn't about to let her go. "You will not take another step until you tell me."

She glared at him, her cheek throbbing.

"Tell me, Katalin."

She tried one last time to twist her arm out of his grasp. He didn't let her succeed. Not until he saw her start to shake. Anger? Fear? Sadness? He didn't recognize what he was seeing in her.

Had he forgotten her so completely? Or had she changed so completely? Whatever it was he was seeing, it stopped him. Made him drop her arm, slowly. Gentle.

How had he forgotten she needed calm? She needed to not feel trapped.

Her eyes narrowed at him, startled by his release, but she didn't move away.

"Tell me, Kat." He forced his voice soft. "Tell me."

She took a deep breath, and it eased the shake in her chest. Her head went down, not looking at him. "I do not know the details. What I know is that there was an ultimatum given to my father by a man named Daunte—he was the one that had provided the targets and letters of marque to my father. My father refused the request, and the man has rescinded his support. Destroyed all evidence that the last English letter of marque I sailed under ever existed. He has effectively made my actions when we took the Rosewater piracy. And he has threatened my father with witnesses that will testify to my piracy."

"Bloody hell. Who is the bastard?"

She did not look up at him. "I do not know. My father refuses to tell me more than the name Daunte. But he did reach out to my mother for help. She is the one that concocted the plan to have me married. She believes it will keep me safe. I do not know the laws, but she says if I marry a peer, I will be afforded the privilege of peerage that comes along with a title."

Jason gave a low whistle. "And to speak slander against a peer is punishable. That alone would stop most from such accusations."

Katalin nodded, still keeping her head down. "Beyond that, she believes if I marry a man above reproach, with enough power, it is additional insurance to my safety. My father has settled a respectable dowry upon me—large enough to draw the right attention, but not overly large to attract the wrong sort of man, or so my mother tells me."

Niggling thoughts of suspicion entered Jason's mind as he looked at the top of her honey-red hair. Was it even possible that she knew he was alive? That she knew who his sister was? How to get to him? The coincidence of her showing up at Curplan was suspect, and he could not attribute it to fate.

Fate was not something he believed in anymore.

"Your mother is unusually canny."

Katalin shrugged, the fire gone from her voice as she finally looked up at him. "Is she? I do not know her very well. At all, truth told. I do not know anything about any of this, Jason. All of this is happening to me and I have no control. But I have no other options. So I am doing what I am told. This is your world, Jason, not mine. The customs, the laws, the social mores—all of it is foreign to me, and I am trapped. Trapped and just trying to survive in it long enough to protect what is most important."

"You are correct—you do not know what you are dealing with, Katalin, which is all the more reason that telling my sister and your cousin about your past was a mistake. There is no arguing it. What would happen if others knew? The truth of your past? If it spread?"

Her eyes turned worried. "Is your sister not to be trusted?"

"Of course she is."

"And my cousin, is she not to be trusted?"

"I do not know. Southfork I trust, but I do not know his wife that well. All I care about—" He cut himself off, not able to finish his sentence. Not with all the doubts in his head. Not with memories of her past actions still haunting him.

"All you care about is what, Jason?" Ire immediately flashed back into her eyes. "What could you possibly care about? You have made it perfectly clear that it is not me you care about. So is it you? Are you afraid I told them of us?"

"Yes, but not—"

"Not to worry upon that, Jase. As I told you, they know nothing of us. And I have to get inside for another fitting." She began walking away.

Jason stared at her retreating back. "So you can just move onward like that? Callous? Cold? You need a husband so go and find a husband?"

She stopped.

Seconds passed, but she did not step forward, did not turn around.

But at her sides, her hands stretched back and forth from straight, to fists, to straight.

The fists won.

She spun, flying back to him, arm waving in a wide arc and voice harsh. "What happened to you, Jason? What happened? Who are you? What the hell did you turn into?"

She stopped in front of him, eyes blazing, chest heaving, her anger palpable.

Blast it. All he wanted to do was grab her, throw her on the ground and take her. Take her in broad daylight. Take her hard. And leave no mistake about whom she belonged to.

But he couldn't. He couldn't shake the feeling he was about to be consumed by her—one small spark away from hell.

"What did I turn into?" he asked.

"You ask what? How about the willow?" Her arm flew wide again and Jason had to duck so he didn't get hit.

"You say cold, callous, Jase? What you did to me the other night under the willow—that was not the man I used to know. You never would have humiliated me so. Used me. Then left me like that. You never possessed that cruelty. You used to be even, Jason. Even. I loved that about you. You were always solid. Through everything you had been through. What we went through. You were even. A rock. You let nothing beat you. You were calm, always moving forward, even when you had nowhere to go."

She stepped into him, closing off the little space that was still between them. Chin tilted up to him, her voice went low, accusing.

"You lost your peace, Jason. You lost it. And you are not the man I knew."

"What the hell do you expect, Kat? You took my peace. You. Do you think I wanted to finally get back to England and then drink myself nightly into the gutter? You had already destroyed me, and then I arrived here only to be greeted with atrocities. My father was murdered. My mother had gone crazy. And my sister had been shot and was kidnapped. And all of it was my damn fault."

Katalin gasped, falling back a step, her face immediate concern. "What? Your fault? But Aggie never said...how?"

He rubbed his forehead, the heavy guilt that had weighed on him for the past two years surfacing. "Things happened, Kat. Bad things."

"What? Why?"

He pondered not telling her, but she would probably find out from Aggie eventually, as they were getting on so well. "Do you remember the men I told you about that had me thrown into the ship hold—the men I was gathering evidence of treason against?"

"Yes."

"Before they got to me, I had sent the evidence to my father. My father was killed when the leader went after what I had sent. Aggie watched him die. And then the bastard went after her. Were it not for the duke, she would be dead as well. All of it—my disappearance, my father's death, sent my mother into a catatonic state. Mother has never recovered."

"Aggie told me about the man that was after her, but she said nothing of your involvement. Nothing that it was your fault."

"Yes, well, it was."

She moved to him, her fingers light on his forearm. "Jason, I am so sorry. That you had to go through that alone."

His eyes whipped to hers and he didn't bother to tone down his voice. "Alone. Exactly. I was alone. So yes, I lost my peace. What my family suffered because of me. What you did to me. Why would I not want to forget it all? What else am I to do?"

She blinked hard, sympathy slipping away from her face as she took a step backward and crossed her arms under her chest. "So rather than be productive, you have felt sorry for yourself for two years? Two years of drinking yourself to death? Of not moving on?"

His eyebrows arched at her.

"Yes, your sister mentioned that is all you have done for years. Which is killing her to watch, by the by. You have been standing in one spot—bitter and angry. And now you feel the need to chastise me for wanting to move on, for wanting to protect myself?"

"You seem to be particularly eager to move forward, Katalin."

"And you seem to be particularly eager to be rid of me, Jason." Her hold on her body tightened. "Since the day I thought you died, not an hour has passed that I did not wish to be back on that island with you. Back in your arms. But I have not had the luxury of stopping. I have had to move forward, one minute at a time. But while I have never forgotten you—never stopped loving you—you have let bitterness consume your soul."

She paused, shaking her head. "Either that, or maybe I was always wrong about you. Maybe you have always been like this, and I never recognized it. Selfish. Cruel. Maybe I was just a fine dalliance for you while you were stuck on an ocean, but now that you are home and an earl, it is best to be rid of me? We were married, Jase. I was your wife. Your wife. What of that?"

"Was it real, Kat? Our wedding?"

"Does it matter?"

He shrugged.

Did it matter if they were lawfully married or not? He still loved her, even with all of his suspicions. But her past actions and her current goal of a titled husband forced him not to trust her.

He truly had no answer.

"Exactly. So you are clear of me." Her voice cracked, all fire gone. "You refused to claim me, so what we had together never happened. I understood you perfectly under the willow, Jase. Perfectly. I know when I am not wanted, and I would be a fool to allow you to treat me this way. To use me and throw me away. I will not allow it."

"Katalin, you misunderstand—"

"No. No, I do not think I do. You do not want me. And I cannot make you. So I will never admit to knowing you before this time. I believe that should ease your worries on the matter. Please excuse me."

This time she didn't walk away, she ran.

Ran, and there was no stopping her.

# CHAPTER 16

Katalin stood in the entry of Lord Southfork's London home, her gloved hands smoothing down for the hundredth time the emerald silk of the most exquisite gown she had ever seen. Exquisite—and it was on her body.

As difficult and overbearing as her mother had been over the past two weeks, the woman did have one outstanding trait—impeccable taste. That, and she was a maven of propriety. After the first rough week—rough because of her mother and because of Jason and because of the combination of them both—Katalin settled into a week of numbly doing exactly what her mother asked of her.

No questions. No complaints. Just regurgitation of all she was taught. With that, her mother's constant judging did ease, even if the woman did not truly warm to Katalin.

Katalin still didn't know what her mother thought of her. A burden? A mere inconvenience?

She tried to keep in mind what Reanna had told her. That her mother was cold, but that did not mean she didn't feel. But if her mother did have any kind feelings toward Katalin, she hid them well.

It hurt, but in all reality, Katalin had never had a mother, so the sudden presence of one that didn't care for her didn't bother her nearly as much as the situation with Jason had.

Jason she had once had.

Jason she had loved more than life itself.

So how he had ripped her heart out under the willow had left a gaping wound in her soul. A wound she was having a hard time healing. Or at least ignoring.

But he did not want her. And what was she to do, except figure out a way to not want him? She had to for her own sanity, but she was having a devil of a time doing so. No matter that he humiliated her. No matter that he discarded her. She still wanted him and hated her own lack of pride in the matter.

She was grateful when he finally left Curplan the day after their last encounter. She did not think she could continue to see him daily, continue to be drawn into conversation with him. It hurt too intensely.

The only bright spots in her days had been Reanna and Aggie. Katalin knew she had been peckish, but her two new friends asked no questions, finding their only duty to make her laugh. And she did manage to laugh.

So now she stood, polished—the product of all of their hard work in making her a presentable lady—waiting to finally be judged by the masses.

"You will be fine, lass." Her father's voice made her jump. "I regret I cannot accompany you tonight. Witness what you were always destined to be."

She watched him hobble heavy on his cane into the entryway, his good eye shining bright on her.

"You have more faith in me than mother."

"Aye. But I know you have never not accomplished what you set out to do, lass." His hands went on her shoulders. "This has been hard on you. I seen it. But you will do this, and you will protect your own. Just remember what is at stake."

Katalin nodded. She knew. Her heart ached it knew so well.

"You are ready?" Her mother's voice preceded her down the stairs.

Katalin looked up at her. Perfection in dress, in hair, in spine.

"Yes, if I meet your approval."

Her mother glided down the stairs, her hawk eyes on Katalin the entire time. In the entryway, she did a slow circle around her daughter. For weeks Katalin had been unnerved by these inspections, but was now able to patiently take the scrutiny without fidgeting.

Completing the circle, her mother announced her verdict. "You will do well. I dare say you are even more exquisite than I was at my debut."

Katalin held her shock at her mother's words in check, offering only a slight smile. She knew relieved laughter would be frowned upon.

She went up in her slippers to kiss her father's cheek goodbye, and then, within ten minutes, they were on their way. Her cousin and Lord Southfork had taken an earlier carriage, so Katalin was alone with her mother.

It was silent in the coach, the constant clip clop of the horses' hooves the only thing keeping Katalin's mind from spinning into complete nervousness. She knew her gloved fingers had begun to fidget on her lap when her mother's voice cut into her thoughts.

"Katalin, I understand your father told you long ago that I did not want you. That it was the reason I sent you to him, abandoning you." She cleared her throat, drawing herself impossibly straighter, but her voice was softer than Katalin had ever heard it. "I have already had it out with your father about that time period. About what he told you. I cannot fault him for doing what he did. He did what was needed. I do, however, wish you to know he told you the exact opposite of the truth. I wanted you. I was prepared to leave my life for you. To keep you. To leave with your father. But then I was told you were dead."

Katalin's eyes widened, her throat closing. "Mother…"

"I did think you should know the truth of the matter. I did want you. It is important to me that you know that."

Katalin blinked hard. She had no idea her mother possessed her own heartache—her own memories that haunted her. But before Katalin had a chance to respond, her mother's voice resumed its usual clipped pace. "I am confident my plan to marry you well will work. At this moment, you are the epitome of what makes a darling of the ton. You have a vivaciousness that will intrigue many. Pair that with your dowry, and you will attract a flurry of initial attention. But be careful, child, once you are in the throes of it, you must keep your tongue. It is your only lacking feature."

"I will remember."

"But if my plan does not work, know that we will find another way. Another way to hide you. I will not allow you to be in danger. Your father and his poor choices may be the cause of all of this, but I am the end of it."

"Mother, I know you disagree with what he let me do, but I cannot allow you to speak ill of my father. Please, moth—"

"Lady Pentworth—from hence forward, you will have to address me as Lady Pentworth. The story I have concocted has us four relations removed, so it is a necessity. It will be easier if you get into the habit." Her cheek twitched, almost to a smile. "As for your father, your defense of him is admirable, but unnecessary. He did you well in the important traits—you are kind and loyal—even if he was misguided in certain aspects of your upbringing."

Once more, Katalin was shocked into silence. The carriage slowed.

"Back straight, dear, we have arrived."

~ ~ ~

Jason saw it when it happened—his eyes had been glued on the swirling skirts—but it was also hard not to miss the gasps emanating from the dance floor.

"Jason, you need to save her."

His sister popped up in front of him, and Jason tore his bleary eyes from the widening circle on the dance floor to Aggie.

"Save who?"

"Who? Are you that drunk? Did you not see?"

He shrugged his shoulders.

"Really, Jason, I have had it with your imbibing. Miss Dewitt, of course. She was just cut by Lord Vutton. He was the exact type we were trying to avoid—Katalin's observations are entirely too keen for a delicate man such as he—but he somehow made it onto her dance card and has now abandoned her on the dance floor. Disastrous. I would send Devin or Killian, but they are married and all would know it is a pity save. I need a bachelor." She grabbed his arm, tugging it as her rapid words flew. "Jason, come, we only have seconds to save this."

She turned, pulling him, her head bobbing up and around the tall shoulders in the crush before her. Jason kept his feet planted.

She whipped around. "I swear to God I will have Devin cut you out of every investment from here to eternity if you do not do this, Jason. You have been a drunkard for well too long, but I still think you know he is the only one keeping the estate intact."

"You would not dare."

"No?"

"Do not force me, Aggie."

"Do not test me, Jason."

Her hand tightened on his arm, her face set hard against him.

Jason stared at her, will against will.

Another murmur swept through the crowd, and Aggie's eyes flickered over her shoulder to the dance floor. Relief flooded her face.

"Thank goodness. Even better."

Jason looked above the plum-colored feathers on his sister's headdress. It took some couples moving out of his way on the dance floor before he found Katalin again. A tall man—Jason could only see the back of him—had stepped in and clearly saved Katalin from complete ruin on her first night in society.

Aggie's hand dropped from his arm. "Excellent. This should take care of the situation quite nicely."

"How?"

"That is the new Duke of Letson. I have never met him, but as I understand it, he has impeccable taste." She continued to watch the dance floor, hope bubbling in her eyes. "No one has ever seen him dance, so that he has just saved her more than outshines the cut she just suffered. Very nice. He is splendid."

Jason looked from his sister to the dance floor once more. A turn, and he could see the man's face. For the first time that night, jealously stung his spine. Tall, dark hair, solid build, and a damn duke. The bastard was handsome.

Jason took an instant dislike to him. Mostly because the duke's hands were on his wife—bloody hell—had he just called Katalin his wife in his mind?

He clearly wasn't drunk enough. Tipping back his wine glass, he downed the rest of the burgundy liquid.

But he couldn't stop his eyes from drifting back to the dance floor. Blast it. Could Katalin truly fall for a man like that? He seemed to meet her requirements—a title, a cache of power, a willingness to save her from harm.

"My apologies, Jason." Aggie was looking up at him, watching him with slightly narrowed eyes. He recognized the look. She was trying to figure something out about him. "I did not mean to threaten you so. It was all I could think to do in the moment. The cut on Miss Dewitt needed immediate interference and you were most handy."

"All ended well." Jason lifted his empty glass to the dance floor.

His sister's face turned even more calculating. "Why did I have to threaten you? It was just a simple dance. A simple step-in to save her reputation. Even as a drunkard, I have not known you to lose your spirit of generosity."

Jason didn't like where Aggie's thoughts were taking her.

"So why not? Why not save Miss Dewitt? Do you not care for her for some reason? Past your odd meeting, I did not think you talked to her but a sentence or two at Curplan."

"I did not like being threatened, Aggie."

She stared at him for a long moment, her eyes still shrewd. "No. It was not that." She shook her head. "I do wonder on your refusal, though. You did not want to dance with Miss Dewitt. Her specifically. Is there something between you two that I do not know of?"

"No. Your imagination runs away with you, Aggie. One, you did not need a drunkard like me tripping his way to Miss Dewitt. Two, I simply did not wish to be bothered at the moment. My refusal had nothing to do with Miss Dewitt. You may drop the matter."

"Very well." His sister looked to the open swath of dancers where the duke was accompanying Katalin off the dance floor. "As they are already chatting like old friends, I have new things to worry about."

"Such as?"

"Mitigating all of the jealous eyes shooting daggers in the direction of Miss Dewitt right now. The duke is quite the catch, and there are too many young chits and mamas plotting against her at this very moment."

Jason scanned the crush. Aggie was spot-on about the jealous eyes and tongues flying.

"God speed, Aggie," he said dryly.

She slipped away from him, bright smile on her face, ready to do battle.

~ ~ ~

After encountering the Duke of Letson at three separate affairs in the last week alone, Katalin had begun to harbor the smallest hope that her mother's plan would work.

She found the duke incredibly nice, handsome, and witty. Everything in a suitor she had hoped for. Given his title, and that he was secure with his own fortune, he was also everything that her mother had hoped for.

The duke liked her, or at least found her interesting. That, Katalin could easily discern, even with the limited conversations that were afforded to them on the dance floors and in the presence of her mother, Aggie or Reanna.

So on the fourth evening her new friends had managed to position her in front of the duke, Katalin was relieved to see it was a smaller, more informal gathering. Hopefully, it would allow more than casual conversation with the duke.

She was anxious to delve deeper into his personality. After all, if she had managed to manifest an incredibly poised veneer at the larger parties and dinners, she imagined he was very capable of doing the same.

After dining, the duke crossed her path and offered to accompany her to the outside veranda for a breath of fresh air.

Stepping into the cool dampness, Katalin snapped her fan closed, taking a deep breath of non-stifling fall air. The roof overhang above the veranda saved them from the slight mist coming down.

After a quick glance over her shoulder, she looked up at the duke. "You will forgive me, your grace, but I must stay within sight of Lady Pentworth. She is a stickler of propriety, and she is not about to fail in her duty as my chaperone."

"Of course, Miss Dewitt," the duke said. "I would not dream of compromising your reputation."

"Thank you." Katalin walked to the wrought iron railing, gloved fingers resting on the cool metal. The slight wetness on the rail soaked through the silk to her skin. A small garden below, edged with neat boxwoods, drew her attention and she couldn't help the pang of homesickness that struck her—she missed the wilds of the island vegetation. Even in the gardens on her father's estate, things grew rampant, untamable no matter how much attention the gardener put forth. It was always best to let things flow, rather than control. Nothing like the gardens here in England. Precise. Crisp. Beautiful. Untouchable.

The duke stepped next to her, and Katalin could feel his eyes solidly on her.

"I must admit, Miss Dewitt, this is a pleasant change from the normal."

Katalin looked up at him, arching her eyebrows in question.

"I am more accustomed to mamas conveniently 'encouraging' their daughters into improper situations with me."

"If you cannot catch a duke one way, any old devious way will do?"

"Yes. Too spot on, I am afraid." His hand went on the railing next to hers as his eyes went down to the crisp hedges.

"You do not care for the ladies of the ton—or their mamas, your grace?"

He shrugged. "I have experienced a few, and they do not suit me well."

"Why not?"

He looked at her, his astute dark eyes studying her. "The young ones have fanciful notions of love. The older ones are desperate."

Katalin laughed. "Make no mistake, your grace, I am desperate."

For a second he looked appalled, and Katalin bit her tongue. The tongue that her mother was convinced was going to sink Katalin.

But then the duke chuckled. "That is honesty I am unaccustomed to, Miss Dewitt."

She gave a hesitant smile. "And I am unaccustomed to absolutely everything about this world. I do apologize. I tend to say the most dreadfully wrong things. As you have already witnessed—and saved me from."

"What did you say to Lord Vutton that first night?"

Katalin shook her head. "No. I repeated it to Lady Southfork, and she made me swear to never speak those words in polite society again."

His eyebrow cocked, slight smile on his face. He was waiting for an answer.

Katalin found it entirely interesting that he was not going to ask. Just wait. He truly did expect that he would get an answer. That must be the natural arrogance of a duke. Arrogance that would come in handy were pirate hunters to someday show up at her door.

And then he surprised her. He asked. "Your integrity is admirable, Miss Dewitt, but I already think ill of Lord Vutton. Why do you think I was so quick to save you that night?"

"Ah, so it had nothing to do with me?" For some reason, that fact alone pleased Katalin, although she wasn't sure why. "You have a slight vengeful streak, do you not, your grace?"

"Possibly. And I am still curious as to what you said to him and would like to know, but I do understand your tight lips."

Katalin met his gaze, squirming against what her own intuition told her to say. So very opposite the words her mother would have her speak. She hid a sigh. The duke may as well know the magnitude of missteps she was capable of.

"I must first report that my comment was merely a reaction to a noxious question he asked. He inquired as to how far below my lace my nipples were." She braced herself as the word "nipple" left her mouth. This conversation was spinning into complete vulgarity. "I may be new to this society, but even I recognized the sheer audacity of it."

He nodded, his manner unfazed. "Defense stated. Vutton's words do not surprise. And you replied?"

She cringed before the words even left her mouth. "I asked him if he took a wicked deep lick of a horse's ass before he arrived, as his foul tongue was exacerbating his foul breath."

The duke laughed—loud—not bothering to hide the sound, not bothering to hide from the attention it gathered. "Well done, Miss Dewitt. Whoever brought you up should be inordinately pleased with his or her self."

"My father. And yes, I imagine that had he heard what I said, he would be proud, but possibly a bit disappointed I held myself somewhat in check."

"I will be curious to meet your father."

Katalin smiled, unsure what to say to that. Was this all it took? A few conversations? A few lively laughs and she would be married off to a man for the rest of her life? A man she barely knew.

A lump forced its way into her throat. A man that was not Jason.

Her eyes slid down to the railing. Dammit. Damn that Jason continued to burst into her head at the worst possible times. She had seen glimpses of him here and there at the soirees over the past weeks. Usually with a drink in his hand. Usually teetering. But he never approached her. Never smiled. Never even inclined his head in her direction.

And each and every time, it felt like he was leaving her under the willow tree again. Disposing of her from his life. Tearing out her heart. Damn him.

Her hand came up, the wet glove covering her mouth as she coughed, trying to clear the lump.

"If I may say, Miss Dewitt, I have watched you for days now, and at this moment, that particular look on your face is striking. Do not take offense, for it does not mar your beauty, but you have the look of a person that has lost someone dear. Someone you do not wish to replace in your heart."

She couldn't look up at him. She had been too obvious. Not in control of her emotions. Her mother would be horrified.

Honesty was her only ally now. "Yes. You read me correctly, your grace. I apparently do not hide it well."

The wind shifted, blowing drizzle in at them. Katalin dropped her other hand from the railing, turning fully to him, meeting his dark eyes. "But I do wonder at your observation, your grace. You seem to recognize what is happening in my heart too easily. Like you know the feeling well yourself."

"I suppose I do, Miss Dewitt."

Sadness touched her voice. "We are of like mind in this regard, are we not?"

He nodded, slowly, looking like he was accepting a truth he was troubled to acknowledge.

Katalin shook her head, curious. "Why do I suddenly like you even more than I did a moment ago?"

# CHAPTER 17

She could feel the seam splitting. First, one thread popped, then another. And she was sitting through the most excruciating dinner she had ever experienced.

A small affair at the Duke of Dunway's home, Katalin was in awe of Aggie's abilities as hostess. Flawlessness that had somehow positioned Katalin into a seat directly between the Duke of Letson and Jason. Aggie knew nothing of Katalin's past with Jason, so the seating arrangement only made sense.

For hours, Katalin had not only had to keep up bright conversation with the duke—as Aggie had concocted the whole affair solely for the purpose of putting her and the duke in more private, close proximity—she also had to ignore the copious amounts of wine Jason downed next to her.

Three, four, five, six—Katalin counted the threads popping loose down the side of her ribcage. How many stitches could she lose before her breasts spilled out of the tight top of her burgundy gown? Her left upper arm clamped down even tighter to her body, pressing the fabric as hard as she could to her ribs.

She just needed to make it to the end of dinner without showing nipples. That was all. She took another shallow breath, afraid to actually fill her lungs.

As awkward as it was to finish the meal with one free hand, Katalin succeeded, and then positioned her palm casually on her chest, holding the fabric tight to her breasts as she stood. The second the ladies were free of the males and in the drawing room, Katalin shot to Aggie's ear, leaning in with a whisper. "Aggie, might you assist me? It appears I am in need of a needle and thread."

Aggie looked down at Katalin's well-positioned arm at her side and the hand still over her chest. "I thought you were looking a touch more full on the top tonight." She gave a sympathetic smile. "The seam split, I presume?"

Without waiting for an answer, Aggie put her arm behind Katalin's waist, steering her out of the room.

Katalin groaned as they stepped into the hallway. "It is all this food during the past few weeks. I have never in my life eaten so much. My mother would be mortified that I just busted this seam."

"Let us be grateful she took the night off." Aggie pointed to Katalin's breasts. "And that you managed to hold them in during dinner. That would have been most awkward. The extra fullness does seem to land in your bosom. But do not fret; you will get better at the dinners. It is a skill to eat just enough to satisfy the host, yet to not gorge yourself."

After delivering Katalin to her chambers, Aggie left Katalin with her maid and a needle and thread. Within fifteen minutes, Aggie's maid had the seam secured and, breasts back in place, Katalin made her way down the stairs to the drawing room.

Turning right at the bottom of the staircase, Katalin started down the dark hallway and bumped smack into a chest that appeared in front of her.

Jason.

Her hand at her chest covered her slight gasp. "You scared me."

"You have never been scared in your life, Katalin."

She looked up at him, eyebrow arched, as the alcohol permeating him filtered into her nose. "Never?"

"Save that once. It is not in your nature." He grabbed her shoulders, steering her backward into the dark nook at the curvature of the staircase. "You do not get scared, Kat. You survive. That is what you excel at."

His hands were hot on her bare skin, squeezing. She gripped his forearms through his dark jacket, yanking them off of her. "Jason, I told you, time and again. I thought I was saving you. I cannot continue to apologize for it. I have to stand by what my choice was. A choice to save you." She stared at his glassy eyes, not buckling under his glare. She was tired of having the worst mistake she ever made thrown in her face. Tired and mad.

She had gone through the excruciating pain of his death. The pain of knowing she sent him to that death.

But he had lived, and then never came for her. He had been alive, and he never came for her.

Anger pricking the hairs on the back of her head, she didn't think she could stand to be near his drunk self another instant. She stepped around him, moving down the hall.

"And you are busy surviving right now, as well." His words were drawn out, poking, taunting.

Katalin spun. "What is that to mean?"

Jason kept his back to her, allowing only a slight look over his shoulder in her direction. "The duke. Your plan to capture a title. You would survive quite nicely with him, would you not?"

"What the hell do you want me to do, Jason? Hang? Lose my head?" Voice hissing, she stepped closer, almost touching his back. "Would that be enough penance for you? My head on a stake? Would that prove my love?"

She saw his eyes close, but he did not turn to her.

"It is not going to happen, Jase. There are more important things than you, and I pray that you will let me do what I need to without this constant interference. Just leave me alone, Jason. Leave me alone. Do not show up at balls—dinners—parties—and drink and stare at me. I saw you at every one of those blasted affairs. It does you no good and does nothing but further shatter my already shattered heart. Do not find me under trees, in hallways. Do not talk to me. You do not want me, so let me go."

He did not open his eyes.

Even though she knew it was a mistake, she reached out and touched his arm. Instant fire in her hand. Her breath caught hard in her chest and it took a moment to continue, her voice raw. "You will always own my heart, Jase, but I cannot lay waste to your hatred of me. I cannot let it consume me. I cannot die because of it. Let me go, Jase."

His head tilted down, but his eyes remained closed to her.

Her hand heavy, it dropped from his arm, and she turned, her slippers soft on the wood floor as she moved down the hallway, wiping fresh tears from her cheeks.

~ ~ ~

"I do not hate you, Katalin." Jason whispered it, even though he knew she was gone, knew she couldn't hear him.

"What?"

His eyes snapped open. His sister stood in front of him, speculation on her face.

"What did you hear, Aggie?"

"Only the last few words you spoke." She gripped his elbow, pulling him from the hallway into the empty front drawing room. "Jason, I do not understand what is between you and Katalin. While I thought you were nothing but a casual acquaintance to her, I am beginning to suspect that is not the case. Am I wrong?"

Jason refused to answer her, his chin jutting stubbornly out.

She waved her hand. "You may not answer, but your closed mouth tells volumes, brother. I may not understand whatever it is between the two of you, but I do know one thing."

"Which is?"

"You are running out of time."

"Time for what?"

"The duke is set to propose to Katalin. And from what I have found out about him, he is not one to wait once a decision is made."

Jason bit his tongue, thrusting the tip of it clearly into his cheek.

Aggie's eyes narrowed at him. "Hmmm. Fine. I think I just told you what you needed to know. I will not ask questions. Not yet."

"Give my regards to your husband, Aggie. My night is over." With a slight bow, Jason stepped past his sister and down the hall, ensuring Aggie stayed true to her restraint with questions.

"You look gorgeous, Katalin." Aggie leaned forward, smiling as she pulled the mask over Katalin's eyes slightly away to peek at her face. "That is you in there, is it not? You do not know how many people I have already mistaken here tonight. This is more extravagance than I am accustomed to in the little season."

Aggie turned from her to survey the large ballroom. Moving in line with her friend, Katalin adjusted the mask that covered the upper portion of her face, from mid-nose to forehead, so she could see clearly again. It was then she realized the wide feathers of her and Aggie's masks had tangled. Laughing, she took a step away as she attempted to delicately untangle the wily feathers.

"I must admit, Aggie, this is bizarre, these masks. Fun, I suppose, but bizarre. Such a production."

"The production is precisely the point, Katalin. The grander the production, the more the attendees are invested in the success of it. Masked balls do tend to be the highlight of the regular season, so it is not surprising that one would be thrown now. And while I have no need of it, there are plenty of ladies and gentleman who delight in "accidentally" flirting—or more—with those they would not normally associate with were they not hiding behind masks."

Katalin shook her head, rolling her eyes. "For all the rules of propriety, the ton truly does enjoy breaking them."

"An abundance of entitlement will do that." Aggie went to her toes, searching the ballroom. "Beyond all that, I am having a devil of a time finding your duke in this crush. Not to mention Reanna, Killian and my husband. There is not even proper space for dancing."

It was thick—too thick. The familiar feeling of suffocation was starting to tighten Katalin's chest.

"Can we make our way to the back balconies?" Katalin asked. "There looks to be more air there."

Aggie glanced at her. "Of course, from what I can see of you, you look like you are near to passing out."

Past Aggie's mask, Katalin could see the instant concern in her friend's eyes. Aggie grabbed Katalin's wrist, quickly dragging her between the wall and the crush of bodies to the row of arched doors in the back of the ballroom.

Katalin felt the duke step in line behind them halfway to the doors—or at least she thought it was him—but she could not look back to verify. She was having a hard enough time trying to breathe, trying to control the panic that had seized her chest.

Five steps from the open doors, Katalin swayed, her wrist slipping from Aggie, and would have fallen over had it not been for the sudden strong arm about her waist.

The duke's hands completely inappropriate on her body— and completely saving.

He lifted her, half carrying her on her toes out the double doors.

Aggie spun once they were free on the balcony, both of her hands clutching Katalin's arm. "Your grace, thank you so much." She leaned over Katalin's shoulder, peering at the man's face. "That is you, your grace?"

"It is."

"Good." All of her attention went back to Katalin. "Dear, you still look woozy."

Katalin could only nod.

"Here, over here." Aggie pointed to the steps going down into the gardens. "The air will be much cooler down there."

The duke kept his hands around Katalin, and they trailed Aggie down the short flight of stairs to the garden. The first bench they came to, the duke gently set Katalin down, keeping a hand lightly on her shoulder for stability.

Aggie's eyes moved from Katalin to the duke. "I do not know how long it will take to find Lady Pentworth or Lord Southfork and have a carriage brought about. Will you please sit with her, your grace?" Aggie looked around at the many couples moving to and from the gardens to the ballroom. Her bottom lip slipped under her teeth. "Lady Pentworth knows she is with me, so I do not believe anyone will question Katalin's whereabouts. This area is well-travelled."

"Go. We will be fine," the duke said.

Eyes closed, Katalin tried to force her breath into a normal pace. Several minutes passed, and the duke waited for her, patient, his hand not moving from her shoulder. A warm comfort against the tight clamp squeezing her chest.

When she finally regained control of her breathing and mind, Katalin opened her eyes, looking up at him. "I apologize I made such a fuss. I do not do well in tight spaces. And that was tight."

"It was no bother. And not so much of a fuss."

"You are exceptionally good at saving me."

"I have merely been at the right places at the right times. Plus, this was fortunate. You made it convenient for us to be free of the crowd inside and out into the night air. You look like you have gained your equilibrium." He held out his hand. "Walk with me?"

Katalin looked up into the glowing ballroom. Even from this angle, she could tell the crowd had only thickened, and Aggie had long since disappeared out of view. Her mother had been on the other side of the ballroom, and Katalin already knew how difficult it was to make it anywhere in there. Time was on her side.

She put her white-gloved hand into his. "Of course. I think it will do me well. But I believe I will need a hand on you for stability."

The duke held out his elbow, and Katalin stood, putting her hand into the crook of his arm, but was surprised at how solid her legs were. Moments ago they had felt like liquid.

They walked along the outer wall of the garden, high evergreen hedges on either side of them. Several minutes into the quiet stroll, the duke motioned with his free hand towards an arbor that led into a small garden room.

"I have been interested in speaking to you in private, Miss Dewitt. The opportunity has happened to appear. Would you mind?"

A curious glance up to him, and Katalin nodded, letting him usher her into the small square area surrounded by tall, evenly shaped boxwoods with thick grass blanketing the ground.

Katalin went to the stone bench on the side, sitting. "None can see us here—would you mind if I dispensed of this ridiculous mask?"

"Please, but only if I can remove mine." The duke joined her at the bench, his tall frame easing down next to her.

Katalin untied the ribbon at the back of her head, setting the mask on her lap, taking care not to crush the feathers. "This is such a help. Thank you for helping me escape the crowd without making a complete fool of myself."

The duke removed his simple black mask, holding it in his hand as he shifted on the bench to face her. "I doubt even a fool would have been noticed in that fray, but I was happy to oblige."

"What was it you wanted to speak to me about?"

"I am hoping you would do me the honor of marrying me."

Katalin froze, blinking hard at his dark eyes. Had she truly just heard that right? Had he just bluntly asked her to marry him?

"What?" she croaked out.

"Will you marry me, Miss Dewitt?"

"Oh." Katalin knew she looked like a simpleton, but had no control to stop it. "I am afraid I was not prepared for that question. Here in England, do courtships not take longer?"

The duke laughed. "Yes, usually they do take longer. Sometimes years. But I am not usual. I do not wish to drag such things out. I have learned in life that action is better than non-action. So I am not one to pander about once I know what I want."

"And you wish to marry me?" She had to ask it one more time to make sure she was not mistaking his intentions.

"Yes."

Katalin fiddled with the mask in her white-gloved hands, running her fingertips along the long bright feathers. She was beyond shock. But shock in that it had happened so quickly. Her mother had been right. Her plan worked.

But instant guilt gripped Katalin's mind. Where were the butterflies? The pounding heart? The stolen breath?

She felt none of it.

Her mother had said love would never be a part of this endeavor, and Katalin realized in that instant what her mother's words had truly meant. They meant a gaping hole.

"Katalin? I do realize this was abrupt, but I am hoping for some sort of response." He didn't say it unkindly, just curious.

Katalin cleared her throat, stalling. "I have all the respect in the world for you, your grace. And I do consider you a true friend. But before I can answer, there are things of me you must know. Things that may make you wish to rescind the offer. And if that is so, I will fully understand."

"Miss Dewitt, you do not need to tell me anything. My offer of marriage stands."

She shook her head. "That is kind, but I do need to tell you. I was married once."

He didn't blink. "What happened?"

"He died."

The duke's large hand slid around hers, squeezing it. "I am sorry for your loss, Miss Dewitt, but why would that threaten my proposal?"

Katalin drew in a deep breath. Why was he making this so hard? She had to tell him. She was not about to start a marriage with a foundation of deception. "Your grace, I have done other things. Things I am not proud of. Things that may eventually destroy me."

"Stop, Miss Dewitt, stop." His hand on hers tightened. "I do not wish to rehash the past. Not yours. Not mine. I doubt either of us is innocent—not in my past life—and I do not judge you on yours."

She glanced up sharply at him. Jason had used that word. This life, the next.

"What is that look?" Confusion crinkled the duke's brow.

"You said past life. It is just...it is just that those words..."

"Past is past, Miss Dewitt. There is no use in walking back in time. I understand there will always be parts of you I do not know."

"And there will be parts of you that I do not know?"

He nodded. "I am at peace with this. You may keep what you need to. As long as I may keep what I need to."

"Is it that easy?"

"It can be."

Katalin tilted her head back to look at the dark sky. A half-moon hung just above the eaves of the ballroom. "I want to believe you. Want to believe this is the right thing."

Her eyes swung to his. "Forgive me for saying so, but we are not attracted to each other. There is no passion. I consider you an entirely kind and dear friend, your grace, but there is no fire between us. Do you disagree?"

"No." He laughed. "I do not disagree. You are incredibly honest, Miss Dewitt, but that is exactly what I wish. I do not wish deception. I do not wish fire. I wish peace. Someone I can trust. But within that—make no mistake—you are definitely beautiful enough for me to create children with, Miss Dewitt. I hope you can stomach the thought—that I am not too hideous to make children with."

Katalin chuckled, rolling her eyes. "Your looks are not the problem, your grace, and you very well know that. I am sure I can find some enjoyment in that. I just do not wish to disappoint you. I count you as an important friend—with or without a marriage proposal."

"We are of like mind on that account. A marriage of friendship is completely agreeable to me. I do respect you. Do wish to see you happy. You will make a wonderful mother. And I need heirs. You can bear children, correct?"

"Yes."

He leaned in, his dark eyes searching hers. "Then what is it you are afraid of? Are you afraid I cannot pleasure you, Miss Dewitt? Afraid our friendship will get in the way?"

A thick blush instantly colored Katalin's cheeks. "No. It is not that."

"Let me assure you, I can pleasure you, Miss Dewitt. Can create fire where there is none."

Before Katalin realized his intentions, his fingers were moving in along her bare shoulder, cupping the nape of her neck as he drew her closer.

Closer, and directly onto his lips.

She had touched no man since Jason, and curiosity immediately mixed with guilt. The duke's lips—soft and warm and gentle—it was amazing how very much like Jason he was.

And how completely he was not.

The duke's other hand came up, his thumb sliding along her chin, and he deepened the kiss, parting her lips, his tongue exploring. Katalin angled her head, closing her eyes as she acquiesced to his insistent exploring.

Within a moment, she was lost. Lost in his kiss. Lost in her intentions. Lost in thought.

The kiss only awakened things that she had thought long since dead.

It hadn't been bravado—he truly could create fire where there was none.

"No."

The word filtered into her mind. Hard. Angry. Hazy.

In the next instant a hand gripped her arm and ripped her from the duke. A yank to her feet, and she stumbled, her silk-clad feet slipping on the wet grass.

"No, Katalin." Jason spun her, his rage grip tightening painfully on her arm. "I will not allow another's hands upon you."

It took a moment for Katalin to realize Jason had appeared out of the darkness, his black mask pushed up onto his forehead, and he had manhandled her away from the duke. In the next moment, her own anger spiked.

She found her footing. "Why? You have no claim on me, Jason. You have already made that perfectly clear."

His face went into hers, his teeth in a growl. "You are mine, Katalin. No other hands will touch your body."

The duke forced himself between the two of them, shoving Jason and ripping his grip from her arm. She stumbled backward, but the duke grabbed her left flailing wrist, righting her.

"You have no business here, Clapinshire. I suggest you take your leave." Voice seething, the duke moved his wide frame, blocking Katalin from Jason's view.

"She cannot marry you, Letson." Jason's words were suddenly calm—deathly calm.

No. Hell no. Not now. He was going to do it. Jason was going to ruin everything.

Panicked, Katalin tried to move from behind the duke, but he had his arm up, keeping her locked behind him.

"Why the hell not, Clapinshire?"

"Miss Dewitt is already married."

Katalin swayed on her feet, the world concurrently slowing and spinning.

"To whom?"

"Me."

"Preposterous. What kind of a farce are you concocting Clapinshire?"

Moving through the fog of shock, Katalin ducked under the duke's arm, stepping between the two of them, her hand on the duke's chest. Good, because the duke looked ready to attack. She attempted to make her voice as light and calm as possible. "Please, your grace, Lord Clapinshire is merely a misguided suitor, nothing more."

"He is much more, Miss Dewitt."

"He is?"

"Yes, he is a man about to sully your reputation."

Katalin gave a serene nod. "Yes. And also misguided, and may I say, somewhat delusional. But there is past with him, your grace. Past that needs to be set to rest, before I can move onward."

She cleared her throat, hoping against hope she was not about to go too far. "I know it is entirely inappropriate, but I must call upon the kindness of our friendship—please, your grace, let me talk to Lord Clapinshire in private."

"I cannot do that, Miss Dewitt."

"Please, your grace. I am in no danger from Lord Clapinshire. You know I am with him, so it is assured he will do nothing to harm me. I merely need to speak to him. To bring peace to the past."

The duke's eyes flickered from her to Jason. Katalin did not dare a look back over her shoulder at Jason—she could only watch the duke's face to read her fate.

Seconds ticked by and just when Katalin was sure the duke was to refuse her, he gave one crisp nod, his eyes falling on her.

"I do not believe you will be missed for a few minutes, Miss Dewitt." He pointed to the tall hedges lining the garden walk and then turned away, picking up her fallen mask from the grass. "But put your mask on before you disappear into the gardens. I will not allow a breach upon your reputation."

Katalin took the mask from the duke's hand, wiping away the slight dew and setting it to her face. Feathers were already matted to ruin, their colors running and mixing and bleeding onto her white gloves. She felt Jason's hands instantly at the back of her head, tying the ribbons tight. "Thank you, your grace. This is the utmost in generosity."

"We will discuss this at a later time, Miss Dewitt. Please be back at the ballroom doors within ten minutes. I will provide interference with the duchess if she has already rounded your carriage and is looking for you."

"Thank you, your grace. I will be there."

His eyes shifted to Jason. "Do not make me regret this, Clapinshire. Ten minutes. And you do not touch her."

Katalin held her breath as the men eyed each other. But then Jason nodded, lips tight.

They all stood, rooted in spot, awkwardly staring at one another for a moment. The duke was being overly generous allowing this to happen, but he was clearly not about to let them have the privacy of this small garden nook.

Her ten minutes quickly dwindling, Katalin glanced at Jason. "Please, let us stroll, Lord Clapinshire?"

Jason held his palm out wide, motioning her through the arbor entrance. Katalin stepped out, looking down the garden pathway, and then quickly moved to her right between the tall evergreen hedges. Tall torches lit the path in even intervals.

Jason fell in step beside her, his mask now down over his eyes, and his hands were solidly at his sides.

They walked in silence for a while, until Katalin glanced over her shoulder to make sure the duke didn't trail them. Alone with Jason, she stopped, looking up at him.

"You cannot do this to me, Jason."

"Bloody hell, I want to kiss you."

"What?" She waved her hand in fury before his eyes. "Jason—you do not want me. We have already gone through this, and I will not allow you to continue to use me like this—prey upon my heart and then rip it to shreds. I will not go through you refusing me once again. Do not ruin the peace that I am so close to. Please. Please upon all that we once were. You do not want me, so let me be another's."

His hands went behind his back, her words making no mark on his countenance. He leaned slightly over her, using his height to his advantage. He wasn't touching her, but she sure as hell felt his body heating hers.

"I know exactly how you got the notion that I did not want you, Kat, and for that, I am sorry. That is my error to own, and I am sorry for everything I did to set your mind on that path. To set your mind away from me."

He went silent as another couple approached, arm in arm, and he stepped to the side of the cobblestone path to let them pass. Katalin watched Jason as he watched the backs of the couple until they walked an appropriate distance away.

Safe from ears, he stepped close to her again.

"Make no mistake, Kat," Jason's deep voice had gone low, raw. "I always wanted you—I always want you. As much as I denied the fact to myself, that has never changed."

If the heat in his words could win her over, Katalin would have melted right then. But her mind, her logic would not allow it. Could not allow it.

"You want me, but you do not wish to claim me as yours. I understand it, Jason, and I refuse to accept it. I cannot be your mistress. You cannot ruin my chances with the duke just because you want to bed me. I will not—"

"Stop, Katalin, do not go off again. I rather thought claiming you as my wife in front of the duke would let everyone involved know just where I stand on the matter."

"What?" She went to her toes, her face next to his, sniffing. "Are you drunk?"

"No. God no." He took a direct step backward. "And do not put yourself that close to me, Kat. I cannot handle it. Not without shoving you back into the bushes and taking you like I should be this very second."

"But if you are not drunk…" Her hand went to her forehead behind the ruined feathers, rubbing it. She was starting to truly grasp what he was saying. Starting to actually believe what he was saying. But she could not let hope rise. She knew too well that hope was only disguised torture.

"I have not touched alcohol since the night at my sister's dinner. Aggie sobered me. She made more sense than I have possessed in the last month."

"What did Aggie say?"

"She simply told me the duke was about to ask for your hand in marriage." He swallowed the distance between them again, his hands still firmly behind his back. "Nothing has ever been more sobering. You are my wife, Kat, and against all the hatred I harbored for you during the past two years, I damn still love you. I. Need. You."

Katalin drew a shaky breath, her defenses slipping from her control. "You have already destroyed me again and again, Jason. How can I put myself through that once more?"

"I have no right to ask after what I did to you, but you need to trust me. Please, Kat, please. I was dead, you were dead to me, yet somehow, across an ocean, we found each other again. Do not let my stupidity become the end of us." He moved even closer, his hand rising to her arm, but not making contact. "Hell, I need to touch you, Kat."

The nearest lit torch sent swaths of light across his face, and Katalin stared past his mask, searching his eyes. Searching for intention. For honesty.

He could ruin everything. He could use her, toss her aside, and she would have nothing. The duke would be gone, and she would have nothing. Nothing to protect herself. Nothing to protect her family.

Damn herself. Damn her love for this man. Damn that she wasn't strong enough to hate him. To deny him.

Damn it all.

She closed her eyes, her chest rising with a deep breath. Her face tilted upward, and she opened her eyes to him slowly, meeting his burning stare. "So touch me."

He jerked a step backward.

Away from her. The epitome of cruelty.

She lost her breath.

"No, do not look at me like that, Kat. I promised the duke. I am not about to ruin you in this garden—scar your reputation. And our time is almost up."

"Time be damned. I do not know if I can trust you, Jason—not without touching you. Feeling you. I do not care if I am ruined."

"I care. And you do too. You need to get to the doors, Kat."

"But we are not done."

Jason closed his eyes, and a deep breath of what looked like relief vibrated through his body. "You do not know how badly I needed to hear you say that." He opened his eyes. "We are not done. So meet me. It is still early. Aggie was rounding the carriage for you?"

"Yes."

Immediate concern crossed his face. "Are you ill?"

"I am fine. It was just the crush. The tight space. The duke saved me."

"Of course he did. He most certainly has not let an opportunity to save you pass him by." He waved his hand. "Go. My sister is no doubt waiting for you, guarding the prize she is incredibly proud of."

"The duke is not a prize, Jason. He is a decent man. A friend. And he has been nothing but gracious to me. If you could stifle your jealousy for even a moment, you might realize that I needed a friend, and that he has been very kind to me."

"I prefer to keep my jealousy sharp when it comes to you."

"Jason—"

His palms came up. "I am done. I appreciate that he is a man with exquisite taste in women, if nothing else. And I am thankful he has been a friend to you. I did nothing but create the situation myself. But please, tell me you will meet me? I will follow your carriage and will be waiting a block south of Southfork's residence, if you think you can sneak out from under your mother's watch? Tell me you can do so."

Katalin cocked her head, a feather dropping in front of her eyes. She brushed it away. "I do not know, Jase. Maybe. I will try, but I cannot promise anything."

"I will wait, regardless."

# CHAPTER 18

Her black cape wrapped full around her darkest gown, a deep purple, Katalin pulled the hood further down her forehead. If she was wrong about this. Wrong about Jason. This would be her death sentence. She would be ruined to society. To all titles. To all the safety it could afford her and her family.

But she needed this. Needed Jason. And if this was her last chance at having him, then she had to take it. Had to have faith the fates would not put them together to only cause more pain for her.

She tried to soften the sounds of her boots on the cobblestone walkway as she turned the corner at the end of the block. She had waited for her mother to retire to her chambers, and then another hour before she dared to slip out the back entrance of the Southfork townhouse. It took so long, Katalin half-expected there to be no carriage when she rounded the southern street.

Instead, there were two waiting carriages. At the first carriage, the coachman stood next to the front wheel of his coach, and at the other, the coachman was on the driver's perch.

Awkward. How many midnight rendezvouses were happening on this block? Katalin pondered for a moment about how she could she discretely find Jason's carriage—if one of these was even his. She had no idea what his coat-of-arms even looked like. A pang of so completely not knowing who Jason truly was hit her. She really knew so little of him. Who he had really been all this time?

Was she being an absolute idiot?

She set her head further down, hopeful that the shadow of the hood covered her face. She slowed her pace, watching the first coach out of the corner of her hood. The driver stood, tossing back a flask to swallow from as she passed. In the darkness, he looked to take little note of Katalin. She kept walking.

She passed the driver on his perch of the second coach, and was almost past it when the driver coughed, and then she could swear he said, "Captain."

She froze, turning slowly in his direction.

"Captain?" he repeated.

She glanced at the windows of the coach—dark curtains were drawn, but a lantern clearly lit the interior.

Katalin looked up to the driver, already hopping down off his ledge. "Yes."

He nodded, and pulled the stairs of the coach, opening the door.

Heart thundering, Katalin stepped up into the carriage.

It was empty.

She turned back to the coachman, still trying to hide her face.

"We be there in the swish of 'e horse's tail." He closed the door, and within a moment, the horses jolted forward.

After a courtesy glance about the plush interior, Katalin leaned to the window, cracking the curtains so she could see the passing buildings. Minutes later the carriage stopped in front of a large brick townhouse, one of three on a block. It looked eerily dark inside, as if no one was home.

Before she could pause to think on it, the carriage door opened and the driver looked up at her. "This be it." He pointed with his thumb over his shoulder. "I 'ave me an umbrella, if'in ye'd like to be discrete. But yer cloak should do ye fine."

"My cloak will do." Katalin stepped down the carriage steps, pulling the cloak as far forward about her face as she could. She hurried up the marble stairs and stopped at the wide red double-doors. Her hand rose to the gold knocker, and then she paused. Should she knock? She assumed this was Jason's home, but she truly did not know what this place was. For that matter, she assumed that was Jason's carriage, but what if she was wrong?

She shook her head. He had said he would wait for her, but he was not there.

But who else other than Jason would send someone to her and have him call her "Captain"? The man named Daunte couldn't possibly know she was in London with her father. Couldn't possibly know her whereabouts.

Just as her guard flew up, the door opened in front of her, and a hand reached out, grabbing her wrist and dragging her through the door into the darkness inside.

She instantly fought the grip on her arm, instinct taking over. The grip only tightened, and she was spun around, arms clamping hard around her body. She went wild, kicking, trying to free herself.

"Kat, Kat, it is me. It's me, Kat." The voice made its way through her hood and it stilled her.

Jason.

One arm stayed tight around her, holding her to his body, while his other hand went to her hood, pulling it off her head.

"What is happening with you, Kat? Why were you so terrified?"

Her head fell back on his chest as she tried to quell the panic that still raged through her body. Where she could have been—who could have had her, and the repercussions—too severe. Unbearable. She had too much to lose.

She kept her eyes closed, the back of her head pressing into the hard muscles of Jason's chest. "Nothing. It was nothing. You were—" She spun out of his one arm and smacked his chest. "You were supposed to be there. Waiting. But the carriage was empty. And this house is dark. And then you grabbed me."

Jason snatched her hand before she could swat him again. "I did not want to take the chance of being discovered with you. I am trying to do the right thing, Kat. I am trying to keep your reputation above reproach, so that if you decide…"

"Decide what, Jason?"

"Decide that what I have done, how I have treated you, is unforgivable. Decide that you would rather have the duke." His words came out hard, vicious against the possibility.

Katalin let her arm drop, and he released her hand. "You are trying to be honorable? Now? On my account?"

He shrugged. "Asking you to meet me is not exactly honorable, Kat. But I can at least protect you where I can."

She stared at him. A loose white linen shirt covered his torso, open wide at his chest. His dark trousers curved well around his thighs, and he was barefoot. She crossed her arms over her chest. "You realize you just scared me half to my grave."

"I do. I apologize. Grabbing you off the step was a bit extreme, but you were standing there for far too long. I cleared the house of everyone, but there are a lot of snoops in the other houses on this block."

Katalin's head tilted up as she scanned the entryway they were in. She could see up two stories, and above them, there was a room with a door slightly ajar, fire flickering light into the entry. "Is this your home?"

"Yes. One of them."

"One of them?" She shook her head. "I really do not know anything of you, Jason. All of this. You told me nothing of this. Of who you are."

"Would it have mattered? I told you of my family. You knew me. The me without all of this. I never lied. And you never asked."

"How would I even know to ask this, Jason?" Her arm swung wide. "All of this makes you who you are. Everything you are is built upon this privilege."

"No. Everything I am is built upon my family. Upon the people who raised me, supported me, loved me. Upon seeing the world. Upon pain. Upon torture. Upon meeting you." He moved closer to her. "That is who I am. Not houses. Not money. Not a title. If I had told you then, would it have mattered? Would you not have been my captain?"

Katalin looked up at him, the familiar heat in his dark green eyes already searing her soul. Her head went back and forth. "No. Nothing like this matters on the sea."

His hand came up slowly, nearing her cheek, almost touching her skin. But then he stilled, hand suspended in mid-air, neither touching nor drawing away.

Katalin wanted desperately to lean into his hand, to feel the warmth of his palm on her cheek, to feel her skin tingle as his fingers went into her hair.

But she held fast. She knew she was desperate for him—ready to give up the world for him—ready to give up too much. She still had responsibility.

He drew a deep breath, his hand twitching. "Before I touch you, Kat, you need to know. Under the willow, you said I did not wait for you—wait for this next life. Do you remember?"

She swallowed hard, not flinching from his stare or the pain of the memory. "Yes."

"You appeared out of thin air, Kat. And you found me when I was living between two lives. I was stuck between the old life I was trying desperately to forget—the life with you—and the new life I did not want to move forward into it. Not without you. For two years I was stuck in that purgatory. And then I saw you by that pond."

"And I saw a ghost."

"Yes. That was exactly what you saw. I was stuck. Stuck in what happened—what I thought happened. What I blamed you for. But I should have known. You would have never done that to me."

Katalin's knees went weak. Weak in the relief that he finally believed her. That he didn't blame her. His hand still hovered by her head, and she could stand it no longer.

She reached up, her fingers slipping along the back of his hand, pressing it to her face. The instant his palm flattened on her skin, she leaned into it, closing her eyes, tears slipping out.

Jason's other hand came up, cupping the opposite side of her face. "Tell me you waited. Tell me you did not give up on us. Tell me we can still be." He tilted her chin upward. "Look at me, Kat."

She opened her eyes.

"I am ready, Kat. Ready. I am fully here in this next life. Fully ready. You are my wife, and I desperately want to never have to deny that again. Please, Kat."

The reality of his words, as true as the sun, made it into her mind, her heart, and Katalin swayed, but only for an instant. An instant that coiled her legs, and in the next she sprung on him, arms tight about his neck, both legs wrapping around his waist. She buried her face in his neck, her lips on the salt of his skin as he staggered backward, catching his balance.

Laughing, one arm tight around her waist, clamping her body to his, he grabbed the nape of her hair with his free hand, pulling her head back to see her face. "Tell me this means you forgive me. Tell me I have my wife again."

"Yes—God yes—you have me, Jase." She met his lips hard, tasting him, remembering what it had been to be his, the heat of him, his strength. His lips parted, taking her in, just as hungry as she was.

She jerked away, eyes wide. "But wait. I still do not know if we are legally married—not with your laws."

"I will marry you a thousand times over, Katalin, but we cannot do anything about that in this moment." His lascivious smile followed his eyes as they shifted down to where the white skin of the top of her bosom peeked out from under her cloak. "But we can do other things. I will wait—dammit it to hell—I will wait if you want to, Kat. Until we can marry again with no possibility of it not being legal. But then you sure as hell need to get off me."

"I am not getting off of you for the life of me, Jase."

His mouth captured hers as he took a step forward, propping her back onto the wall by the door. Supported by the wall, her legs still tight around his waist, Jason pulled back, leaving her lips plump and raw. Both hands free, he worked the front clasp on her dark cloak, and by the time it dropped from her shoulders, exposing her chest, he growled in impatience, his fingers slipping under the front lace trim of her dress.

"Tear it. Just tear it, Jase," she whispered, her breath trembling.

He glanced at her, pure carnal smile crossing his face. In the next instant, fabric ripped and he yanked the front ribbon of her short stays, freeing her. He grabbed her hips, lifting her higher to pull her left nipple into his mouth, his teeth capturing, tongue teasing.

Katalin's hands went into his hair, gripping, holding him hard to her body even as she arched on the wall.

"Damn, I am an imbecile—I waited far too long for you— for this—these." He shifted to her other nipple, already taut with the cool air.

Her face went down, burying into the top of his head. "And I have waited far too long to have you deep in me."

"You are ready?"

"I have never stopped being ready."

Hands still on her hips, he pulled her from the wall, spinning them and stalking across to the stairs. She pulled up on the back of his shirt, yanking it over his head as he walked.

He stopped, setting her on the third step up of the mahogany stairs, and he shrugged the white linen shirt off his arms. Leaning over Katalin, his hands went under her skirt, moving up past her boots, fingers trailing along the outside of her thighs. Mid-thigh, he stopped motion, and with a wicked grin, he slowly—too slowly for Katalin—veered inwards, leaving wakes of prickled skin behind his fingertips.

Hands roaming his chest, the hard lines on his belly that she had never forgotten, her arms slipped to his back, fingers running over the lines of scars. He was still perfect. Her perfect.

Deep under her skirts, a finger, then two, slipped into her folds, and Katalin almost lost control, buckling. He plied her as she strained into his hand, gasping against the years without him. Years she had dreamt of this. Of him.

He chuckled. "You truly are ready, Kat."

"Did you expect me to lie about this? Never this. Never you." Katalin worked the buttons on his trousers, searching for the skin underneath, searching to free the bulge she could feel pulsating.

In one swift motion, his trousers fell, and he was naked in front of her. She was only half naked, the top of her dress ripped open, but it would have to do. She dragged up her skirts as her fingers went behind him, pulling him into her.

Hands landing on the stairs, he braced himself above her. "You looking like that, I am not about to last long."

"I am not either. Too long, Jase. Too long."

He came down on her mouth, his lips open, tongue slipping into her, tasting her, just as he moved the last of her skirts and slid into her. Full into her tightness, he groaned.

He started slow, gentle, and she could feel him shaking, vibrating against his own harsh needs. Katalin would have none of it. She grabbed his hips, drawing him into her hard, fast, not giving him the slightest pause in his movements. Each stroke she drew him deeper, screaming, begging, opening wider to him until he set a rhythm that matched her guttural need.

Her hands flew up, grabbing the ledge of the stair above her, holding herself solid against his thrusts.

Jason slipped an arm behind her lower back, shielding it from the step cutting into her spine as he drove faster, not allowing her body to gain space from his.

Her screams melded with his deep growls, even more fervent than hers.

His lips still hungry on her skin, the haze of his voice slipped past her screams. "You are mine, Kat. Mine. Always. Come with me. Now, Kat."

Breath gone, she arched even further, driving her hips into him, swiveling for contact. Eyes closed, her head hit the stair above and she writhed, reaching explosion as her nails dug into the wood of the stair above her.

Her body in spasm around him, a savage scream heated her neck, and Jason erupted within her.

His arm tight around her, Jason would not let their skin part for minutes, and she gripped him, eyes closed, breathing him in and refusing to give up the moment as well.

When she felt his back muscles flex under her arms, she tightened her hold, willing him into stillness.

He chuckled as he relaxed his face into her neck once more. "I do not want to move either, but the stair is near to snapping my arm in two." He nuzzled her neck. "Besides, you do not know how I have dreamt of having you in a proper bed. I just want to move us up into my chambers."

"To your bed, and that is all?"

"I swear. My bed. And then I am going to take you again. You do realize I am going to be insatiable tonight? Probably for the next fortnight. Probably for the next six months."

Katalin laughed, swatting his backside. "It better be longer than that."

He went upright on his knees and slipped his arm under her legs, picking her up as he stood.

"I would have said lifetime, but I did not want to scare you," he said, starting up the staircase.

"Have you ever known me to be scared, save that once?" she asked, smirking.

"No." Jason kissed her forehead and pushed open a door with his bare foot. "But I wish you were scared more."

"Ridiculous. Why?" She looked around the room. This was the space that she had seen that was lit earlier, a fire burning brightly in the fireplace opposite an enormous four-post bed.

"It would keep you safer." He tossed her onto the bed and grabbed her skirts, pulling her deep purple dress down, stripping her of the last bits of offending cloth.

Katalin stretched, her naked back burrowing onto the coverlet. "Ready so soon?"

"Preparing." Jason sat at the edge of the bed, taking one of her legs into his lap, removing the boot, and then repeating with the other.

He scooted up next to her, and Katalin turned onto her side, one hand propping up her head, and the other going to his face. Tracing his jawline, she stared at him, still only half-believing this dream she was currently in. There was still so much to say.

Still so much that could go wrong.

"What?" He grabbed her hand, sweeping a kiss across her knuckles. "I do not like that frown that just appeared on your face."

She gave a small shake of her head, eyes not meeting his. "It is just the past. I do not wish to revisit it, but I need you to understand what happened."

"You told me what happened, Kat. I believe you."

"But there is more."

"More?" He slowly fingered a tendril of hair loose on her cheek, brushing it behind her ear. "Tell me."

Katalin took a deep breath and moved closer to him on the bed, slinking her top leg between his calves and setting her hand on his waist. She stared at her thumb rubbing along the ridge of Jason's muscle from his hip-bone, watching the fire light dance off his skin, debating about where and when to start.

He was silent in front of her, not asking, not demanding. As patient as he had always been with her. Steady. He was back. Real and alive and himself.

She took a deep breath, her eyes meeting his. "You have always been my captain, Jase. You always will be. When you were on trial I knew I would not get a chance to talk to you again, and I needed you to know that. If I could leave you with nothing else, I had to make you know that one thing. Even if it made you hate me. Even if you believed it was a betrayal. It was all I could do at that time, claim you as my captain."

"Why?"

"I had no choice, Jase. I knew I was never going to see you again. The deal I made with my father—I would never see you again, and he would get you out of there. That was the deal. He promised."

"And you believed him?"

"Yes. It was my only hope to free you, because I could not do it myself. I had to save the one thing that was more important than you. More important than me."

"Your father?"

His words were soft, but lined with remnants of bitterness, and they cut into her soul, pulling bare all the regret she had harbored in the past years. A tear slipped down her face as she shook her head.

"No, not my father, Jase. My child."

"Child?" He whipped upright, sitting on the bed.

Katalin followed suit, keeping her watery eyes on his. "Your child."

He moved away from her, standing from the bed, staggering backward as his palm went up to her. "My child?"

Katalin moved to the edge of the bed, her toes touching the wood floors. "Your child, Jase. I was pregnant. I figured it out when we were in those cells, and I could not tell you. Not with a stone wall between us…Not with what could have happened. If I had died, and you had known and survived…I could not do that to you…I could not…" Her hand went to her throat as it collapsed in emotion, the long past terror still taking a hold on her.

Jason turned from her, facing the fireplace.

She watched his back, watched the stillness of all the scars lining his skin.

"I had to get out of there, Jason. At all costs, I had to save my baby—your baby."

Not turning around, his chin went on his shoulder, his profile to her, but he refused to look at her. "I have a child?"

"A girl." Katalin stood, slowly approaching his back. Watching his profile carefully, she stopped just shy of touching him.

"What…Where…Alive?"

"Yes."

He still did not turn to her, but his eyes lifted and he caught her gaze. "How could you not tell me, Kat?"

She needed to touch him. But she did not dare. She could see the rage pulsating along his jawline, his muscles that were beyond taut. "Your honor. After what happened under the willow. After you denied me. I could not tell you. I could not have you pitying me, being with me just because of her. Nothing would be crueler. Trapping you. Trapping you with your own damn sense of honor. Not when you hated me."

She swallowed the hurt the words caused. "I was not about to do that to you. To do that to me. Nor was I going to take the chance she would be deemed a bastard—not after everything I have learned about English society. I would not do that to her."

His eyes didn't veer from hers. "What is her name?"

"Josalyn."

"Where is she now?"

"Safe. She is with her nanny at the home of one of my mother's friends, just outside of London. No one knows of her except my mother. We could not risk her safety. We do not believe Daunte knows of her existence, but my father is not sure. Daunte has only threatened me, and I could not risk him knowing of her. She is my life, Jason. She is why I even came to England. To keep her safe. I could not let her grow up without a mother—not like me..."

"Which was why you were so desperate to marry." The words were slow and measured, and he finally turned to her.

Katalin held her breath, waiting for judgment, praying that its harshness would not destroy them. He had every right to hate her for not telling him of their daughter.

In the next instant, he encapsulated her into a hard embrace. "God, Kat. What you have been through. Hell. What I put you through. You did this for her. For our baby."

At that, Katalin broke.

All of the fear and pain and worry that she had denied herself for two years rushed from the pit of her stomach, sending her body into racking sobs, clutching desperately to Jason's chest.

"I miss her so much, Jase. I miss her." Her words choked out between shudders. "She is my life and I have not seen her in so long and I miss her. My baby girl...I just miss her..."

"Damn me, Kat. Damn my stupidity. Damn me for believing you could have betrayed me. Damn me for not coming for you. For not knowing. You have been too damn strong—you always have been—and I was not there for you."

Her legs buckled. But Jason had her, and he picked her up, bringing her to bed.

He didn't let her go, didn't loosen his hold on her. Just laid her down, his hand cradling her head to his chest as her sobs soaked his skin.

Taking her tears. Taking the weight of all she had gone through.

# CHAPTER 19

The harsh knock came out of the darkness, pulling Jason from the deep thoughts he was immersed in. Deep thoughts of imagining Katalin and a little girl that looked just like her in the gardens at the Clapinshire estate.

The pounding echoed up through the house again, but Katalin was still asleep on top of him. She had cried for an hour, and Jason could not blame her. Only hold her. And take comfort in the fact that she clung to him, not willing to give him up, or to rail at him for what he put her through.

For that, he was beyond grateful. Her sobs eventually petered out, and she fell into a hiccupping sleep, which eventually turned into her back rising and falling in peaceful rest. Peace that Jason prayed could be sustained. Peace he needed to give to her.

He rolled to his side, settling Katalin's limp form on the bed, and pulled the coverlet over her nude body.

Grumbling at the intrusion, he yanked on a robe and thundered down the stairs.

The last thing he wanted to see greeted him at the door.

His sister, brother-in-law, Southfork, and his wife. The four of them, all standing with accusing glares on their faces.

Jason cleared his throat. "What, Aggie? I was sleeping."

"I doubt that." Aggie pushed past him, and the other three followed her in. "Do not even try to feign innocence on this one."

Shutting the door, Jason turned around to the small mob.

"Is she here?" Aggie asked, arms crossed over her chest.

"Who?"

"You know exactly, who, Jason. When Reanna stopped in to check on Katalin, she was missing. We are worried sick. Is Katalin here? Tell me she is here. That looks like her cloak on the floor."

"I am." Katalin appeared in the balcony above the entryway, one of Jason's linen shirts haphazardly tossed atop her small frame, a grey sheet wrapped around her lower half and dragging. "I am so sorry to have worried you all. Does my mother know?"

Reanna ran up the flight of stairs, her hands going to Katalin's shoulders. "No, she was sleeping, and I did not want to wake her and worry her if we could find you. Are you well? Injured? Why would you disappear on us?"

"I truly am sorry to have caused such a fuss. It is just that…" Katalin's voice trailed and she looked down at Jason.

Even in the low light, he could see the distinct flush filling her cheeks and spreading across her forehead. She knew how to explain this even less than he did.

Jason looked at Aggie. "We have some explaining to do. But first, afford us the dignity of some clothes. Please, the lot of you into the library. We will be down in a moment, and will answer any and every question you have."

"I have a number of them," Aggie said.

Jason hid his eye roll. "I imagine you do." He looked at Devin. "The staff is gone at the moment, so if you could light a fire, that would be helpful."

Within ten minutes, Jason and Katalin had dressed and made their way to the library. Jason had found one of his mother's simple muslin dresses for Katalin, since hers was torn beyond any and all modesty.

They had been silent upstairs, and Jason had watched as all color, bit by bit, had left Katalin's face. And now, standing outside the library doors, she looked like she was walking to her execution.

He grabbed her hand, squeezing it as he leaned down to her ear. "We have done nothing wrong, Kat. You are my wife. You are the mother of my child. We merely have to explain the debacle I have created this past month."

She looked up at him, eyes huge, and nodded. His words did obviously little in assuaging her panic at how the four people on the other side of the door would regard her now.

Not dropping her hand, they stepped into room, now lit by
a bright fire. Devin and Killian had already helped themselves
to glasses of brandy, and Devin, good man that he was, handed
Jason a full glass as he and Katalin walked to the center of the
room.

Jason sat on the leather tufted sofa, tugging Katalin to sit
down next to him.

"Please, sit," Jason said.

All but his sister did. She was too busy pacing in front of
the fire. She paused in her steps when everyone was seated and
pinned Jason with her eyes. "You need to tell me this instant what
is happening here, Jason."

Jason dropped Katalin's hand, leaning back on the sofa and
putting his arm around her shoulders. "The short story is that
Katalin and I are married."

"What? How?" Aggie's face skewed to shock. "You better tell
us the long story, brother."

He sighed, taking the smallest sip of the brandy. "We met a
bit more than two years ago after I had been captured and tossed
onto that first ship—forced into captive labor. I was on a ship
called the Rosewater that Katalin and her crew took when she was
privateering. She kept me."

"Kept you?" Devin asked, eyebrow cocked.

"She sent the lot of the crew—my captors—to the sea in a
long boat, but kept me aboard as an extra hand. She saved my
life, even if it was not her intention."

"What was your intention?" Reanna asked, her eyes swinging
to Katalin.

"My intention was that Jason was strong, and he took up
arms against his own shipmates, so I took the risk that he was
not a threat to my crew. I figured his hands would be helpful on
the Windrunner, and in exchange, I would get him to dry land. I
never imagined..."

Jason squeezed her shoulder as her voice faltered. "She never
imagined we would fall in love. We married. But soon after,
we were captured by pirate hunters. I was on trial for being the

captain of the Windrunner, and Katalin's father saved her from the noose, but I was left behind. I thought I had been betrayed."

Aggie's hawk look veered to Katalin, instant protector of her brother. "You betrayed Jason?"

Katalin didn't flinch from the question. "No. And yes. I thought I was saving him, but in doing so, yes, I betrayed him. I never would have left Jason had I known what was to happen. Never would have said what I did. And then I thought he was executed. It is why I acted so oddly when I saw him at Curplan— why I fainted. For near two years I believed Jason was dead. And he was not."

"Jason, this is too fantastical, even for you," Aggie said. "Why have you never told me any of this?"

"It was not something I wanted to remember. It was something I was trying to forget. Trying to black out with copious amounts of alcohol."

"You two hid all of this at Curplan?" Reanna asked.

"Yes," Jason said. "I did not understand what Katalin had tried to do—how she had tried to save me. And I was still too angry with her to even want to acknowledge her."

"So you thought to be an ass to her instead? Do you know what she has been through—what we all have been through trying to land her a title, and you were sitting there all along— married and you wouldn't acknowledge it?" Aggie asked, hands on her hips. "Really, Jason, this is beyond—buggers, the duke. Buggers, buggers, buggers. That is going to take some explanation."

His sister started to pace again, finger tapping her chin. She stopped abruptly. "Who married you?"

"A man of God on one of the islands—but he is self-proclaimed," Katalin said. "It would be as legally binding as anything else in that part of the world, but here..." She shrugged. "I am not sure."

"We are married, Kat." Jason's arm tightened around her. "Do not question that."

Aggie went back to pacing. "We will need to smooth this the best we can. You have already been to too many functions at the same time, but apart. So it is awkward. We will have to float the rumor that there was a marriage ceremony in the Caribbean, but neither of you believed it to be truly valid. That will have to suffice as the reason Katalin was now seeking a match."

"That is dreadfully thin," Reanna said.

"I know—but what are we to do? We have to save Katalin from scandal somehow." Aggie looked at Jason and Katalin. "But then you both had a change of affection, and realized you were meant to be together. Which is true and a love story, and the gossips adore a tantalizing love story. But we will need to marry you two again. A large affair. It is not usual, but we need an event that gives not the slightest hint of embarrassment or scandal in your past. A proud wedding that no one will be able to question."

"Will that work?" Katalin asked.

"No. Not fully. But I am at a loss." Aggie shrugged. "If we create enough bravado about it, it will be harder to pop pins into the narrative."

"We are married, Aggie, we need not do this," Jason said, leaning forward. "I defy anyone to tell me we are not."

"This is not about whether you two are truly married or not; this is about keeping Katalin's reputation above reproach, since the threat of Daunte and his accusations of piracy have not disappeared."

Katalin nodded, looking at Jason. "It is true. He is still a real threat."

As much as it irked Jason to admit it, Aggie was right. Katalin was right. Daunte was still a very real threat. And not just to his wife. To his daughter as well. He needed to ferret out the bastard and end him.

But first things first. He looked at his brother-in-law. "We need to get married as soon as possible. You have been through this—can you help with the special license?"

Devin nodded. "Yes. It may be a day or two."

"Good. Thank you. Aggie, can you pull a wedding together in that time?"

"Yes. As long as you do not continue to steal Katalin away from Killian's townhouse."

Katalin grabbed Jason's knee, looking at him. "I would like to speak to the duke. I owe him an explanation."

It rankled him, but Jason knew that Katalin smoothing this over with the duke would be vital. He gave a crisp nod.

"Excellent," Aggie said, clasping her hands together as she resumed pacing. "That will do well. Reanna, can you serve as chaperone tomorrow as Katalin visits the duke? I imagine he will not be pleased, but a direct explanation from Katalin may help curb the stickiness of the situation, or at least keep him from becoming an enemy. That is the last thing we need, the Duke of Letson out for vengeance."

"Of course," Reanna said.

"And I will be staying here tonight," Aggie announced, stopping her pace.

"That is not necessary, Aggie," Jason said.

"Yes, it is. You know as well as I that Dowager Delray does nothing but sit at her window all night recording the comings and goings of this block. She has done it since we were little. Four came in, so four must go out. That means, Katalin, you will need to leave now with Killian, Reanna, and my husband. Take my cloak and keep your head down. I will leave from here in the morning, and be obvious in the process. She would not think twice on my presence in the house."

Jason stood, sighing, holding his hand down to Katalin. "I am afraid we are now utterly powerless, under Aggie's ever-exuberant guard until the wedding." He looked to Aggie, eyes narrowing. "And I pray that your conniving mind will never be used for evil, dear sister."

~ ~ ~

Katalin sank onto the settee in the front drawing room of the Southfork townhouse, staring blankly out the window. She and Reanna had just arrived back from their meeting with the duke.

It went well, as well as could have been expected. True to his title, the duke was a gentleman about the mess, but she knew her actions were inexcusable.

She could see that quite clearly now. Putting herself out as marriageable—when she was nothing of the kind, especially in heart and mind—was despicable. Thinking she could deny the truth of the past, of her impossibly unyielding love for Jason—it had been a fool's quest, and she had dragged not only the duke down with her, but her new friends as well.

She leaned back on the turquoise settee, her head resting on the top curve of the sofa as she closed her eyes. Adding the duke's meeting to her very difficult conversations with first her mother, and then her father, earlier this morning, did nothing to help her mind set.

Her mother had coldly listened, then silently left the room. Her father had railed at her for an hour—but her father's tirades she was used to. She had listened to him her whole life. But her mother's coldness, she was not used to. She never would be.

At least she was alone at the moment. Alone and able to wallow in the muck she had created.

The sudden hand on her forehead should have made her jump, but she had no energy. She cracked her eyes open instead.

Jason stared down at her, the flecks of brown in his green eyes shimmering in concern.

"It went poorly?" He didn't move his hand from her head, tracing a tendril of hair along her brow until he freed it from a pin and could spin it around his forefinger.

"I do not know if it could have been anything but awful. But I apologized profusely until Reanna kicked me to get me to stop."

He chuckled. "She did? In front of the duke? You must have been making quite the spectacle."

"I am sure I was. But he was gracious. He said I may still consider him a friend, and for that, I am grateful."

"I will have to reconsider my ill thoughts of him. He could have easily made this very difficult for us."

Watching Jason, his face upside down, Katalin reached up, her fingers landing on the back of his hand, sliding up past his wrist and under the cuff of his dark blue jacket. She still was not accustomed to seeing him dressed in finery. "Aggie would kill you if she knew you were here. She wants us as apart as apart can be until the wedding."

"My sister would like a lot of things to be her way. This is not one that I will grant her." He rounded the sofa, and Katalin's head came up as her breath caught. This was harsh. Too harsh. She was so close to touching him, to having him be hers again, but she had to wait—last night had been nothing but a tease. Glorious in the moment, but a tease.

Jason stood in front of her. "I have to meet her, Kat."

"Josalyn?"

He nodded. "Even if we do not tell her right away who I am. I do not want to scare her. She is still young, so I am not worried about the future. She will not remember a time when I was not her father. But I have to see her. I have thought of nothing else since last night. I know she needs to stay hidden—safe until we wed. But can you bring me to her—safely?"

Katalin stood, her exhaustion falling away. "I can, and I so want you to meet her, Jason. She is only about an hour outside of London, in a cottage on the estate of Lady Timlad. Do you know of it, where it is?"

"No, but I will."

"But I do not know how I will escape from here for the time needed." Katalin looked over her shoulder in the general direction of the rest of the household. "Not without a proper chaperone."

"Aggie will be of no help, but maybe you can ask your cousin to chaperone? Can she keep the secret?"

Katalin nodded. "I believe she would. Was it a mistake to not tell everyone last night about Josalyn?"

"I think the news of our past was more than enough last night." Jason shrugged. "We will tell everyone come the day after the wedding. But I need to see her, Kat. This afternoon? Can we leave an hour from now?"

Katalin took a deep breath. There was nothing she wanted more in the world than to have Jason meet his daughter. Than for her to see her little girl again—it had been far too long, and the gaping hole burned by not seeing her daughter everyday weighed heavy on Katalin.

"Yes. I will talk with Reanna right now. But we will have to take the Southfork carriage. Even I know we are skirting wide on the outer fringes of propriety as it is."

~ ~ ~

Hours later, Katalin heard threads snap as she twisted the white gloves in her hands. She looked down at them, mangled beyond ever being worn again. She needed to see Josalyn so desperately, she hadn't known how badly until they pulled onto Lady Timlad's estate.

"There, there it is. Stop." Katalin looked at the short row of seven cottages, her eyes focusing on the second-to-last cottage.

Jason knocked on the ceiling of the carriage and it slowed.

Katalin looked at Reanna. "Would it be rude—"

Reanna instantly patted Katalin's hand, cutting her off. "Nonsense. This is a private affair between the three of you. I am merely here to ensure there is no chance of gossip before the wedding. We are far enough from London that you can be seen without me in tow. Go." She glanced down at Katalin's white knuckles. "Go before you tear those gloves in half."

With a grateful smile to Reanna, Katalin followed Jason out of the carriage.

They were a few steps from the carriage before Jason spoke. "I talked to your father today."

Katalin stopped, looking up at him. "You what?"

"When you were with the duke this morning, your father and I had a discussion."

Katalin's eyes went wide. She knew what a brute her father could be. "How did that go?"

Jason shrugged. "He was still livid from when you spoke with him—you should have left it for me to explain to him."

"He would have killed you if you had explained it."

"No, quite the contrary. You apparently did not take him to task for lying to you after the trial. He had no choice but to calm once I pointed out the fact that had he never lied to you—never told you I was dead—all of this could have been avoided. If he had only told the truth and had me delivered to you after Roland broke me out of my cell, we never would have been apart."

Katalin's bottom lip went into frown. "I have wanted to rant at him since you showed up alive, but I could not confess who you were, not after…"

"After I would not claim you as my wife? I know, Kat. I have not made this entire affair easy. Lies on top of lies."

"But his lie. I know he thought he was doing what he needed to protect me, but two years, Jason. Two years we lost because of the lie. Years you lost with your daughter. You did not get to see her born. You never got to see her as a baby. Her first steps. Her first words. Her baby giggle—it sparkled. You missed all of that because of my father's lie." Tears slid down her face, stopping her words.

Jason's arm went around her shoulders, and he prodded them forward, walking down the row of cottages. "I get to see her now, Kat. That is what is most important. Today. The future."

"She was beautiful from the first. She always had your eyes. From the moment she opened them, you were all I saw in her."

The front door of the second to last cottage swung wide open, and Josalyn's nanny stepped out, waving at Katalin.

"Annette, how are you?" Katalin leaned forward, kissing the cheek of Josalyn's nanny.

Annette smiled, conspiratorially, and pointed into the cottage. "I saw you coming so I popped out here—she is in the back room and she has not seen you yet. This is such a surprise—I cannot wait to hear her glee."

Katalin stepped past Annette into the cottage, and in the next moment, a squeal beyond compare filled the small rooms.

"Mama! Mama! Mama!"

Josalyn stumbled into the main room, running as fast as her awkward toddler legs could carry her. Katalin stepped in, scooping her up, smothering her in her arms.

Katalin would not let her squirm out of her hold for minutes, overwhelmed at how much she had missed her little girl. She hadn't known how long it would be before she could be with Josalyn again—she had been guessing months—so to hold her again so soon was a gift in itself.

Josalyn did eventually manage to squirm enough to wiggle her red-blond head up next to Katalin's cheek, kissing her with loud smacks again and again. And then she spied the man in the doorway.

"Mama. Who?"

Katalin spun, having for a moment forgotten just why she was here. Josalyn turned her head so she could still see Jason.

"Who, Mama?"

Katalin looked at Annette and Jason by the doorway. "Annette, could you please excuse us for a few minutes?"

"Happy to, Katalin. I need to fetch water." She gave a quick glance from Jason to Katalin, and then grabbed the bucket by the doorway. "Josey, I will be back in a moment."

Josalyn smiled at Annette, waving a little goodbye to her.

Jason stepped into the cottage, letting Annette by. He closed the door after her.

"Oh, how I have missed you my little melon." She squeezed Josalyn, drawing a tickled giggle from the little girl.

With a quick glance to Jason, Katalin cocked her head to the chairs set by the hearth, and walked to them. She sat in the rocking chair, Josalyn in her lap. Jason took the seat opposite them.

Arms still secure around her, Katalin took in her daughter's beaming face. Big green eyes still twinkling with mischief. Wavy red-blond hair, pulled back with a ribbon from her face and a little longer than Katalin remembered it. Her pudgy cheeks still pudgy. Katalin ran a hand over her head, kissing her forehead again.

Josalyn was busy trying to turn around to eye Jason.

"Josey, do you remember all the stories I have told you about your daddy?"

Josalyn's face turned to Katalin.

"How he was big and strong and so very handsome? But that he was gone?" Katalin continued.

Josalyn nodded.

"Well, I did not know it, sweetie, but he was alive. He has been found."

The little girl clapped, squealing.

Katalin laughed. "I know. It is very exciting. Do you remember how Poppy is my daddy?"

"Poppy?" Josalyn looked around, searching the room for him.

"No sweetie, Poppy is not here right now, but your daddy is. He is right there."

Josalyn wiggled to fully face Jason, her eyes narrowing as her mind worked on the man across from her.

Katalin whispered in her ear. "He is still the same big and strong and handsome daddy that I always told you about, sweetie. Don't you think?"

Slowly, Josalyn nodded, her eyes not leaving Jason.

"You can go over to him if you want to, Josey. He is your daddy and he is so happy to meet you."

Josalyn watched him for a very long minute, deciding what she wanted to do about this strange man. Katalin studied her profile, waiting with held breath.

Her daughter had never been cautious around any of the myriad of characters that came through her father's estate on the island, and all of them were much scarier looking than Jason. Of course, Katalin had never told her daughter that any of them was her daddy. Katalin guessed cautiousness was inevitable in this situation. Even for an almost two-year-old.

Jason watched her, the look on his face just as serious. And then he slid down off the chair, going to his knees on the rug in front of the hearth.

"Your mama is right, Josalyn—Josey. I am very happy to meet you. More than happy." His voice had gone incredibly thick, and Katalin was surprised his words managed to come out.

Josalyn bit her lip, sucking on it hard. And then she slid from Katalin's lap, toddling slowly to Jason. She stopped an arm's length away from him, and her thumb went into her mouth as she stared at him, eye to eye.

"I understand you have a birthday coming up, Josey? Two years old, correct?"

Josalyn's eyes went wide and she nodded, her face even more serious.

"Turning two is a very big deal," Jason said.

Josalyn nodded again.

"I thought you might like a little early present for the occasion."

Josalyn looked over her shoulder at Katalin, and Katalin gave her a reassuring smile but said nothing.

"I wanted to get you more things, but I first want to hear from you about what you like. In the meantime, I want to give you this." Jason reached into his jacket and pulled out a small brown and black spotted stuffed horse, the size of his hand. The mane and tail were real horse-hair, glossy black.

Josalyn's thumb instantly left her mouth, and she reached for the horse with both hands, giggling. She held it up, turning back to Katalin to show her the prize. "Mama, look."

"It is beautiful, sweetie. Maybe your daddy can tell you where he got it."

Josalyn looked back to Jason, and Jason switched positions, sitting on the floor, legs crossed. Josalyn teetered a step closer to him.

Jason kept up steady chatter to her about how the horse was made, what to name it, where it could go on adventures, and within minutes, Josalyn was in his lap, laughing and copying her father's neighing sounds for her new horse.

But most important, she beamed at her father. Jason kept his voice light and fun, even as Katalin watched his eyes water and the slightest tear slip out onto his cheek.

She swallowed hard. She was watching exactly what she had hoped for herself when meeting her own mother. Tears. Joy. Disbelief.

Katalin had had none of that when meeting her own mother. But this was everything she had hoped for. Her own mother could not give it to her, but Jason gave it all willingly to their daughter, holding nothing back.

She hadn't imagined she could love this man any more than she already did, but in that instant, her heart expanded ten-fold.

He was exactly where he was always meant to be, how she had always imagined him to be. A father. A husband.

A family complete.

# CHAPTER 20

Katalin looked in the silver-framed mirror on the dressing table in her room at the Southfork house. Her hair still drying from an early morning bath, she pulled at the damp tendrils, tousling air into them. For as nervous as both Aggie and Reanna had been the entire day before and this morning, Katalin had felt none of it. Any nervousness, any doubts she had of her marriage, of her life with Jason, were put to rest when he had met their daughter.

They belonged together, and the wedding—only hours away—was merely a quick obligation that had to happen in order for them to move on and live the life they were always meant to live.

But she still wanted to put on a proper show out of respect to Aggie and Reanna and all the hard work they did in pulling together a wedding in three days.

The door to her room opened, and the maid that had been assigned to her, Mable, came in. She stepped behind Katalin, looking at her in the mirror. "Your hair 'bout ready for plaiting, miss? I be itchin' to get a go at it. Oh, but first." Her head went down as she rummaged in the front pocket of her apron. "There be lots o' congratulations rollin' in downstairs, miss. But the man below that delivered this to Mr. Albertson was insistent 'bout this one getting into your hands right off. Maybe from his lordship?"

Mable smirked as she pulled the note, sealed with red wax, from her pocket and handed it to Katalin.

Katalin took the letter, cracked the seal over the dressing table, and then turned on the stool so the maid couldn't peek over her shoulder. She didn't know if Mable could read or not, but the girl looked rather interested in the contents. Katalin scanned the handwriting she did not recognize. Only four words were on the thick cream vellum: Look out your window.

Folding the note closed, Katalin stood, going to the window in her room. Had Jason sent some sort of surprise for her? She looked down to the street, noting it was busier than usual, horses and carriages and lots of vendors walking along the street in the bright sun of the day.

Eyes searching the scene, she noticed the one thing that was not moving below—a carriage that was parked, and a lone figure in front of it.

Breath catching, Katalin leaned closer to the window, nose touching the glass. It looked like—no—it couldn't be.

She squinted.

Annette.

Josalyn's nanny stood in front of a carriage, stone still, with a trail of blood running down her cheek from a swollen left eye.

Katalin went deathly calm.

"I need a dress on this instant, Mable," Katalin said, her stare not leaving Annette.

"But it be too early fer your wedding dress, miss. I still have to do your hair. Or do ye mean another dress? Which one do you want?"

"I do not give a damn which dress, Mable, just get me into something this instant. And a cloak with a hood. Go."

Within two minutes, Katalin was flying down the back servant stairs and out into the street, hood tight over her head.

Across the street in a flash, Katalin stopped in front of her, raising her hood so Annette could see her face.

Annette's petrified eyes widened in relief.

"Katalin, thank God." Her hands were shaking. "Thank God."

The carriage door behind Annette opened, and a hand came down, grabbing Annette's arm and yanking her up into the carriage.

Katalin jumped up into the carriage after her, instantly regretting that in her haste she hadn't grabbed a sword, a knife—anything to kill whoever was in that carriage.

Annette landed sprawled on the front bench next to a brute of a man—clearly a hired thug. Katalin found the other person in the carriage—a man—and started to pounce, ready to choke the life out of him.

His hand flew up. "Stop, Miss Dewitt. You will note your daughter is not in this carriage."

Katalin froze, standing, but bent over him, fingers twitching in rage. "Where the hell is my daughter?"

"Sit, Miss Dewitt. I find it curious you brought no weapon with you, what with your history."

"Where the hell is my daughter?"

"Sit."

Katalin took a step to the side, sitting on the very edge of the bench the man sat on, her feet still at the ready to push off and kill him. No matter that he was twice her size.

"Where the hell is my daughter?"

"I have her. She is fine. Not here, of course."

"Daunte?"

He nodded, a tight smile on his face. The man was older, grey hair, but still lean with only a slight bit of paunch. He was also wealthy, if his clothes, carriage, and hired thug were any indication.

Her breath sped, her heart out of control, but Katalin managed a veneer of steel. "You will deliver me to my daughter this instant."

He waved her words off with a flippant toss of his hand. "The most interesting thing happened to me the other morning. I was skimming through The London Chronicle, but then I was interrupted and had set the paper on my desk. When I looked down, the paper was open to announcements of weddings, which I usually ignore for all the flip-floppery of them, but then, in the middle of the page, a name popped out at me. A Miss Katalin Dewitt. To marry the Earl of Clapinshire, of all things."

He clasped his gloved hands together in his lap. "What a fortunate moment in time for me. That you were even on English soil was preposterous. I stared at the paper for minutes, bewildered. And I, mind you, am never bewildered. But then I realized your plan, and I realized I had greatly underestimated your father. Marry a peer, gain the privilege of peerage. Convenient for you, what with your colorful past."

He nodded to himself, a hard smile on his face. "You father always was a canny one, which was why both he, and you, were so valuable to me. But once I knew you were here, you were quite easy to find. Even easier to follow. And you led me directly to the one thing that I know is quite valuable to both you and your father. Your daughter. The one thing that will ensure I get what I want."

No. No. No. Katalin's mind screamed, horrified that she herself had led Daunte to Josalyn. But she forced cool calmness into her face, into her words. "What do you want, Daunte? You must want me for something, or I would already be in the gallows."

"What I have wanted for the past two years. What your father has refused me. I want the Wake Ripper brought down. Sunk."

Katalin gasped, not able to hide her shock.

Daunte laughed. "He never told you? The bastard. Maybe you would have liked the challenge."

Katalin reeled at his words. The Wake Ripper was a notorious pirate ship that had wreaked havoc in Caribbean shipping lanes for years. Neither Katalin nor her father had ever dared to skirt near the Wake Ripper. She shook her head. "But that is…You want the Wake Ripper? That is what all of this is about? Why?"

"We used to do a brisk business together, the Wake Ripper's captain and I, but it ended on a sour note. Much like my association with your father."

"So? Why would you even care about the Wake Ripper now?"

"I need the shipping lanes open, and the Wake Ripper has been targeting my ships, no matter which flag they fly under. Every ship I have hired to sink the bastard has failed. I was incredibly close to owning those shipping lanes, and now my competitor has taken over. That will not do."

"But this is my daughter, Daunte. We have nothing to do with you. You cannot do this."

"I can. It is unseemly, but if taking your daughter is the only way to make you go after the Wake Ripper, so be it. I need that ship, that crew, that captain taken down, and you are the one to do it."

"No, but I cannot. I have not been a captain in years. I do not know where all of the crew is. I have no ship. I—"

"You will do it if you want your daughter back."

Katalin's open jaw snapped shut.

"My fastest ship, the Black Falcon, is leaving port tonight. I renamed it, but I think you will recognize the vessel. I procured it quite cheaply at auction."

Katalin eyes went wide. "You took the Windrunner?"

"It was available, and I am no fool. The Black Falcon sets sail on the high tide. I suggest you be on it."

"And if I am not?"

"I do not think you would dare to put your daughter in that danger. Nor would you dare to tell another soul what you are going to do. The consequences of that would be severe. I think you forget that I now know exactly where you are. Exactly where your father is. Exactly where your daughter is. Exactly whom you are to marry. One way or another, you will be on that ship when it sets sail tonight." Daunte leaned forward, drawing the closed curtain open a crack. "As I see you have another engagement to attend to, I am magnanimous when I say, I do not care what you do between now and tonight. Put your affairs in order, child. But be on that ship."

He pointed at Annette. "Although we had a regrettably rough start, I am sure this fine lady will take excellent care of your daughter under my watch until you sink the Wake Ripper and return. Am I correct in that?" He raised an eyebrow at Annette.

Annette nodded before Katalin could even begin to beg for her help. Annette was part of the family, adored Josalyn, and was beyond loyal to Katalin. Katalin abhorred having to put Annette in this awful situation, but she had no recourse.

Katalin mouthed the words, "Thank you," to Annette, not able to impart the enormity of her gratitude. Her eyes went back to Daunte, turning icy.

"I will get her back—unharmed—when I return?"

He nodded.

"Swear it."

"You will get her back when you return."

"And if I fail—if I do not return, you will deliver her to the Earl of Clapinshire?"

Daunte shrugged. "I recommend you not fail. I do not know what the earl would want with a bastard baby, but yes, I will do so upon your death."

He leaned past Katalin and opened the carriage door. "The tide is rising, Captain. It is time for you to set your affairs in order."

Katalin pulled the hood of the cloak over her head and stepped out of the carriage, her legs numb and almost dropping her to the ground.

Sheer force of will brought her shaking limbs upstairs to her room, and she collapsed, sitting onto her bed, the shock not subsiding enough for tears.

Her door opened and Katalin turned her head to see Mable walk in. She sat up.

"When is high tide, Mable?"

Startled, Mable cocked her head in confusion. "High tide, miss?"

"Yes. High tide."

"I don't rightly know, miss."

"Go—go now. Find out the answer, and get back here as quickly as possible with it."

"But, Miss Dewitt, your hair—"

Jumping to her feet, Katalin pointed at the door. "Go now. Now, Mable, now."

Katalin knew she was sharp with the girl but could not bring herself to care. She would have to be sharp if she was to captain a ship again.

She had no choice.

~ ~ ~

The most miserable moments of her life snarled with what should have been the happiest. Time ticked by slowly with Katalin's mind in a thick haze. The wedding, the small celebration afterward, the early dinner. Aggie and Reanna had made sure the day was magical.

Magic that Katalin could not feel. Not through the pain of her little girl missing. Not with her being unable to tell Jason what had happened.

And now Katalin was half-naked, facing Jason, her now unquestionably official husband.

He stood shirtless, staring at her. He had put on ragged old trousers—slops—slung low from his hip bones, loosely tied with white rope—rope from a ship, and bare feet. Exactly as he was when she had first met him. The nostalgia of it made her heart ache, that he would do this to bring a smile to her lips.

She faced him, but her eyes kept flickering over his shoulder to the ticking hand of the clock on the bureau behind him.

Four hours left.

Four hours to make Jason feel everything she ever needed him to know. Make him feel how intensely she loved him.

She would sink the Wake Ripper. She would get her daughter back. But once she disappeared on Jason, she knew he would never be hers again. She had sworn to trust him. But she could not trust him with this. Not when it meant Josalyn's life. Not when it could mean his life.

She sacrificed her husband once. She would not do it again.

Even if she failed, Josalyn would have her father. Daunte would no longer need Josalyn, and Jason would find a way to their daughter. That was the part she had to trust him with.

Her eyes swung from the clock to Jason's face. Light from the fireplace across from his bed danced on his cheek, the shadows much like it used to be late at night on the deck of the ship. A shiver ran down her spine.

The past. The future. Both loomed, suffocating her.

She had to live in this moment. Live in every second they had together until she had to disappear. It was the only way to honor what Jason meant to her. What he would always mean to her.

She stepped to him.

"I am almost afraid to touch you, Kat."

She took another step, closing the distance between them and letting her thin, dark blue night rail fall open in front of her. It skimmed her nipples—the only part of her body that remained hidden. "I have never seen you afraid of anything."

"This. That this is real. That you are real in front of me. That this is not a dream. A dream where I will touch you and you will disappear and I will wake up in the dank hold of a ship again."

She set her fingers on his chest, letting them slowly spread wide until her palms were on the heat of his skin. His heart-beat pulsed under her hand. Solid. Even. Chin down, her eyes went up to him. "Did I disappear?"

The smile spread slow, lazy across his face. But then his hand shot out, grabbing her behind her neck and dragging her up to him, their lips colliding. Not lazy. Not soft.

He pulled back, his deep voice rough. "You do not know what this means to me. You are mine and the whole damn world now knows it. Never again do I have to hold my hand at my side when I need to touch you. Bow my head instead of looking at you, hungry. Hide my every thought of you from the world."

"I do. I do know. It means the same to me, Jase. More than. This moment. This is the moment I want to be in—the moment I have always needed to be in. No past. No future. Just you and I."

Her hands went down, working loose the rope that held his trousers. "I like the rope."

"I thought you might. Homage to our early days on the ship—the moments that made me fall in love with you."

The rope came loose, and Katalin tugged it free from the trousers as her lips went to his skin, tasting the crease in the middle of his chest. His trousers fell, but Katalin kept the rope in her hands. "And useful beyond holding your trousers up."

Jason chuckled. "I cannot wait."

"But that is the point." She pushed him backward until his thighs hit the bed. "We have never truly had the luxury of time. You are always so quick to attend to me, but I want this. Time for you to feel every caress, every breath, every lick. This will merely ensure that. "

She gave him a slight shove, and he landed on the bed. Katalin straddled him, knees on the bed, and grabbed his wrists. She leaned forward, kissing him, even as her hands worked a tight weave of the rope in a figure eight around his wrists.

Pulling up, Katalin looked down, seeing Jason was already more than ready for her, pulsating large. Which was exactly why she needed to do this. Needed to slow time.

Snapping the rope tight, she took the free ends of the rope, tugging him to the end of the bed, and tied him to the bottom right bed-post.

"Take care you do not make this too exquisite, Kat, or I am liable to have to pay you back for this."

"First, I want to see your back." His arms above his head, she flipped him over so his stomach was flat on the bed. She sat on his backside, her legs on either side of him. "I did not get to see this up close the other day."

It was as she had thought. Scars she did not recognize on top of the ones she did. Her fingers slid along the newer ridges. "These are from after we were captured?"

"All of that was a long time ago, Kat. They have long since healed."

"They are new to me. Suffering because of me. Because you needed to save me, when you should not have."

"I would do anything to save you from harm, Kat. How do you not know that?"

But she did know it. Know it, and it terrified her. If she did not leave England without Jason knowing, there was no limit to what he would do to save her.

And then who would save Josalyn?

Tears sprang to her eyes, and Katalin was grateful Jason could not look at her directly. The present. She had to concentrate on the present. She bent over, her fingers, her lips trailing over the new scars, the taste of his skin mixing with the salt of her tears.

When she had thoroughly kissed every bit of his back, her tears had finally dried, and she slipped her hands along his hips, wedging them under him to caress his front side.

"Agony, Kat. Agony. Tell me it is time to flip."

She leaned forward, trailing the tip of her tongue along his neck until she reached his ear. Her voice a whisper, she offered one word. "Flip."

Katalin didn't think it possible with his hands tied, but he spun around with ease, sending her flying off of him onto the bed.

Laughing and knowing she had his eyes full well on her, she went tall on her knees, stripping off her night rail, shoulder by shoulder, letting the silk slip down her skin.

"Time to untie me, Kat."

"No. Not nearly." She snatched his closest ankle, her lips going to his skin, and she worked her way up his calf and then veered inward to his thigh.

A low groan escaped him, vibrating his chest as Katalin worked slowly upward until her lips met his very solid member. She grasped him, her tongue working the length of him, the ridges, until she took him deep, sucking a tormented grunt from him.

His hips arched with the strokes of her head until he buckled away from her mouth, shaking, straining. Katalin looked up to his face, and she could see he was at his breaking point.

"Kat. Dammit." He grimaced. "Dammit. You need to untie me this instant, Kat."

Her fingers released him, but then she moved her hands achingly slow up his body, her lips following along the hard lines of his stomach, to his chest where she bit, teasing each nipple, to along the stretched muscles of his shoulders and his neck. Stopping at his mouth, she hovered over him for long seconds, her eyes intent on his.

This. This was how she needed to remember him. Love. Lust. Wonder. All of it in his eyes as he looked up at her, the heat vibrating out of control between them.

"Kat—"

She met his mouth, halting his words, taking his tongue into her mouth. Their lips bruising, hard, and she reached up and worked free the knot she had tied. Tied much too well—and she swore at herself.

In the same breath his hands were untied, Jason clasped an arm around her and flipped her onto her back, his body covering hers.

"Kat, I need—"

"Yes." Her word said it less than her eyes did, and she reached up to grasp his neck.

It was all the invitation Jason needed, and he slammed into her, driving to full hilt.

Filled with him, gasping for she hadn't realized how insane she had just driven her own body as well, she swore as he pulled out, demanding him deep, sating her voracious need for him.

Gently, slowly, he slid into her, his hand going to her right breast, rolling her nipple in his fingers. The combination sent Katalin into a wicked arch against him, and she was instantly begging, instantly contorting her body to get closer to his.

Fingernails deep in his shoulders, she thrust upward, meeting him repeatedly as he crashed into her. He paused in his rhythm, his fingers going into her folds, plying her, and Katalin shattered, convulsing under him as her body came hard, her core shocking her nerves with fire.

Unable to stop, Jason used her arching back to his advantage, grabbing her hips and pulling her up from the bed, driving into her fast, his own body going taut in a harsh yell as he sank deep, emptying into her, his rigid muscles quivering in spasms.

Jason collapsed on top of her, burying her body deep into the soft bed. Even with the spent muscles in her arms, she managed to wrap her hands onto his back, fingers splayed on the sheen of his skin.

She had never been so exhausted. So safe. So loved.

A moment in time that was exactly what she needed to hold onto.

# CHAPTER 21

Before he even opened his eyes, a smile touched Jason's lips. He was the luckiest man alive, and he knew it. Not only was Katalin finally, truly his, but he had never dreamed he would so enjoy not only being tied up himself, but tying Kat up and giving her a taste of her own wicked actions last night.

He would definitely be keeping that rope handy.

They had fallen asleep, Katalin curled deep into him, her heart beating on his. Jason had not had such a restful night in years—not since well before he was bound and gagged and tossed on that first ship years ago.

His hand twitched into the air. Why wasn't her heat still next to his?

He opened his eyes, fully expecting a naked Katalin to be draped on the bed next to him.

Empty. An empty bed.

He rolled over, expecting her to be by the fire. No Katalin.

Maybe in his adjoining chambers?

Loath to get out of the warm bed, and wanting his wife back in it with him, Jason cleared his throat. "Kat?"

No answer.

"Kat?"

Silence. She couldn't be dressed and downstairs already, could she? How long had he been asleep?

Tossing the coverlet back, he stepped from the bed into the chill of the morning, and checked his adjoining dressing chamber. Empty.

Dressing in her rooms? Jason knew some, but not a lot of her possessions had been moved into her chambers the day before. He walked over to the door between their rooms, opening it slowly.

All was still—no Katalin. A quick check into her attached dressing room, and Jason turned around, frown on his face. It looked like nothing in the room had been touched—open trunks sat on the floor with her clothing overflowing like a maid had started, but not finished, putting away Katalin's wardrobe.

And then he saw it. On the neatly made bed, a cream envelope sat propped on the plump pillows. His name was scrawled across it in large cursive. Even from his distance to it, he could see it was fat, holding several sheets of paper. Dread flooded his chest.

Each step to the bed heavier than the last, he was out of breath by the time his fingers picked up the envelope.

He sank onto the bed, shoulders hunched, staring down at the envelope he held in his lap. Unable to move for minutes, he bargained with himself, telling himself he could handle whatever was in it.

Maybe Katalin just wanted to write him a love letter.

Maybe she went for a visit at the Southfork home and left him with a list of chores.

Maybe.

Courage worked up, but breath held, he opened the seal on the back of the envelope and unfolded the sheets of paper, the crispness of the thin vellum crinkling under his fingers.

*My love,*

*By the time you are reading this, I will be gone. I was to tell no one of this, but now that I am away, I need you to know. I cannot bear the thought of you wondering, questioning our love, what you mean to me. I could not leave this land, this home, without telling you why.*

*While I would never choose this, the choice is not mine. Josalyn has been taken by Daunte, the same man that has threatened me. Annette is still with her, and I have to trust that she is safe for now. To have her returned to us, Daunte demanded I return to the Caribbean and captain the Windrunner once more. He has ordered me to take down a pirate in those waters.*

*I do so willingly. If this is the only way to get Josalyn back, I do it without hesitation or fear.*

*I never understood why my father lied to me about you, not until the moment I found out Josalyn was taken. It is a primal force to protect one's child, and I am no different than my father. What he did to protect me—who he hurt along the way—I understand it now. I understand it because I must do it to you. I must leave. Even with the hurt I will cause.*

*I will do everything in my power—till my breath is no more, to see that our little girl is safe and returned to us—to you, should I fail.*

*Please trust that I would never lie to you, nor could anything ever tear me away from you, save for her.*

*If I fail, Daunte can demand no more from me or my father, and you must find a way to get Josalyn back if he does not deliver her to you as he promised. I know you will. I know you will protect her as you would me.*

*And if my baby girl ever asks about me, simply tell her that I loved her very much, but do not tell her why I disappeared. I do not wish for her to carry the burden of the truth, not when she is innocent.*

*I do not know if you will understand. I can only pray that you will find a way to forgive me for leaving you. It shatters me to think I will cause you more pain.*

*I am so sorry.*

*But know I will wait. Wait until the next life.*

*Maybe then, then will be our time.*

*I love you. More than life.*

*Always,*

*Katalin*

Jason's breathing became harsh, the sound filling his head before he read the last line.

He sat, heaving for long minutes as his eyes went over her words repeatedly.

Gone...Protect...Fail...Understand...Forgive...Wait...Love...

The last calm thing he did was to neatly refold the vellum and tuck it back into the envelope.

And then he lost all control.

It started with the lamp on the side of the bed, thrown across the room and shattering on the fireplace mantel. The nearest chair smashed into the wall, followed in quick procession with tipping over the armoire, ripping the coverlet in two, and hurling every possible item that could be picked up.

When Katalin's room was destroyed, feathers from the bed still flying in the air, Jason stormed into his room, punching his hand through the plaster wall along the way.

And then he repeated the process of destruction in his own room.

Two rooms demolished, and still, his rage was palpable, threatening to burst through his skin.

Jason stood in the mess in heaving silence, staring at Katalin's blue night rail in tatters, pieces of it littered in front of the fireplace.

Her father.

He had to get to her father and find a way to stop this.

~ ~ ~

Pounding on the grey door of the townhouse Dewitt had been renting, it took long minutes before the door cracked, and Jason shoved it wide, sending the maid flying backward.

"Where is Dewitt?"

Trying to catch her feet, the maid pointed to the room opposite the stairs, more scared than annoyed. "He be in the study, sir."

Jason stalked by her, slamming into the study. Dewitt was by the fireplace, feet on an ottoman, hands folded across his stomach. He hadn't moved from his relaxed position, even though Jason knew full well Dewitt had to have heard the ruckus as he came in.

"She is gone, Dewitt."

Katalin's father sat up, looking in Jason's general direction, his posture suddenly interested. "That is you, boy? I thought we came to the understanding that we avoid each other."

"I damn well wish I could do that, Dewitt, but your daughter is gone. And your granddaughter has been kidnapped."

Dewitt shot to his feet, his large form teetering off his bad leg, and he squinted his one good eye at Jason. "What abomination is this? What do you mean Katalin is gone? And my granddaughter? What is the meaning of this?"

"That is why I am here. To get some answers." Jason pulled Katalin's note from the inside of his jacket, his fingers quickly slipping out the sheets and handing them to Dewitt.

Dewitt grabbed them, holding the paper up to his nose. Jason could see the writing was upside down.

"You know I can't read this with my sight, boy." He thrust the papers back at Jason.

Snatching the letter back, Jason looked down at Katalin's words, loathing the fact that he would need to read them out loud. But he cleared his throat and started, running through it as quickly as he could, skipping over the parts that were for him alone.

Dewitt fell back, collapsing onto the chair he had been sitting in. At the silence following Jason's last words, his head fell into his hand.

"No. This cannot be. Not Josalyn. Not the baby."

Jason had no time to allow Dewitt to wallow in the news. "Who has her? Who has my daughter, Dewitt?"

"His name...his name is Daunte."

"I already damn well know that—Katalin told me—who the hell is he? And what the hell did he set Katalin to do—take down a bloody pirate—what sort of madness is this?"

"The Wake Ripper." Dewitt's head came up from his hand, his voice haunted. "He wants the Wake Ripper brought down. He has tried repeatedly, but none he has hired to do so have been successful."

Dewitt's head fell, shaking as he stared into his lap. "I cannot believe he would do this...for two years, Daunte has demanded me crew take down the Wake Ripper. And for two years, I have refused. I have refused to send Katalin out—she be a mother now—and I will no longer allow that life for her, much less put her onto the tail of the Wake Ripper. Nor will I put my crew in danger like that."

He looked up at Jason, his good eye seeking out the figure in front of him. "It is a mission of suicide to go after the Wake Ripper. Pure suicide. And even if there be a chance, the crew has not been out on waters since they were captured with you, boy."

"The rest all survived?"

"Aye. They did. But we were done. We were all done—for good. And that has driven Daunte mad. Over the years he has become more insistent. More desperate. And that was when he threatened Katalin with piracy to force us to go after the Wake Ripper. And then I became desperate and contacted Katalin's mother for help."

Jason's jaw flexed. He needed to punch this man, his frailties be damned. "But instead of helping, you only put both Katalin and my daughter in danger."

"I am sorry, boy, I thought I had hid the fact of Josalyn's existence from him. I never would have put the babe in danger, never—we both—Katalin and I—be doing this, coming to England for that wee one. For that wee one to have a safe future."

"Who the hell is he, Dewitt? He must be here in London to have gotten to Katalin. To have gotten to Josalyn."

"He is the one that has provided us the letters of marque, some real—some fake I now know. For years, too many to count, he would deliver me a list—ships to sack. Me and me crew would comply."

He rubbed the leathery skin of his forehead. "We never asked questions. And then when I could no longer see enough to captain, Katalin took over. I did not like it, but she is a canny one, my daughter. And she did well as captain. By then we were all wealthy, but Daunte would still insist on the ships he identified being taken down. And heaven help me, by my orders, we complied. But then you were captured and we were done. We were all done."

Fists digging into his own thighs, Jason shifted on his feet. He didn't need a damn history lesson, he needed to find out who Daunte was. "Get to it Dewitt, who the hell is he—why would you do his bidding—what sort of power does he have over you?"

Dewitt sighed, his crooked weathered fingers scratching the back of his neck. "He is my brother, boy. My damn brother. The eldest. Baron Walton. Five sons of our mother, and we are the last two."

"Blast it. Your brother?" The name exploded in Jason's head. Baron Walton—Lord Walton—the bastard that had sunk one of Devin and Killian's merchant ships. "Does Katalin know?"

"No. I never told her. Never told her where my orders came from other than the name Daunte. I never thought he would go this far. Be this desperate. I will kill him for this."

"Please do so. But I need to get my daughter back first. Where is he now? Where would he have Josalyn?"

Dewitt shook his head. "He is well guarded. If I tried to kill him, my damn eyesight would have me a dead man before I got near him. And I do not know where he might be keeping a stolen babe."

"Then I will kill him. And torture his men until they tell me where my daughter is."

Dewitt heaved another sigh, a beaten man, and went to his feet. A half-head taller than Jason, he looked down at him with his good eye. "Aye. You know my terror now, boy. What wouldn't you give to keep your daughter safe? To get Katalin back in yer arms? A deal with the devil is a small price to pay for their safety—it was what I did on the island to save Katalin from the noose. Sent you to hang instead of her."

Jason's voice went icy. "You know nothing of my terror, old man. You have brought this down upon your very own blood. You. You sent your daughter to her death, and have lost your granddaughter. You. Your greed. Your weakness." He stepped in on him. "You know nothing of my terror."

The bluster on Dewitt's face fell, and he turned from Jason. "Aye. I have chosen this life, and now I am paying for my deeds."

Jason stared at his humped shoulders, pity blending with disgust.

Dewitt was no blasted help to him. But his brother-in-law would be.

Swearing a string of incoherent blasphemies under his breath, Jason grabbed Dewitt's arm, dragging him out of the house.

# CHAPTER 22

Katalin's father sank onto a side chair with a heavy glass of brandy in his hand, while Jason turned to face Devin and Killian in the duke's study. Devin sat behind his large mahogany desk, and Killian stood by the sideboard, pouring himself a glass of brandy.

"What is going on, Jason?" Devin asked. "Sneaking us all in here without Aggie knowing must mean something drastic."

"Action is needed, and I need your help. But this is danger my sister will have no part of, and if she hears of it, she will no doubt insert herself." Jason cleared his throat. "I do not wish to rehash at great length, so I will be short. Katalin is gone, forced onto the seas to captain a ship again."

Killian spun from the glasses in front of him, decanter in hand. "What in the bloody hell?"

Jason held his hand up, stopping Killian's questions. "First, you need to know Katalin and I have a child. A girl, almost two. Her name is Josalyn. We were going to tell you after the wedding. I only found out about her days ago. And this is where I need your help. The man, Daunte—the one that has been threatening Katalin with piracy charges—he has now stolen my child. Daunte is actually Lord Walton. He stole my girl and then used her to get Katalin to go after some rogue ship, the Wake Ripper, that has been terrorizing his vessels in Caribbean shipping lanes."

Devin and Killian glanced at each other.

"The Wake Ripper?" Devin asked.

"Yes. Have you heard of it?"

Devin glanced back to Killian. Killian gave him a crisp nod.

Standing up and walking around his mahogany desk, Devin stopped and leaned on the edge of it, watching Jason. "We employ the Wake Ripper to ensure safe travel for our ships in those waters. Although we pay handsomely for that privilege, we have no say in what the captain of the Wake Ripper does with his ship or crew, though we are aware he has taken several of Lord Walton's ships."

"It seems Lord Walton has had enough," Killian said. "He has been trying to push us out of trade in that vicinity, and the Wake Ripper is one of the few things stopping him from control in the area. We have been locked in this battle with him for years."

Killian took a swallow of his brandy, shaking his head. "He is making a desperate move with this and using your wife and daughter in the process."

Jason looked at Devin, forcing out through clenched teeth the question foremost in his mind. "The Wake Ripper—how brutal are they? What sort of a chance does Katalin have?"

Although Devin tried to hide it, Jason could see a split second of pity flash on his face.

Devin's voice was solemn. "It would be best to stop Katalin before she reached the Wake Ripper."

"She does not stand a chance?"

Devin shook his head.

"Bloody fucking hell." Jason tried to control the fists at his sides. He couldn't destroy another room. Not when he needed to get his wife and daughter back, and time was slipping against him.

"How long has she been gone?" Killian asked. "Can we catch her?"

"At least a half day," Jason said. "She disappeared in the middle of the night. I would guess before the tide went out. I do not know on what sort of vessel she would have left on."

"She be on the Windrunner."

The three men turned to Dewitt, who had been silent thus far.

"What?" Jason stalked to Dewitt. "The Windrunner still exists?"

Dewitt nodded. "She does. My brother bought her at auction. He has been keeping her for just this purpose."

"Dammit," Jason said. "Then Katalin is fast escaping us. With a strong breeze, the Windrunner is uncatchable. She would do anything to save Josalyn and the threat of death is not about to stop her."

"She still has to gather the crew, boy, before she hunts down the Wake Ripper," Dewitt said. "And it will take days to round the mates."

"Will they go with her?" Jason asked.

"Aye." Dewitt's bad eye went aimless, landing on the window. "They will do anything she asks, for she has never truly asked them to do anything. And it is for the wee lass, and for her... for the wee one, they would all march to a watery grave without question."

Silent, Killian's and Devin's eyebrows arched at Dewitt's comment.

Dewitt's face went red as he squinted at their faces, and he jumped to his good foot. "What? You think there be no honor among my kind?"

Killian and Devin remained silent, still.

"There is," Jason said softly. "There is. They will do anything for their captain."

"Aye, boy. You understand the way of it."

Jason turned to Devin. "I have to go after Katalin, but I have to get Josalyn back first. It is the only way she will stop this course of madness. Can you get me in front of Lord Walton?"

"No." Devin crossed his arms over his chest. "Can I get you in front of Lord Walton—yes. But I will do no such thing. You will kill him the instant you are within reach, and we cannot have that."

"Do not pull any ridiculous code of honor into this, Devin." Jason words seethed out. "I do not care if he is titled—this man has no honor. He has stolen my family from me, and he will pay."

Devin didn't flinch. "I do not speak of honor, Jason. I speak of a better way."

Devin glanced at Killian, and Killian offered a quick nod.

"We have spies in his organization. He is our main competitor, and we have spies with him—he has spies with us—it is a game that is played," Devin continued. "But this is no longer a game, this is our family. And those spies may very well know exactly where he is keeping Josalyn. We also have people that watch his every move. We have since you were drunk at the Horn's Rooster with him. Let me get to my men before we flat out kill the baron. It will be safer for Josalyn if we get to her before Walton even knows we are searching for her."

"That will take too long—I have to do this quickly, Devin. Katalin is sea bound and slipping further from me every second."

"So then you need to trust us to get Josalyn back for you," Devin said. "You need to go after Katalin and stop her before she reaches the Wake Ripper. Her situation is more dire."

"I cannot leave with Josalyn in Walton's clutches."

"This is when you need to trust me, Jason," Devin said. "You need to trust someone aside from yourself. It is the only way. We will get Josalyn back. I have no doubt we will find her one way or the other—believe me when I say I hold no honor when it comes to pain and getting what I need from a sniveling coward that would steal a baby."

"But—"

"Jason, you are in an impossible situation—your wife or your daughter—so it is damn well time you accept help from your family." Devin stood tall from the desk. "Can you truly afford to stay around here to get Josalyn back, only to have to tell her that her mother is dead? Do you want her to grow up without Katalin? For her to ask you one day why you did not save her mother? Did not protect her?"

Jason's fist was flying at his brother-in-law before he had a thought to control it. But Killian was just as quick, grabbing Jason's wrist before it made contact with Devin.

"Devin can do this, Jason," Killian said, dropping Jason's wrist. "You know he is in the best position to get your daughter back. And you are in the best position to stop Katalin—do you think she would stop her course of action if anyone but you told her Josalyn was safe?"

Jason heaved a sigh, a sad attempt to rein his anger. Chin jutted out against the truth, he shook his head.

"Trust us, Jason. Trust me," Devin said, his voice deadly. "What I think you do not understand is that Josalyn is now family. Family. And no one threatens my blood. I will treat getting Josalyn back no different than I would treat going after my own son, were he in that situation. No mercy."

Only letting it slip for a moment, Jason could see livid fury spill with Devin's words. It was chilling to see, and Jason was instantly grateful Devin was on his side.

He would have to thank his sister for that when this was all done.

"Fine. You get my daughter back, Devin. You keep her safe."

Face set in stone, Devin nodded. "I will. No mercy, Jason. None. Trust I will get her back."

Jason stared at his brother-in-law for a hard moment, and then nodded. "So then, I need a ship."

Dewitt cleared his throat, drawing the eyes of the three men. "For that, boy, I have the perfect ship for you."

~ ~ ~

His forearms cutting into the wooden railing, Jason's eyes swept across the western seas before them. The ship had reached a decent pace now that they were on open waters and a strong wind had their sails.

The breeze kept a solid chop on the tips of the waves, and Jason sucked in salty air, shaking his head as he tried to calm the rage that had not subsided in the slightest during the last day. The one thing he had sworn to himself years ago was that when he reached England, he would never set foot on a blasted ship again.

Yet here he was.

And not only had he boarded willingly, he was now wishing they were much further into the empty vastness of the ocean.

Katalin had forced him into the one thing he swore he would never do. But then, he had also never thought to have her again. So if fate demanded he prove his love by doing this, then, hell, he'd never set foot on land again if it meant he could keep Katalin safe.

"If we be lucky, an' the winds keep right like this, we will get her, lad."

Jason's eyes didn't leave the horizon, but he did give a slight nod to Captain Roland as the man grasped the railing next to Jason. It was the Rosewater that Dewitt had requested stay in port after delivering him, Katalin, and Josalyn to England. So it was the Rosewater that Jason had boarded. They had been lucky, just setting sail with the tide after spending hours rounding up the crew.

"Thank you for helping to find her, Captain Roland. It is appreciated more than you know."

"Aye, no need for thanks, lad. It be for Captain Kat. That is all I needed to know."

They stood for a moment in silence until Jason turned to Captain Roland, leaning his hip on the railing, arms crossing his chest.

"Why did you do it?"

"Do what, lad?"

"Save me from prison, only to lie to me?"

"I lied?" Roland stroked his beard. "I don't recall a lie that day. Not that I be above it, matey."

"You lied about Captain Kat. You said she left me there to die."

"Hmmm. I be saying that?"

"You did. You said she wanted to be rid of me."

Roland suddenly nodded, scratching his chin through the thick of his beard. "Aye. I did say that, I reck'n. There be much goin' on that day, what with the explosions and the pillaging to be had."

"Yes, I can see where it may have slipped your mind. But in doing so, you set me on a path so very wrong for where I should have been. Away from Katalin. Away from my child." Jason's hand swept aimlessly over the sea. "All of this could have been avoided."

"Ah, I understand now." Roland laughed, a booming sound that echoed up off the water. "Lots in life can be avoided, matey, but some things ain't meant to come forth. The lady o' luck decides that. Plus, you misunderstand me integrity, matey."

"How so?"

Roland clasped a heavy paw on Jason's shoulder. "I have no loyalty for what is right, lad. Me loyalty is for the code. And the code tells me I do what Cap'n says."

"But you are a captain."

"Aye. But I will always bow to the wishes of me true cap'n, matey. Always."

"And that is not Captain Kat, is it?"

"No, matey, it ain't. Cap'n De will always be me true cap'n. He be the real reason we are headed to hit the Wake Ripper, matey. Orders from me true cap'n. I not be draggin' yer arse clear cross the ocean were it not for the cap'n. Tis a fool's erran' it be. We all know the Wake Ripper is nothin' but black death for all o' us."

Roland's hand dropped from Jason, and he walked off, voice still booming. "Come death or glory, I follow me cap'n's orders, matey."

# CHAPTER 23

Clipping along the waves, Katalin looked down at the main deck before her, her hands sweaty on the wheel. The crew was silent, and gone was the flurry of preparing for battle. All eyes were trained forward, all hands itchy on the hilts of their steel.

The Wake Ripper had spotted them early—too early. Their sails had unfurled in full force, and now the Windrunner was forced into the unfortunate position of pursuer.

It had only taken a week to find the Wake Ripper once they had found the trail of what waters the ship was currently haunting. Much faster than Katalin had guessed, but still not fast enough.

The Windrunner cracked a wave hard, and water flew through the air, spraying across the decks. The back of Katalin's hand dragged against her eyes, clearing the salt water. She blinked away the sting, focusing through the bright sunlight on the far-off ship.

At least now she could see it with the blind eye, and not only with the spyglass. That meant they were still gaining on the Wake Ripper. And that it ran was telling, as it looked to be loaded heavy with some bounty they would rather not have to defend.

Hope sparked. If they had lost crew in the capture of whatever booty they had, that could bode well for Katalin. Her own crew was leaner than she would have liked—she had only gathered the mates that were childless or had grown children, fully avoiding the few men that had wee ones.

She did it, even though she knew it would cause discourse among the men—the ones left behind would be furious, but she was not about to allow their children to grow up without fathers.

That decision left her without the most virile men she could have used in the fight. To a one, the rest had joined her without the slightest cough, without the slightest hesitation. Admirable, for she knew they were sailing into destruction—that death awaited them. Worse, the crew knew it.

But the actions of the Wake Ripper were promising, for Katalin had never heard of the Wake Ripper's captain not heading straight into a battle with full force.

So Katalin held onto the tiniest nugget of hope, letting it bolster her confidence. She knew very well that confidence could mean all the difference in the upcoming battle.

The gains on the Wake Ripper were slow in coming, but they did gain on it. Five hours had passed. The first four hours the crew had been alive—steel clanking, loading pistols, and positioning ropes. But now, except for the tweaking of the sails, they were still, their knees bucking and swaying with the heavy chop they cut through.

Katalin had planned on a quick attack—the less time for the crew to think of their fates, the better. The less time for her to think of her fate, the better.

She had been on the sea for five weeks now, and she was sick of it. Five weeks away from Jason, away from her girl.

She had been so very close. She had Jason. She had been mere hours away from having her girl back with the two of them. So close to the family she never dreamed she could have, but always needed, deep in her soul.

A soul that had shriveled, day by day, hour by hour, the farther she sailed from England.

And here it was. Destiny to be decided within the next few hours.

Her father had always said she was effective as a captain because of one outstanding trait. She didn't care. Didn't care about the squabbles, about the vices, about the pride that brought down so many men.

But now she cared too much. Too damn much, and she had too much to lose. Her life before Jason had been so easy— nothing to lose, and everything to gain. And now she was in the exact opposite position—nothing to gain and everything to lose.

Her only comfort was that, either way it turned out, she would be at peace, or at least she hoped. Her soul could very well end up rotting away in purgatory for all she knew, but at least this would be over. She would either be sailing back to Jason and Josalyn after today, or sinking to the bottom of the ocean.

So on it went for hours. The Wake Ripper ran, taunting them, and the Windrunner pursued.

And then, before her unwavering gaze, a skull and crossbones flag unfurled from the main mast, and the Wake Ripper rounded, heading straight toward the Windrunner. That, Katalin had not expected.

This must be where they rammed head-first into battle, she surmised, and within minutes, the Wake Ripper would be within striking distance.

Katalin steeled herself, but she did not have to order the crew into readiness, the frenzy on the deck below far out-paced her commands.

"Poe—the cannons be ready starboard? We sink her before reaches us—ready them."

"Aye Cap'n," Poe yelled, dropping his body half down the opening to the gun deck below. He popped back up. "They all be loaded and right for firin'."

"We be on approach, ready with the fire."

Just before she opened her mouth to have the fuses lit, the Wake Ripper cut a sharp south in front of them—well beyond what she guessed the capabilities of the ship were.

"Bloody hell." Katalin spun the wheel hard, following. Now on the Windrunner's port side, the damn Wake Ripper just avoided ten cannonballs in its hull. She had taken a chance on approaching them starboard, and now they would be engaged before the crew could ready the cannons port side.

The two ships sailed in tandem for minutes, their speeds now equal, and Katalin slipped the wheel to ease the Windrunner closer and closer to the Wake Ripper.

"Fire at will," she bellowed forth, and could hear the command repeated up the string of men to the bow of the ship.

And then it happened.

The first shot cracked through the air.

Within minutes, boarding hooks went flying from both ships, flintlock pistols exchanged fire, and with a sufficient cloud of blasted gunpowder, Katalin's crew started swinging across the chasm and landing on the deck of the Wake Ripper.

Katalin held the wheel hard on course, but the second the ships collided, wood tearing, she was thrown from the wheel half across the quarterdeck.

She scampered to her toes, her feet slipping at the now skewed pitch of the deck. Reaching the wheel, she turned the Windrunner a hard starboard, easing the space between the two ships. She just hoped the Windrunner was not on the losing end of the screeching damage she heard.

At the wheel, Katalin searched her deck, and then through the smoke onto the deck of the Wake Ripper. Most of her crew was now on board the Wake Ripper, engaged in full, bloody battle.

Steel crashing. Screams of pain. Screeches of attack.

Katalin couldn't see if her crew was holding its own or if it was a massacre.

Checking to make sure the cutlass, three daggers, and two flintlocks strapped to her body were secure, she yelled at Fin, who was still high on the main mast. "Fin, down here. I need you."

"Aye, Cap'n," he yelled back, and scampered down the mast like a lithe boy a quarter of his age.

Fin scurried up to the quarterdeck, stopping next to Katalin.

"Fin, take the wheel—keep her solid."

She gave him a quick glance, and before he could protest, Katalin dropped the wheel, ran to the side of the deck, and grabbed a free rope. She wrapped the rope once around her wrist, jumped to the railing, and swung.

Landing hard on the Wake Ripper's main deck, she dropped onto her side, skidding across the deck in a tumble. She only stopped when she rammed into the booted calves of a very large man who glanced down at her.

Blast it. Not in her crew. She smiled up him, and before he could react, Frog used the man's second of confusion to attack, his sword going high at the man's head. The brute tried to spin away, but tripped on Katalin, falling backward onto the deck. Frog's cutlass cut into his arm on the way down, and Frog jumped over Katalin, knocking the man hard on the head with the thick hilt of his cutlass. The man went still.

"Cap'n, ye shouldn't be o'er here," Frog yelled at her. "Get back to the Windrunner."

"And let you all fight my battle?" She jumped to her feet. "I don't think so, Frog."

"Dammit, Cap'n. Ye ain't our kind no more. Ye be a mother."

She pulled a flintlock, aiming it over Frog's shoulder at the wild man bearing down on Frog's head with a scimitar. She pulled the trigger, making Frog jump.

"Which is exactly why I am needed over here. No one will fight harder for my girl than me."

Frog looked over his shoulder at the man rolling in pain, holding a bloody shoulder. He looked back at Katalin. "That be a might close to me head, don't ye think?"

"His blade or my bullet?"

Frog shrugged. "Both. But yer still as true a shot as ever, Cap'n." He picked up the scimitar at his feet. "Now stay by me side, Cap'n, or yer father'll have me dragged on the ship's hull."

Frog stepped in front of her, his body wide against the melee, and he moved forth, picking off pirates that had them outnumbered two to one. So much for hopes of a small crew.

Not five steps into the thick of the battle, Katalin peeled away from Frog, her cutlass coming down hard on a sword that was about to slide across Jay's throat.

When the pirate finally looked down and found where the cutlass had come from, he sneered a laugh upon seeing her, pulling a long knife from the sash at his slops. He rushed her, swinging both his cutlass and the knife at her. Katalin hopped backward, avoiding the blades, until her backside hit railing.

Snarling in victory, he thrust his long knife straight at her heart, but Katalin dropped, her cutlass swinging in a wide arch. His blade caught her shoulder, but it didn't stop her motion, and she rolled toward his feet, her cutlass dragging along the skin of his left arm.

His blade dropped, and Katalin pulled a short knife from her calf, digging it into his foot until it hit wood. The scream was palpable, and Katalin rolled away from his grasp, away from his anger, leaving him to try and pull the blade from his foot.

Feet in motion all around her, Katalin checked her shoulder—bloody, but she lost no movement in her arm, so that was good. She scanned the cloudy combat around her, suddenly realizing there were a lot of her men down on the deck around her. Some still. Some writhing in pain. Locke. Jeb. Claw. Poe.

Too damn many of her crew.

Her heart thudded. They were losing this battle. Losing it quickly.

She took a deep breath, steeling herself. She had to go back. Go back to the place where she could maim—kill if necessary. A place where she was cold and did not care. No mercy. She had to be Captain Kat again, through and through.

She spotted her next fight. Zed was just barely holding off two attackers steps from her. Gaining her feet, pistol in one hand and cutlass in the other, she made it two feet to Zed before the ship jerked wildly, pitching severely toward the Windrunner.

She fell onto her backside, sliding on the deck. Damn. She hoped Fin hadn't left the wheel of the Windrunner.

But then she looked across the far deck and realized the cause of the Wake Ripper's violent lunge.

Holy hell. Another ship.

Another ship that had just sidled along the Wake Ripper, sandwiching it.

Where the blast had that ship come from?

But before she could see through the battle to figure out the bizarreness of the new ship, she noticed Frog on his back, two attackers bearing down on him with steel tips.

Katalin scampered to her feet, firing her one shot as she moved forward, cutlass high above her shoulder. One fell, and the other brute turned, stopping her swing with his own cutlass. In quick succession, he showered down blows at her, pushing her to the wall below the Wake Ripper's quarterdeck.

Solid wood hitting her back, she spun away from his next blow, but his sword still caught her side, and hot agony sliced through her skin on the side of her belly.

She crumbled in half, cutlass still up to block his next blow, but ended stuck in a corner between the wall and the staircase leading to the quarterdeck.

The brute moved in, easily blocking any escape path Katalin had. He grabbed her raised wrist, slamming it against the wood wall, and her fingers lost her cutlass, the blade clattering to the deck past his feet.

He didn't send his sword through her immediately, like she thought he would, instead, he reached out and ripped off the scarf that covered her head.

He chuckled. A mean, from the depths of hell chuckle. "Well, ain't that be a kick. Ye be look'n too purty fer a boy. We be hav'n new booty." His hand let her wrist go and he grabbed a mass of her braids, yanking her up off her feet.

It was the last thing he did.

A hair from Katalin's cheek, the tip of a blade stopped, and the man froze. It took Katalin a split-second to realize the rest of the blade disappeared into his chest, having run him through.

She strained to see around him, but could only see the brute's chest, blood seeping onto his dirty shirt around the blade.

The silver disappeared back through his body, and he dropped to the deck, his thick paw still tangled in her hair, and Katalin went down with him. She landed half under him on her stomach, his weight crushing her open wound.

Agony pierced her body, and she screamed through gritted teeth, shoving, trying to roll him off of her.

But then hands went under her arms, pulling her out from under the dead weight. Set onto her feet, the hands propped her up in the corner.

She looked up.

Jason.

Hell.

Jason. Here. On the Wake Ripper. About to die with her. About to make Josalyn an orphan.

Double hell.

She hit him hard, squeezing past him as she went after her cutlass still on the deck. "What the blast are you doing here, Jase? Get off this damned ship."

She started to dart forward into the battle, but Jason grabbed her around the waist, his fingers digging into her wound. She cringed in pain as he shoved her back into the corner, wrapping his hand over hers on the hilt of the cutlass.

"You're not getting past me, Kat."

"Dammit, Jase. Get the hell off this ship." She tried to push past him, but he threw a leg up, trapping her to the corner. She shoved at him again, but he was an immovable wall. "I bloody have to fight, Jase."

She tried to claw up him with her free hand, her eyes wild as she watched more of her crew drop behind Jason. Heard their screams. Smelled their blood.

"No, Kat. Stop. You don't." He grabbed her other hand and pinned it to the wall.

She forced her eyes from the battle to his face. "They are falling, Jase. Falling. They are dying and it's my fault. So let me the hell out there."

He dropped her hands, gripping her shoulders and shaking her. "This is not your fault, Kat."

"I have to do this, Jase—I have to or we will not get Josie back."

His hands stopped shaking her, but his fingers dug deeper into her skin. "Kat, you have to trust me—Josalyn is safe."

"No, I have to do this, she is not safe until—"

"Stop. Kat. Just stop. Look at me." He shook her again. "You need to stop. You need to trust me. Trust me, Kat. Trust me. I would not put our daughter in danger."

Her eyes found focus on Jason's face again, and she searched his blood-shot eyes. "What? How?"

"You need to stop. Josalyn is safe. She is with Devin and Aggie."

"What? She is?"

"The duke has her locked away from any threat."

"But Daunte—"

"We all know who he is, Kat. Devin, Southfork, myself. He has been trying to monopolize these shipping lanes for too long, and now we have proof."

Katalin shook her head. "But he will know if I don't do this. He will know and he will take her again."

"He will not. There is no way he can without sacrificing himself. There is no way he can without me killing him. Or the duke killing him. Or Southfork killing him. Or your father killing him. Josalyn is safe, Kat. Safe."

"Safe?"

He nodded. "Safe. I swear it."

"Ain't this be sweet, now."

Katalin heard the bellow before she saw him. In horror, she watched as the heavy air, thick with exploded gunpowder, parted, and a pirate in full blood-red regalia appeared, two flintlock pistols aimed at them.

One at Jason's head. One at hers.

Jason spun around, crushing Katalin into the corner as his arms and body went wide in front of her. "Captain Gallif, I presume?" he asked coolly, not giving the slightest concession to their precarious position.

"Aye. I hear there be the captain of the Windrunner back here. I be waiting to meet the lass fer years. And then the lass attacks me ship. Ballsy beaute, she be. Also, a dead beaute."

Katalin went to her toes to peek over Jason's shoulder. It stretched her bloody side, but she swallowed the pain. "Aye. I be—"

Jason shoved backward, squashing her and cutting the air from her lungs.

"You will not have her, Captain Gallif. I understand the undue attack on your ship has put you into an irked state, but you will not come near Captain Kat."

The captain's bushy black eyebrows collapsed, sending his eyes into pure viciousness. "Ye be think'n ye be in a position to barter with me, ye scallywag?"

"No. He is not. But I am."

The barrel end of a silver pistol pushed into Captain Gallif's right temple. Katalin's eyes followed the arm attached to the pistol.

"Lord Southfork? What the devil…" she croaked out.

Captain Gallif's eyes veered to his right, his forehead creasing in confusion. "Southfork?"

"Yes, Southfork, Captain Gallif," Killian said, his arm not moving. "I trust you are well."

"I'd be a bloody bright better without yer gun to me head."

Katalin blinked hard, not trusting her own sight. "Lord Southfork, what in the bloody heavens…"

"We are family, Captain Kat. And I do not leave family to die alone on an ocean." Killian answered her above the general din of weapons being lowered throughout the deck. Both crews were starting to realize that all the captains were in one spot, and whatever happened in that spot, happened to all of them.

Killian's eyes did not leave Captain Gallif's head. "Plus, it would seem as though our terms with the captain of the Wake Ripper need to be renegotiated."

"We were attacked, matey. Defense," Captain Gallif said.

"Be that as it may, I think you can lower your pistols, Captain Gallif. I am positive that you will be rewarded handsomely for the inconvenience of this skirmish."

"Ye be calling this a skirmish, matey?"

Killian visibly pressed the barrel into Captain Gallif's skull. "That is all this was, Captain Gallif—a skirmish—no?"

A long, tense moment thickened the heavy silence on the deck.

"Aye. This be a skirmish." Captain Gallif lowered his pistols, shoving them into the belt at his waist. The captain's voice went into a bellow. "Arms down, mateys. Arms down. We be cuttin' the ropes and movin' onward."

The silence was deafening until several began to move, grumbling, and a few sheathed their weapons.

"Onward," the captain yelled, leaving no room for disobedience from his crew.

Katalin let her breath escape in relief, and slumped back into the corner, sliding to the deck.

Blackness overtook her.

# CHAPTER 24

Katalin opened her eyes to a dark wood wall. Lying on her side, she took a moment to identify the areas of insistent, throbbing pain in her body. Her side. Her shoulder. That she was lying on her wounded shoulder didn't help that particular pain.

She slowly rolled to her back. Naked from the waist up. Dark wood above her.

She could tell by the familiar sway that she was still on a ship, but she was in a cabin she didn't recognize. Letting her head flop to the side, she saw Jason, turned away from her, crouched close to the light of a lantern on a small desk. After a moment, he turned to her, the needle he just threaded in hand.

"You are awake."

She nodded.

"I had hoped you would stay passed out for another few minutes." His voice was low, measured, and Katalin couldn't tell if was tired or angry.

"What happened?"

"Not now. I still need to sew your shoulder."

Angry. His biting words left no doubt.

She raised her right hand to the ache on her shoulder. "What?"

"Your shoulder." He pulled a wooden chair close to the bed, sitting. "I did your side first because it was worse, but now I need to do your shoulder."

Her hand went down to the side of her belly, fingertips running over what felt like even stitches along her side. "You stitched these?"

"I spent years on the ships, Kat, so yes, I learned a thing or two about stitching after all the sails I have sewed."

Still angry. Even more so.

"The Windrunner?"

"Dammit, Kat. I do not want to talk about that damn ship of yours. Not now."

"No. I meant the crew—who…"

"Zed and Jay were not saved. The rest will survive."

Katalin closed her eyes. Jay and Zed. Both so loyal. And now their deaths were on her soul. She said a silent prayer for their afterlife and opened her eyes. "Where are we?"

"Safe. Far away from the Wake Ripper. On the Rosewater. Actually, Roland renamed her. It is the Sweetbriar now."

"Pretty." She stared at Jason, his jaw twitching, face set hard.

He reached down to the floor and pulled up a flask. "Roll onto your side so I can reach your shoulder."

Katalin eased onto her side, wedging her right arm under her so the stitched wound on her belly would stay above the bed. Jason waited until she settled and then doused her shoulder wound with rum.

The sting sent her cringing, knees flying up and body curling in a single convulsion, before she clamped down on the pain.

His eyes went to her face. "Do you want some?" He held the flask to her.

She nodded, holding up her head as Jason held the lip of the flask to her lips and tilted it.

He set the flask on the floor. "I would wait, but your shoulder is still bleeding. Can you be still? Can you handle this?"

"I do not think at the moment you care if I can handle this or not."

He paused, angry eyes pinning her. "I care if you are in pain, Kat. But you are right. You did this to yourself, and I am having a devil of a time trying to stay delicate with you right now."

Her eyes snapped shut, stung. "Go ahead. I am fine," she whispered.

He wasted no time, and Katalin flinched as the needle cut through her skin, wishing she was still asleep.

Two stitches in, Katalin couldn't help a grimace from overtaking her face. The needle stopped.

"Can you handle this, Kat?" His words were still hard.

Katalin didn't open her eyes. "I do not have a choice, Jason."

The needle slid through her skin again.

Four more stiches, each one agonizing, and Jason tied off the end of the thread.

"That should hold it." He grabbed a wet cloth and dabbed the skin around the wound. Even with his anger, his touch was soft. "The blood looks to be stopping."

He stood up, going to the bucket in the corner and bent over, silently scrubbing the blood from his hands. He straightened, wiping his hands on his trousers and walked to the door.

"Jase. Stop. Where are you going?"

"I am leaving."

"What? Leaving for where?"

"Dammit, I do not know where, Kat. Just not in here." His hand ran through his brown hair. "All I wanted for five weeks was to see your face, Kat. Your face. And now—right now I cannot even look at you. I would not be in here right now were it not for your wounds. I was not about to let another tend to them."

He spun to the door, hand on the black iron handle.

"Please, Jase." Her voice cracked, pleading. "Please don't leave me. Not now."

He stopped. But he did not turn back to her.

"Please, Jase, I—I do not know what to say." Katalin sat up in the bed, gritting against the pain, her legs swinging over the side. "What do you need from me, Jason? You must have gotten my letter. You know I would never have left you were it not for Josalyn."

He whipped back to her. "But you did leave me, Kat. You did not, for one second, think to trust me—your husband—with the problem."

"I could not think, Jason. He took our daughter—I could not think past the very thing that would get her back."

"No. That is unacceptable, Katalin. I am your damn husband. After everything—how could you leave me? How could you not let me take care of you? Take care of our daughter?"

She shook her head, searching for an answer. "I…I…I have just been taking care of Josalyn, of my father, for so long. I have been alone. Alone. I birthed her alone and I have been alone ever since. I do not know another way, Jason. I have had to do this— life—for years by myself, and I could not think when Daunte took her. I could only react. React like I always had—whatever needed to be done to take care of my baby." Hand supporting herself on the wooden rail of the bed, Katalin stood, taking a shaky step toward him. "The action had to be mine—it was all I could think to do."

"Sit down, Kat."

Her mind did not win over her beaten body, and she sank onto the bed.

He stepped in front of her, arms crossed over his chest. "Why did it not enter your mind to trust me? Do you not think I am a man that can take care of you—take care of our child? Then why in the blasted hell did you marry me?"

"No. God, no, Jase." Katalin reached up and grabbed his forearm, her fingers digging into muscle. The action tore at the stitches in her side. "I know. I know in my soul the man I married. I know you are the only one who can take care of me. Take care of Josalyn. I would not have married you if I did not think that was true."

Her arm went weak, and her hand slipped from his skin as her head bowed, voice cracking. "It is me. I am the failure. I just do not know how to let you. I want to—I need to—but I just do not know how."

Jason knelt, balancing on his heels, eyes at her level. He grasped her chin, tilting her head up. Katalin had no choice but to look at him.

"You are not a failure, Kat." His voice had gone incredibly soft. "You are strong. Too strong, sometimes, and it makes it very difficult for me to take care of you. Especially when you decide to sail an ocean away from me. And that is all I want to do, Kat. Take care of you. Love you."

She looked hard into his green eyes. That was exactly what Jason had been doing to her since they met. Take care of her.

It was time she let him.

Her right hand slipped onto his cheek, rubbing along the rough dark stubble. "I want that, Jase. I need you. I love you. But I need to hear it again—is Josalyn safe? Am I safe? This does not feel over, Jason."

"Dammit, Kat." He shook his head. "Hell yes, you are safe. Josalyn is safe. What can I do to make you believe it? To trust what I am telling you?"

"I do not know. I am trying, Jase, I truly am."

He stood, looking down at her. "Then I will hold you. Tell you it is over. Tell you to trust me. Over and over. Do that until you believe me. Until you trust."

He stripped off his white linen shirt, half of it fully stained with her blood. He looked down at her. "Trust me, Kat."

Moving to sit on the bed next to her, he wrapped her in his arms, pulling her tight onto his chest. Katalin took a deep breath and nestled her forehead onto his chest.

"It is over, Kat. Josie is safe. You are safe." He kissed the top of her head. "You are not alone, Kat. You never will be again. Never again. You need to let me take care of you. It is what I always wanted to do. What I was meant to do. You need to give your worries to me."

He stretched the two of them long on the skinny bed, wedging himself between her and the side wall. "You have to trust me, Katalin.

She nodded into his chest. "I do. I have to. I trust you."

His hand clenched into the thick of her hair. "Good. That was not so hard? Because I know the enormity of those words coming from you."

She laughed and a pain sliced through her side. She ignored it. "No. Not as hard as I thought." She tilted her head up, her chin on his chest so she could see his face. "You look strong, my earl. Useful. I think I will keep you."

He chuckled. "Anything to serve my captain. That is the code."

~ ~ ~

Jason allowed himself to take his first real breath since their ship had approached the Wake Ripper. Katalin was still in his arms, still asleep, as she had been for hours. Her chest now moved with even, deep breaths, and his lips on her forehead told him no fever had started. It was what he had feared since he had seen her wounds up close. She wasn't free from an infection, but all seemed well so far in her body.

He adjusted his arm under her, angling so blood could flow better to his hand. Watching the moonlight cast shadows through the stained glass lining the back of the captain's quarters, he instinctively tightened his hold on her. He knew he should be sleeping as well, but the lie he had just told Katalin weighed too heavily in his mind.

He had no idea if Josalyn was safe. Not the slightest knowledge of her whereabouts.

He hated lying to Katalin, but couldn't bear to tell her that he didn't know if Josalyn was truly safe. He'd had to leave England without knowing his daughter's fate.

Devin had found a trail through his contacts and had been close to finding Josalyn by the time Jason had boarded the Sweetbriar. But then the tide started to move out.

Desperate, Jason had waited for word from Devin until the last remnants of the tide were disappearing. But word did not come.

So he had been forced to leave on faith. Faith that his brother-in-law would not fail him. Not fail his family.

A severe test of his own ability to trust, it had been the hardest thing Jason had ever done—leaving port without knowing if his daughter was safe. Placing all of his trust in Devin and his ability to find Josalyn.

He just hoped his trust was not misplaced.

Just hoped his world was not about to crumble.

# CHAPTER 25

The sway of the carriage into the thick of London helped
with the switch to dry land. Her arm fully entwined in Jason's,
Katalin looked across the rented hack at Killian, who still wore
the buckskin breeches and simple white shirt he had favored
on the ship. Having only known him dressed in society's finery,
she had gotten used to seeing him relaxed in the simplicity of
ship life. And he had dispensed with Katalin calling him Lord
Southfork days into the journey back to England.

Katalin had surmised it was awkward for Killian to be the
only one on the ship with a title, since everyone on Roland's crew
still called Jason either "boy," or if they were feeling generous,
"Jase," even though they all now knew he was an earl. And Jason,
man that he was, let them have their fun with good humor.

Both she and Jason still wore their ship-wear, him in slops
and a loose linen shirt, and her in breeches, and a white shirt
topped with a dark blue vest.

But far from the relaxed ease on the ship during the journey
back to England, Katalin noted crispness in the air of the carriage,
and it was not just the chill of the winter weather. Both her
husband and Killian looked unusually nervous—more nervous
than they had been in the past weeks.

Katalin wondered at it—all was right with the world, they
were back in London, she was about to see her little girl, so why
were they both suspiciously twitchy?

She looked up at Jason, leaning into his warmth. "What is
amiss? You have not said two words since we left the docks." Her
eyes swung to Killian. "And neither have you."

Killian offered up a half-smile with a shrug, but it was clear
his mouth was clamped shut.

She looked back to her husband. "Jason?"

His forearm flexed against her fingers and he patted her hand. "It is nothing, Kat. There were some details that were not worked out before we left on the Sweetbriar to come after you."

Her eyes narrowed. "Details? What details?"

"Details about your father and Daunte."

"Jason. You said I was safe—that Josalyn was safe—is that not true?"

"It is, Kat. Do not fret. You are safe, but we just do not know the full details of what went into that. It is why we are headed to the duke's home. He has the details."

The look that exchanged between the two men did not go unnoticed by Katalin, and the sudden tension in her shoulders only tightened.

They rode in uncomfortable silence until they reached the duke's townhouse. Katalin untangled herself from Jason, ready to hurry into the home, but Jason grabbed her wrist.

"Let us hold here for a moment. We do not know where anyone is. Killian will go in and check on everyone's whereabouts."

Leaning back against the thin cushion of the hired hack, Katalin sighed, trying to hold back sudden tears. All she wanted to do was hold Josalyn, and the last few hours had been agonizing in the wait.

"I do not care for whatever it is you are refusing to tell me, Jase. If this is how you intend to take care of me—by rogue looks among men and by holding things back—I do think I would rather go back to browbeating you for information."

"The wait is just as hard for me, Katalin, probably more so." His hand went her face, turning it so she had to look him in the eye. "Everything I have done—it is to make your world safe. You have to believe that. Believe that for just a few more minutes."

The flecks of brown in his green eyes deepened in color, and Katalin nodded. If this was the trust he was asking her for, she would give it. She had no reason not to trust him.

The carriage door opened and Killian stuck his head in. "They are all here."

Jason jumped to his feet, crouching so his head didn't bang the carriage roof. "Everyone?"

Killian smiled. "Everyone."

Katalin watched Jason's face melt into relief. She spun to Killian. "Josalyn's inside?"

"Yes."

Before Killian got the word fully out, Katalin had pushed past him, jumping from the coach and running up the marble stairs to the front door. A tall footman was quick to his job and had the door open before Katalin needed to slow.

She skidded to a stop in the front foyer and glanced back at the footman.

He pointed. "Down the hall to your left, in the library, my lady."

Katalin took off again, Jason now at her heels. She could hear voices and almost slid past the open door on her left before she realized it was the room the voices came from.

She saw the back of Aggie first, and Aggie turned, her baby boy in her arms, and smiled. Realizing she was in the path of what Katalin needed, she took a step sideways.

Katalin froze.

There, in the middle of the floor, Josalyn laughed, tossing a knitted ball across the floor. Tossing the ball to, of all people, Katalin's mother.

Her mother—on the floor, laughing.

Katalin's jaw dropped. Her mother, on the floor, playing with her daughter. Granted, her mother was on a thick Persian rug, but still—remarkably—on the floor.

Josalyn looked up, seeing Katalin. "Mama!" she squealed.

Before Josalyn could get to her feet, Katalin found her legs and was across the library to her daughter in a second, sweeping her little girl into her arms.

For minutes she squeezed her daughter, her heart bursting, trying to hold in the sobs that she knew would scare Josalyn, and failing at it miserably.

It wasn't until Josalyn had nearly wiggled out of the death grip Katalin had on her, that Katalin opened her eyes. Her mother, now standing, Aggie, and her father sitting in a side chair were all watching her.

She looked around the room. Killian was near to groping Reanna in the corner of the library. Spinning, her eyes found Jason, only to see he was whispering with the duke next to the sideboard. Jason eyes were pinned on the back of her father's head, his mouth a tight line, eyebrows pulled together.

Decidedly unhappy with whatever the duke was telling him. Details.

Jason glanced up, only to see Katalin watching him.

She shook her head slightly in confusion, in question.

It was answered with an obvious sigh, and the tight line of Jason's mouth went tighter. He walked over to her, his hand gently capping Josalyn's head. She oozed charm back at her father.

Jason smiled at Josalyn as he set his lips at Katalin's ear. "There are some things that it would be best for your father to tell you. It concerns Daunte," Jason whispered.

Katalin froze for a moment, tightening, then spun to her father. "Father? You need to speak to me?"

"Aye. There be some things I need to explain to you, child. But they can wait."

"What things, Father?" She stepped to him. "I do not think they can wait."

Her father grabbed his cane, pulling himself up to his full height from the leather chair he sat in. "Please, child, not in here. In the study."

Katalin turned to her mother and knelt, sliding Josalyn to the floor. "Josie, will you stay with your grand—Lady Pent—"

"Meme." Her mother's crisp word cut Katalin's fumble.

Katalin glanced at her mother, startled. She looked to Josalyn. "With Meme for just a moment? I see she has a book to read and I will be right back, my sweet melon."

Giggling, her daughter scooted over to her grandmother. Katalin stood, eyebrows arched at Jason as she walked out of the room, following Devin to his study. Jason's face gave her no indication as to what her father needed to tell her, other than it was serious.

In the study, Katalin stood with arms crossed over her belly, watching her father seat himself in an arm-chair, his hands resting on the top of his thick mahogany cane. Jason and the duke stood at the side of the room in front of a wide wall of bookcases, both their faces stone.

"What do you need to tell me, Father?"

"I will not bandy about it child. Daunte is my brother."

"What?" Katalin staggered a step backward, sinking to the leather settee behind her.

"I could never tell you, child. Not for the things he has made me do. Made you do."

She shook her head, having to repeat the words in her own voice. "Daunte is your brother?"

"Aye. And he remains in the land of the living."

She jumped to her feet, whipping to Jason, eyes wide. "Alive? You lied? You said I was safe. That Josalyn was safe. But Daunte is alive?" She rounded back to her father. "Alive? Bloody hell, if he is alive, then—hell, and he is your brother?"

Her father's hand came up, halting her. "Aye, he is my brother, the eldest. And he is a baron. I never told you child, because I wanted to keep you safe from him. If you never knew of him, then he could never harm you. I was just trying to keep you safe, lass."

Katalin stormed to him. "Your version of keeping me safe, Father, has always been warped. How could you do this? How could you not tell me who he was? How could you let him take Josalyn? All of this." Her arm swung wide. "All of this could have been avoided."

Her father's cane slammed onto the wooden floor. "Silence, child. I will not have you question my authority. What I have done for you. What I have done to keep you from harm."

"Keep me from harm?" she guffawed.

"Kat—" Jason tried to interrupt her.

She didn't even glance at Jason as she cut him off, her eyes narrowing on her father. "No, Jase. No. My father wrought this, and he does not escape responsibility because he tried to protect me. The very damn thing he tried to protect me from, I could have protected myself from—my daughter from—had I known the truth." She stepped a toe to nudge her father's cane. "Keep me from harm, Father? How have you kept me from harm? All this time. How has hiding the truth from me kept me safe? It has not done so—far from it."

"I did not think you would get it in your head to sneak off and commandeer the Windrunner, the crew," he thundered at her, his good eye flashing rage. "You disappoint me, child."

"I...I disappoint you?" She couldn't keep the disbelief from shrilling her voice. "I was dead, Father. Dead the moment I set foot on the Wake Ripper—and I would be at the bottom of the sea right now were it not for Jason."

"He knew as well, child. Before he left for you, he knew who Daunte was. The man left before his own daughter was safe—left it to another to get her back—I would never have done that to my daughter."

Her gaze fluttered from her father to Jason.

Jason made no motion to deny. No words to say it wasn't true.

Katalin straightened, the horror of her father's words filtering into her mind. Jason would not have left before Josalyn was safe. No. He couldn't have. He could not have left their child in danger and then lied to her about it.

But there he stood, accepting her silent judgment. Making no excuse for actions done.

Just as she picked up her foot to attack Jason, an instant of clarity hit her.

Her eyes crept down to her father.

"No. You tore me away from him once, Father. You will not do so again. Whatever Jason did, he did to keep me safe. To keep Josalyn safe. I do not question his choices, Father."

"Your husband entrusted me to get Josalyn back, Lady Clapinshire," the duke said, breaking his silence. "Jason did not want to leave, but I was in the best position to find Josalyn and bring her home safely. He was in the best position to bring you home safely."

Katalin looked at the duke, her face softening. "Thank you, your grace. For that, I will forever be indebted to you. I cannot express my gratitude for my daughter's life."

"You are family, Lady Clapinshire. In a heartbeat, Jason would do the same for Andrew were the situations reversed. No thanks are necessary."

"Your grace, I gather you now know everything about Daunte—my uncle?"

He nodded.

"Why is he not dead?"

The duke kept his mouth closed, but his eyes did slip to her father.

"Father. Why is Daunte not dead?"

Shaking his weathered head, her father sighed. A beaten sigh of sadness. "He is my brother, child. I could not." His voice was low. "The duke gave me the option. The pistol was in my hand. In my hand. And I could not do it. I could not be the death of my own brother. He is blood."

"He is blood? Blood?" Her fist pounded on her own chest. "I am blood. Your blood. What about that? After all you have done in your life—the lives you have taken—this, this is the one you leave alive—the one that can crush me? Take my daughter?"

"I am sorry, child. I have failed you in this. But I cannot kill my brother."

Shaking her head—pity obvious even though she knew her father couldn't see it well enough to recognize it—Katalin took a step backward, drawing a breath.

She looked to Jason. "So that is it? I am to live with constantly looking over my shoulder? Not letting Josalyn out of my sight? Where is the justice?"

"It is not what I wanted to hear, either, Kat, but it is what is right in the situation," Jason said.

"Right?"

"It is a gentleman's agreement, Lady Clapinshire," the duke said. "Lord Walton—Daunte—knows who you are, he knows your daughter, but more importantly, we all know who he is now. What he has done. And we hold considerable more power than he. We all know the story. Any one of us could bring him down—the forged letters of marque would give us a case of treason against him. But we will not. He will not be tried for treason, and you will not be tried for piracy."

"Because if I testified against him, everyone would know who I am, what I have done?"

"Correct. If you will not tell, he will not tell. As much as he can harm you, you can harm him tenfold. The ships you took for him. The list your father has. All of it can be traced back to him. He would not dare chance it, no matter what we take from him—which has been quite a bit, since you have been away. We are slowly and as painfully as possible, dismantling his life. But you are untouchable. Josalyn is untouchable." The duke paused, glancing at Jason before he continued on. "And you should both know that he is not long for this earth. I have learned from several sources, that the blood he has been coughing up has become thicker, more frequent."

Katalin looked to Jason. "I am just to accept this? Accept that this man gets to live after all he has done? I do not care if he is on his way to hell. He deserves to be there now. This is our daughter, Jase."

Jason put his hand up to Katalin, looking to the duke and her father. "Can you two please excuse us?"

"Of course," the duke said, waiting at the door until Katalin's father managed to his feet and stepped out before him into the hall.

Jason waited, jawline throbbing, silently staring at Katalin until the door slid closed.

"I do not care for this either, Katalin," Jason said. "The bastard should be dead. But you talk about the code on your ship—this is no different. This would be the code of the peers. The same code that you wanted to use to your advantage when you came to England. A gentleman's agreement amongst peers is binding."

"And if he chooses to unbind it?"

Jason stepped across the room to her, grabbing her shoulders, and he leaned in, his forehead touching hers. "Then I will kill him myself, Kat. You have given your trust to me. Do not lose faith in it now. I hate that he is alive—more so than you after what he did to you, to us, to our daughter. I will kill him without the slightest hesitation. So believe me when I say I will be vigilant against the slightest threat from him. You are safe. Josalyn is safe."

Katalin's eyes closed, and she took a deep breath, drawing in Jason's essence. She was preparing to argue, but instead of opening her mouth, the calmest feeling engulfed her. Jason's hands on her shoulders, his forehead on hers, his breath against hers.

Peace.

He would take care of it. He would take care of her. Take care of Josalyn. There wasn't a fiber in her being that did not trust that thought.

She stepped into him, her arms sliding around his waist, her nose nestled into his neck. "I trust you. You will take care of us, Jason. I trust that."

The shudder that went through his body at her words sent a lump into her throat, and his arms came around her hard, crushing her.

~ ~ ~

Katalin sat on the leather settee, elbows on her breeches and face in her hands, trying to settle her mind. She had asked for a moment alone, a moment to collect herself after all that had just transpired. So the knock on the study door startled her.

The door slid open before she could answer, and Katalin was surprised to see her mother standing in the doorway. She stood, not moving forward, not moving backward, just standing and staring at Katalin.

"Mother?"

She stared at Katalin for a few more moments before her mouth opened and closed without sound.

It was disconcerting. Katalin had never seen her mother looked so...undecided.

"Are you well, Mother?"

"I love you, my child."

"What?" Katalin came to her feet, jaw agape as her mother took one step into the room.

"I love you. Loved you since the moment you were born. I never stopped, and once I had you back, I did not know how to tell you."

Katalin's head cocked sideways, trying to place the brusque woman she had known with this change. "But you have been so...curt with me."

Her mother came fully into the room, stopping before Katalin. "I must apologize for making you think I did not care. I was abrupt because I was trying to save you, my child."

"Truly?"

"Yes, daughter." Her hand went to a loose strand of Katalin's hair, fingering it, but not tucking it away into Katalin's braid like she usually would. "You need to know you were perfect when I met you. It was a travesty that your perfect would not fit into this society. That it would not gain you the husband you needed. There are so many rules imposed upon us. I know I was cold, but it was so I could be objective—it was the only way I knew how to save you. I was not going to lose you again."

"You were cold to save me? That makes no sense, Mother."

"When I lost you after you were born, it destroyed me." She dropped the lock of hair. "I did not think I could let any emotion manifest when you came back into my life. I could not be destroyed again—not when there was the very real threat of losing you. I could not be that vulnerable."

Katalin frowned, her voice soft. "And then I left."

Her mother swiped an ungloved finger across her cheek where a single tear had slipped. "When you disappeared, Katalin—I lived through losing you once more. And I was destroyed just the same—even with my distance, losing you was even more painful than I remembered." She stopped, swallowing hard. "And I never told you. Never told you I loved you."

Katalin stepped to her, grabbing her and pulling her into a hug. To her surprise, her mother's arms wrapped around her, holding her tighter than Katalin guessed her strength would allow.

And her mother did not let go.

For minutes, her mother held her, held her like she was never going to release her.

Katalin gained control of her voice through her tears. "You are telling me now, Mother," she whispered into her ear. "You are telling me now. It is all I ever wanted from you."

She could feel her mother nod, and then she released Katalin, taking a step backward. Hands smoothing the front of her navy blue dress, she smiled—an actual, genuine, warm smile. "You are still perfect, my child. Since the day you were born, until this moment, perfect." She cleared her throat. "That said, I am fine with your chosen attire if your husband is, but I do hope that the breeches you are wearing will be short-lived." She winked at Katalin.

Katalin could do nothing but laugh, and her mother joined in with the slightest chuckle.

Progress. It was small, but it was progress. Progress Katalin was more than happy about.

"I will set to have all of our items gathered," her mother said. "By the graciousness of the duke, we have all been staying here during your...adventure. We had wanted to surround Josalyn with the security of her new, extended family."

Her mother moved to the study door, then paused, turning back to Katalin. "You have chosen well, my daughter. Your husband. His family. Very well, indeed."

With a crisp nod, she exited the study.

Katalin stared at the open doorway. Magical. How had all of this happened to her? How had she travelled from the depths of near-death, to this? Her daughter. Her mother. Her new extended family? Her husband.

A wonder she would never understand, could only be grateful for.

A smile on her face, she started to the doorway, but then movement outside one of the study's windows caught her eye.

White dots softly zigzagged downward.

Jaw dropping, Katalin walked in a trance to the window, her nose pressing on the chilly glass, fogging it.

Snow.

This had to be snow. She had never seen snow before, only heard of it.

She stood transfixed for minutes, eyes drying for lack of blinks. Breathtaking—utterly breathtaking.

"Our daughter had much the same reaction as you." Jason's deep voice came across the study. "She wants you to see it."

Katalin could not look away from the flakes dropping lazily in front of her. "It is her first time as well."

She felt Jason's presence move deeper into the room but could tell he stopped a distance away from her. Unsure. He was still unsure.

As was she. There was one thing that still did not sit well in her mind, even though she tried to ignore it.

Katalin took a deep breath, turning to him, leaning her head back on the window as her hands grabbed the bottom of the windowsill.

"How could you leave her, Jase? How could you leave here before our daughter was safe? She is everything, and you left her."

One small step in her direction, Jason kept his distance, his face set hard, head slightly shaking as he spoke. "It was an impossible decision, Kat. Impossible. You were both gone, and emotion could not be a part of it. It was impossible. So logic made the decision. As the duke said, I was the better one to go after you, and he had the connections—the way into Daunte's inner realm—and was the better one to go after Josalyn."

"But that means you lied to me on the Wake Ripper. You lied to me. You did not know if she was safe. You asked me to trust you, and then you lied to me."

"Dammit, Kat, I would have told you anything in that moment to get you to stop. Anything. I would have told you Josalyn was on the ship, if it would have made you stop." He moved toward her. "I was not about to let you kill yourself."

"In the very same breath that you asked me to trust you, you lied to me."

"I did. Yes, I lied to you. I will make no excuses for it, Kat. I would do it again in a heartbeat. And if I have to lie to keep you safe in the future, then yes, I will do so again."

She rubbed the worry lines on her forehead. "How can you ask me to trust you to keep us safe—knowing that you would lie to me to do so? How can I accept that?"

"I do not know, Kat." He shrugged. "I guess that is part of the trust. That you trust me to make the right decision. That you trust me to lie to you, if I have to."

He walked toward her, stopping in front of her. "This threat, it is no longer your burden to bear, Katalin. You have carried it for you, for our daughter, for your father, for far too long. It was rightfully mine the moment we married on that island, but I abandoned you. Left you with it. I take this now. It is mine. I never want this worry to be yours again."

She looked away from him, staring at the fire in the fireplace for a moment before she looked back to his green eyes. "But the lies."

His hands went to her arms, sliding downward until he wedged his fingers under her palms and lifted her hands from the windowsill. He pulled them upward, holding them to his chest. "Here are the things I will never lie to you about, Katalin. I will never lie to you about how much I love you. How much I love our daughter. How you two are the very breath I breathe. Every heartbeat. Every thought."

He pulled her to standing. "I will never lie to you about your family. About our friends. About our life. The only reason I would ever lie to you, is to keep you safe. That is the only reason. And that. That you will just have to learn to live with. I can offer no promise beyond it."

"And if I cannot?"

His hands left hers on his chest and he encapsulated her, pulling her tight to him. "You will, because I am not letting you go. Not again. Not ever. I swear to you I will never let another take you or our child again. And I need to hear you tell me that you will never leave me like that again, Kat."

His right hand came up, cradling the side of her face. "I told you once that I will be wherever you need to be. So if that is on your father's island, then I will go with you and Josalyn there, or wherever else you think would be a splendid place to live. But you can never leave me again. Tell me, Kat."

Katalin looked up at him, tears welling in her eyes. "I will never leave you again, Jase. I never could."

He smiled, his grip tightening to her face. "I trust you, Kat. I trust you."

A soft knock on the study door filtered into the room.

Jason turned to the door, answering the knock, his arm keeping Katalin solid to his side.

Aggie poked her head into the room. "I am sorry to interrupt, but my niece wants to go outside in the most dire way, and wants you two. It has been a warm winter thus far, so this is the first snowfall. She is fascinated by the wonder of these flakes."

Katalin smiled at her sister-in-law. "As am I. Do not let her go outside without us. I will not allow her first time in snow to be without me and my first time in snow."

"We will be there in a moment," Jason said. "Can you have a thicker cloak fletched for Katalin?"

"Of course," Aggie said, disappearing.

Katalin moved around Jason to face him, her hands on his thick upper arms. "I did not acknowledge how hard that must have been for you, trusting the duke to go after Josalyn."

Jason nodded. "Luckily, the duke has proven himself time and again when it comes to my sister. I could not allow myself to believe he would perform in any less of a manner for our daughter. Plus, Aggie is on our side, and she is no stranger to searching the dark corners of London, if need be. I knew she would make something happen if it became necessary."

"She is a force, your sister."

"That she is. As are you, my wife."

Katalin smiled, watching the brown flecks in his green eyes. "As are you, my husband."

He came down on her, his lips touching her slowly, softly, taking her in as if there was all the time in the world. Kissing her in the exact way he first kissed her on the deck of the Windrunner. A kiss of exploration. Of longing. Of promise.

She smiled to herself, the memory vibrant in her mind. But here she was today. Still his. Always his.

He was it. He was all.

Her captain. Her earl. Her soul.

# EPILOGUE

Half hidden under Jason's arm, little arms and legs wiggled and Josalyn snuggled deeper below the coverlet between Katalin and Jason. Katalin smiled to herself.

Absolute perfection.

Even if this had been their too-early wake-up notice every day for the past three weeks, and Katalin was dead tired. Absolute perfection.

Josalyn had always been an early riser, but since they had arrived at the main Clapinshire estate, she had been jumping into bed with Jason and Katalin well before dawn.

Her cold toes poked under Katalin's thigh and Katalin twitched, flipping onto her side with a groan.

Jason keeping her up late. Josalyn getting her up early. Still, absolute perfection.

She cracked her eyes open to look out the window—a few rays of sunlight. That was improvement. Her gaze went down to her husband. He was still feigning sleep, and Josalyn was having none of it, insistently blowing into his upturned ear. Giggling. Blowing into his ear. Giggling. It went on for a minute until Jason bear-growled and captured her, squashing her deep into the bed.

The subsequent high squeal of laughter rang in Katalin's ear.

Both Jason and Josalyn were laughing now, exchanging tickles, until Josalyn looked at Katalin, realizing her mother was being left out. She pounced. And Jason joined in.

Katalin spun, squirming in the bed, trying to avoid the wiggling fingers to no avail. They captured her with ease and were merciless in tickling her rib cage and behind her knees.

"Surrender, surrender, surrender," Katalin managed to gasp out through tortured laughter.

With a wicked laugh—too wicked for a two-year-old—Josalyn plopped onto her chest, hands squeezing Katalin's cheeks. Jason flopped close beside her, his head propped on his palm, his hand protective over her belly.

Katalin grabbed Josalyn's hands, kissing the fingertips. "Josie, did you at least let Annette sleep in this morning before you came in here and jumped onto our bed?"

Josalyn nodded, smirk on her face, which most likely meant her answer was really a "no."

"Oohh, sweet melon, I know you are anxious to get outside and plant more spring flowers today, but I have important business for you first."

Josalyn's eyes went wide. "What?"

"Do you remember today is the day Meme is leaving for London with Papi?"

Josalyn nodded.

"So you should go make sure Meme is awake—she will want to spend some time with you before she leaves."

"Yes, mama." Josalyn clambered off Katalin's chest and slipped off the bed, her bare feet pitter-pattering across the wood floor and out the door.

Jason waited until the door closed to let his chuckle escape. He grabbed Katalin's hip and pulled her closer to his warm body. "That was diabolical."

Katalin shrugged as she burrowed her face into Jason's chest, closing her eyes. "Was it? I consider it self-preservation—I need more sleep."

"Are you not well?" The concern was instant in his voice.

"I am. Reanna said she was tired like this in the early days of her pregnancy. It is normal."

"Were you this tired with Josalyn?" His chest vibrated with the low words.

"I have no idea—all that time—those early months—a blur. I do not remember much of those days."

"Well, no need to think on it now." He kissed the top of her head. "We are so firmly into this life, you should never have to look backward."

Katalin drifted into light sleep before his words ended, and was rewarded with five whole minutes of peace.

Peace that vanished the moment Josalyn ran back into the room, leaping onto the bed. "Poppy with Meme."

Katalin and Jason both bolted upright, staring at their daughter.

"What, Josie? What did you say?" Katalin asked. She had to have misheard.

"Poppy in with Meme."

Jason sputtered a cough.

Katalin thwacked his bare chest, but kept her eyes on Josalyn. "Oh. Well, let us give them a moment, then." She tucked a curl hanging in front of Josalyn's eye behind her ear. "Sweetie, can you have Annette get you into some play clothes? I am sure your father would love to get outside with you right away this morning—maybe check out the new foal in the stable?"

Josalyn clapped, looking at Jason.

He smiled at her irresistible glee. "Yes, I am all yours, little Josie. We are going to let your mother sleep this morning. Off you go. Clothes first."

Josalyn scampered out of the room and Katalin sank back into the pillows, staring at her husband, shock still on her face and forehead scrunched. "My father was in with my mother? What blasted craziness is that? Maybe there actually is something to what my father has been declaring for months now."

"That he would be getting your mother to marry him one of these days?"

"Yes. I thought it ridiculous, but...but I guess it is possible."

"They were together once." Jason's hand went to her belly, rubbing. "So if Josie really found them together, and ran back into here, I would venture to say the thought is a bit less ridiculous than you imagined. And it will make Josie calling her 'Meme' much easier to explain."

Katalin rubbed her forehead. "I thought my mother was just accompanying father to London because she had to talk to her solicitor, but—do you think she is actually going with him to see Walton? Which I still do not condone—I do not know why father insists on seeing him."

"Forgive him for sins done?"

"The man does not deserve forgiveness."

"It is your father's choice, Katalin. His brother is on his deathbed. They will always have history we know nothing of, nor could understand."

Katalin shook her head, her hand going to Jason's jawline, thumb caressing the scar. "Always too reasonable, you are. Too steady. I do not care for any of it in regards to Walton."

"I know." He turned his head to kiss her hand. "But you also love me for that very same reason. You keep your opinions on him. Believe me, mine are even harsher. But if Walton needs forgiveness from his brother to leave this world, then I say God speed to your father."

Jason pulled down the coverlet from her chest. "But I do not wish to start the day with talk of Walton, my wife."

"No?"

"No." He leaned over her stomach, his lips on her belly through her blue night rail. "Good morning baby. Grow big today."

He kissed Katalin's belly, just as he had done every morning since they learned she was pregnant. Sitting upright, he adjusted the coverlet, tucking it under her chin. "And you sleep well. I will make sure to wake you before anyone leaves."

Her hand popped out from under the cover to caress the dark scruff on his chin. "I love that about you as well, my husband."

"Me waking you up?"

"You taking care of me. You are only one who could."

"I would never allow another." He kissed her forehead, her lips, and then rolled out of the other side of the bed.

Katalin watched him, smile on her face, until he disappeared into the dressing chambers. She sank her head deeper into the pillow, closing her eyes.

Perfection. Absolute perfection.

# ~ About the Author ~

K.J. Jackson is the author of *The Hold Your Breath Series* and *The Flame Moon Series*. She specializes in historical and paranormal romance, will work for travel, and is a sucker for a good story in any genre. She lives in Minnesota with her husband, two children, and a dog who has taken the sport of bed-hogging to new heights.

Visit her at www.kjjackson.com

# ~ Author's Note ~

Thank you so much for taking a trip back in time with me. The next book in the *Hold Your Breath* series will debut in Summer 2015. And if you missed the first two in this series, be sure to check out **Stone Devil Duke,** and **Unmasking the Marquess.**

Be sure to sign up for news of my next releases at **www.KJJackson.com** (email addresses are precious, so out of respect, you'll only hear from me when I actually have real news).

## Interested in Paranormal Romance?

In the meantime, if you want to switch genres and check out my Flame Moon paranormal romance series, **Flame Moon #1**, the first book in the series, is currently free (ebook) at all stores. **Flame Moon** is a stand-alone story, so no worries on getting sucked into a cliffhanger. But number two in the series, **Triple Infinity**, ends with a fun cliff, so be forewarned. Number three in the series, **Flux Flame**, ties up that portion of the series.

As always, I love to connect with my readers, you can reach me at:

www.KJJackson.com

https://www.facebook.com/kjjacksonauthor

Twitter: @K_J_Jackson

Thank you for allowing my stories into your life
and time—it is an honor!
~ K.J. Jackson

Made in the USA
Columbia, SC
03 September 2023

22434845R00152